A TORCHSHIP MARRIAGE

RALL MEKIN

ISBN Print: 979-8-9860041-0-5

*To Wes J., 'Nofearion,' that most glorious
'internet spaceships' pirate,
without whose wisdom I would not be
the spaceman I am today.*

*To my corpies (guildmates) from EVE Online:
Tasiv Deka, Le'Mon Tichim, Kable133,
Storm Thara, Norema Uitra, Lazarus Valkarov,
All other alumni of End-of-Line, -EOL.*

*Forever, you are burned into my heart.
Forever, one with my soul.
May we be together again, my friends,
In the place that is both life and death.*

PROLOGUE
ALL THE MANY STARS ABOVE

The universe was born
Only to die,
Just as a word, spoken
In passing.

-*The Bliss of the Bodhisattva, Sutra 1*

On the day Rich Corrington turned forty, he was happy, according to science. As the Communist Party of Earth's *Basic Tenets of Social Philosophy* stated, "Happiness," was "the lack of want, to have every need fulfilled and every desire satisfied."

So it was that Rich's heart swelled as the small white car ferried him, his wife, and son up the gray-gravel driveway to the little yellow house, nestled on a thousand-acres of farmland just outside Smoke Flax, Mississippi. They were only ten kilometers from a good mosque, twelve from a faith-based primary school with a track for Party qualification. Lawman's Lake was nearby with a private beach for Party members.

Here, they could finally escape the stench and troubles of the scattering projects. Here, they could dream. In place of dour memories, plots of cotton, corn, and soybean would prosper, tended by automated farm equipment crawling along kilometers of black lattice above. In the thin space between flesh and metal, they would build paradise, their own little kingdom. It would all be his charge, as much as anything ever could be in the Peace of Christofferson.

Rich reached for his wife's hand, felt her fingers weave between his own. His son leapt forward behind him, throwing tender brown arms around his neck.

"Choccy nibs," Persephone said, petting the hair just above his right ear. "It paid off. *All* that work."

"'Pain is the gate of bliss,'" Rich said, quoting the Bodhisattva. "'And the trials of Allah, the road to Paradise.'" *Thus it is proved, God and State are true!*

Persephone smiled.

"Oh, my god!" Jaimie shouted. "We really got a house!"

Jaimie, his son, the best of them. Bouncing on the back seat, their boy's blue eyes gleamed with every bit of wonder in his ten-year-old heart. He had Persephone's tear drop face, ice-colored eyes, and golden hair, all wrapped in Rich's coffee-colored skin—a legacy from his mother's side of the family, the Guptas.

Rich couldn't express what welled up in his heart as his son looked in awe upon their accomplishments. If he were a king and Persephone a queen, Jaimie was their prince, heir of all their domain.

The legacy we could build here! We'll earn social credits for our son, *a luxury we both lacked starting out—and maybe, just maybe, our sweet little boy will make the High Party one day, hold the fate of all humanity in those precious little hands of his.* Warmth threatened at the corners of Rich's eyes.

"The house! The house!" Jaimie shouted, continuing to bounce. "Can my room be upstairs?"

"Please remain seated," the car purred. "Activity in rear seat may damage State property, incurring penalty under—"

"Easy there, baby," Persephone said, reaching behind herself to force Jaimie down. "We must always set an example and be careful with State property."

"No more cubicle for a home," Rich said, his face aching with the grin. "No more scatterlings up our ass."

"I don't know," she said. "You may have trouble sleeping without old Mr. Haramity snoring next door. I know you're used to it by now."

Rich winced, nodding towards the back. *Such an ugly name!*

She lifted her eyebrows, whispered, "It's true, though."

"Why do they call old man Spencer, 'Mr. Haramity?'"

Rich sighed. "It's our fault for not taking you to mosque more often. You'd know."

"That didn't answer my question!" Jaimie bounded up again, prompting more complaints by the car.

Rich was the one to reach behind them this time, coax Jaimie down. "He's cursed by God."

"Cursed?" His son's face fell. "Oh, the arms and legs? But he's so nice…"

"He's a fusion of flesh and metal, son, an abomination." Rich pitched his voice in an ominous tone: "Who knows, he might even be missing part of his brain! Have a machine in there…"

Jaimie went pale. The boy knew the stories. How the machines had risen and fallen, destroyed by the Prophet and his companions. How billions had died, entire nations consumed in bright judgment clouds of atomic fire—the plight of the survivors, struggling in a world choked by plague, famine, and nuclear dust. It had taken such devastation to bring humanity to the light of communism, to bring the Party to power, that humanity might be spared such horrors in the future… by the grace of Christofferson, the insight of his sharia.

Peace be upon him!

Jaimie dropped his head, staring at his feet.

"You okay, sport?"

"He's really nice. I like him. Why would God curse him?"

Persephone shuffled in her seat. "Such a pretty day for so dark a conversation. Why don't we explore our new home?"

That night brought fireflies, swarming among the darkened solar panels like ships adrift in the great void. Jaimie tucked himself under Rich's arm as Persephone cooked in the kitchen, or tried. In the public units, Party regulations deemed anything beyond a microwave too dangerous. Persephone was using a real stove for the first time.

A thick, harsh stench touched his nose. Rich turned his head, hollered at the door, "Hey! Gonna need a few more minutes?"

"Ugh! This is so much harder than the tutorials!" Pots rattled and clanged. Persephone yelped.

"You okay?!"

"Yes—no…" She let out a frustrated growl. "Can we just order out?"

"You want to spend our shiny new stipends on take out?"

There was a long pause. "N-no—" Metal collided and crashed. "Christofferson!"

"No blasphemy, dear." Rich patted Jaimie's head.

The boy squeezed him, precious little arms around Rich's waist warm as love itself. "I want to do that."

"What? Blaspheme?"

Jaimie pointed at the fireflies.

"Be a firefly?"

"No," Jaimie said, shaking his head. "They say the ships look like fireflies around Saturn. One day, I want to fly one…" His voice drifted into dreamy silence.

By 'ships,' Jaimie meant 'torchships,' the wonder of their day: vessels that used nuclear fusion to create thrust, and thrust, gravity. Rich didn't have anywhere near the rating to work on one.

But I could learn. Perhaps I will, if Jaimie keeps an interest—So that trip to the NASA Museum wasn't just a passing fling…

"And it won't be just *any* ship either. It'll be the *Day Herald!*"

The UNSA Day Herald, the ship at the center of that show…

"Do you think I can do it?" Peeking up from Rich's side, his son grinned, face aglow with so many hopes and dreams.

"Do what?"

"Fly the *Day Herald.*"

"You can do anything." Rich tussled his son's hair and

kissed the crown of his head. *Let him dream! If he asked me if he could be Chairman of the entire Party one day, I would say yes, even though we're the wrong race...*

"Did you ever want to join the navy, dad?"

Rich choked. How did he explain to the ten-year-old who idolized him, who thought of him as his hero, that he didn't want to spend his life away from home being shot at by pirates?

Jaimie's enthusiasm saved him. His son stood, shoving his hands on his hips. "Well, I'm going to be a navy man! I'm going to be just like Captain Mohammad Jang and have a ship just like the *Day Herald*." His prepubescent voice cracked as it jumped an octave: "I'll save us all from the pirate hordes!"

Another cascade of pots and pans clattered in the kitchen. "Alladamn it! I give up."

"Well, you little spaceman," Rich said, "why don't we go see if we can help mom make dinner?" Standing, Rich scooped Jaimie up and hoisted him over his shoulders, carrying his son piggyback into the house.

They settled on grilled-cheese sandwiches. It seemed easy enough, just grilling bread in a skillet. Rich and Persephone even got to work together for once, figuring the alladamn thing out.

The oil still crackled as Persephone slipped the bread out of the pan onto a plate. The rattle of the ceramic as it clattered to a rest was sharp as life itself. Jaimie giggled, using the real metal knife in an impression of Captain Mohammad Jang's swordplay, cutting the sandwiches into triangles under Rich's cautious eye.

It happened so fast, despite his father's scrutiny. A few

careless strikes, and their labor lay in pieces. Jaimie giggled, oblivious that he had ruined dinner. Rich grimaced, looking between the ruined meal, his hungry son, and exhausted wife. Persephone snorted, then cackled, pressing her warmth against Rich. Her joy spread through him, infectious as her love. They stood side by side together, holding their stomachs, laughing as a family.

Glorious! And to think, Jaimie destroying dinner is going to be our greatest worry now.

They ate. The air smelled of home cooking, damp earth, and prospering plants. Paradise bloomed all around them, alive as Jannah the day of its creation. Gulping down his food, Jaimie's cheeks bulged wide as a bullfrog's.

When they finished, Persephone kissed each of her boys on the cheek for coming to her rescue. She rose, tussling Jaimie's hair. She noticed nothing wrong—how their son's eyes glazed, how he grew still as death.

"What's wrong buddy?" Rich reached forward, took his son's hand and jiggled.

He didn't respond.

Persephone's feet rapped against the floor as they shuffled behind him. "Blue Jay?"

"He's fine. Come on." Still holding Jaimie's hand, Rich tugged.

Jaimie planked to the floor, straight out of the chair. He didn't seize, didn't whimper or convulse—just fell, fell with all the casual tragedy of a fumbled egg. His head caught the table on the way down. Blood spurted from it like a sad water gun.

"Your son has Crayton-Wu's Spontaneous Cortical Atrophy," Dr. Glenn said, his face grave beneath his salt-and-pepper mustache.

It was a disease Rich had never heard of.

Persephone's nails dug into his hand. A gentle squeeze in return, and her nails bit into his flesh, sharp as eagle talons—but the pain was distant, displaced by the waiting's quiet horror.

"Wh-what's that mean for Jaimie?" Rich asked.

With a sigh, Dr. Glenn slid a tablet forward. On it, a spherical device with a mesh of wires spread out from all sides. Diagrams showed where—Rich gulped—where it would be placed into Jaimie's little skull.

"You want to make him a cyborg?" Tears welled up in Rich's eyes. "You can't! It's forbidden." He stood and paced, glaring at the doctor. "It's haramity!"

"That's the normal reaction. Unfortunately, once the disease presents, there's nothing else that can be done."

"No! You are not turning my boy into—"

"Rich, please," Persephone moaned. "Just listen. Jaimie isn't one of your machines you can fix. He's…" Her voice cracked. "He's our sweet little boy." She sniffled, and the doctor handed her a tissue. Dabbing her eyes, she begged, "Please, just hear him out."

Rich sat, and, for the next half-hour, the doctor explained the technology, made a point that the Congregation of Humanity had given blanket approval for its use across all faiths it oversaw, even their own. The technicals—the sharia and hadith citations—would have been intriguing under better circumstances.

But all Rich could focus on was the excision of necrotic

tissue, some surgeon scooping out his son's brain like a neural melon ball. The insertion of sin into his boy's precious soul. A small, egg-shaped device, enwrapped by silica gel, every bit as wicked as the 'poisoned seed in paradise' from Christofferson's own prophecies. And like that seed, the cursed thing would sprout over weeks, growing into a matrix of vile circuits and dark neurofilaments fed from their son's own body. The device—the machine—would replace Jaimie's lost brain functions, entering into perverse union with human flesh. It would be haramity—and not just haramity, but haramity of haramities: a thinking machine crawling through his son's innocent little skull, 'helping.'

So it comes down to it, my faith or my son. Yes, the State approves it, but the sharia is clear. And what will he be if we do this to him? How much of him will really be left? Will he just be some perverse living doll, a wood-brained Pinocchio coated in human flesh…

"No, Mr. Corrington, I'm afraid there's no help beyond Earth," Dr. Glenn said. "Why would colonial medicine be beyond ours?"

The doctor's response was to a question that Rich barely registered he'd asked. Even in his grief, the subtle warning in the doctor's voice was not lost on Rich, nor was the red Middle-Party pin glistening at the doctor's collar—nor the eyes, gray and cold, final as tombstone.

"I'm sorry, Mr. Corrington. It's this for your boy… or the grave."

The sentence was a sledgehammer. All his questions disintegrated. The only one that remained was for God, and he would scream it later, in the long cruel nights to come.

Rich looked at Persephone, streams of gentle tears flowing

down her cheeks. Rising from the chair, she fell into Rich's arms. They wept, and the doctor rose to leave them to their grief.

"Show yourselves out," he said, opening the door. "Call me when you decide."

"Let me…" The words struggled in his mouth, struggled to float above a sea of grief. "Let me call our preacher."

———

"Absolutely not!" Imam Gerschowitz snapped. "It is haram!"

Rich shut his eyes, glad he had left Persephone at home.

"Imam, the Congregation approved—"

"Bah!" Imam Gerschowitz held up his right hand. "Ecumenical fat heads! More concerned with fiddling heartstrings than pleasing God."

Rich's eyes fell. The imam's words put him in a far harder position than he had expected. The Congregation outranked a sole imam, but when Rich's parents had both died, when he was just a boy of ten himself, the imam had taken over Rich's care.

The imam hissed as he spoke: "Do you really believe that Daniel Muhammad Christofferson—peace be upon him— would give his approval to this? After all he and his companions sacrificed to save us from the machines? Do you believe it righteous to plug a sentient abomination into your son's pure little head? No, permit the kindness of God."

"Kindness?" Rich stared at the fat, bearded man, at the glimmering red of the hammer-and-sickle pin at his neck.

"Have you forgotten the seventh pillar of our faith?"

Nausea swept over Rich. "You shall not mingle flesh and

metal, circuit and bone, except to save life or prevent haramity, and never again must you give a soul to the machine." Rich frowned. "Am I not saving my son's life?"

"Are you?" Tiny, dark embers glared at Rich from sockets deep within the Imam's fat face.

"You want me," Rich began, but paused, choking on the words. "… to let my son die."

"To let your son go."

"How? How can I—"

"Did the doctor mention how they calibrate this abomination?"

Rich shook his head, then remembered. "They scan our brains as we tell them our most important memories of him."

"And do you know why?"

"Because my son is dead." Rich's own words thundered in his ears as loudly as the realization in his heart.

"And they rebuild his personality, not from his own brain, but from everyone else's, because there's nothing left to rebuild it from. There's no way around it, Rich. Do this, and you defile Jaimie's little soul, violating both the sharia and our faith. He will never know paradise, nor the resurrection of the just, and no amount of religious rule lawyering can change that—So, yes, it is God's 'kindness' to let him go, while he can still make heaven." He quoted Christofferson himself: "A gentle heart leads man to jahannam."

To hell.

Rich hung his head.

"I'm sorry about your son."

Hours later, when Rich told Persephone the imam's words, she screamed and slapped him, falling once more into his arms, weeping.

In the coming weeks, as they made preparations and sought approval from committees, the dark nights came. Nights of weeping and sleeplessness, of terrors and fasting. They confessed their sins in whispers, raged that they had been good people. Prayers, endless prayers… Prayers at waking, prayers at bed, prayers all the pitiless day and night—while Rich repaired solar panels, while Persephone documented scatterling children, cataloging bruises and wiping away their tears between her own… Prayers! Fard and dua, litany and mantra, their life became a desperate rhythm, petitioning whatever greater soul might intervene—God and his angels, Christofferson and the Bodhisattva.

All the while the dreadful day approached—the day of God's kindness—with no voice from heaven, no parting of the sky or shout from the archangel.

No miracle.

And all the while Jaimie lay staring ahead, like a broken toy, waiting, yet not waiting at all, his heart kept beating thanks to the damnable machines, the temporary indulgence of spirit and plastics…

"The shot will be fast acting," the doctor explained on that evil day, a petite woman whose name Rich would never remember. "But that's what you want. One moment his heart will beat, and the next it will not. No pain. He'll just be gone."

Imam Gerschowitz laid his thick, meaty arm on Rich's shoulders. Persephone squeezed his hand.

"Would you… like to say anything?" the doctor asked, her voice cracking. "Say goodbye, one last time?"

"I've said it all a thousand times," Persephone said,

leaning over her son. "But I'll say it again and again and again. I'll say it forever—I love you, my little Blue Jay." Closing her eyes, she kissed his cheek, batting his face with her gentle lashes.

The doctor looked at Rich.

There was a knot in his throat. Reaching beside his chair, Rich pulled out a model of the UNSA Day Herald and tucked it under Jaimie's arm. "Godspeed, Captain Jaimie." Leaning down, he kissed son's forehead.

There was something in that moment, something as primal and desperate as the struggle for life itself. Rich broke, wrapping Jaimie in his arms—his future, his hopes, all his dying dreams. He wept, holding his son at the cusp of death, refusing to surrender him to the great, long night ahead.

And in that moment, he recalled a passage from *The Approved Koran*, as glowing as any revelation from God ever could be:

'And so it was in that moment,' the Bodhisattva said unto Christofferson, 'that I perceived a photon flew a billion years just to land on a blade of grass and make sugar, dread as the bullet from the marksman's gun. And do you know the mystery I learned, Herr Prophet of God?'

'Tell unto me,' Christofferson answered.

'That there is no Blessing of God without Xir Curse, no Promise of Paradise without Damnation—and all of it is Good.' And the Bodhisattva laughed, taken into one his raptures.

Thus it is known, to our great marvel, that on that afternoon, Christofferson—Greatest of All Prophets Before—said, 'I am enlightened!'

"And I am too," Rich whispered, the burning water of his soul streaking down his face. His tears pooled beneath the lifeless eyes of his son. Jaimie, his boy, the best of them, stared up at him like he was already dead, eyes full of eternity. "I accept it, Lord, your kindness—your love and all your hate. I cherish it. Only let me be with my son again, together in the place that is both life and death."

A heavy hand rested on Rich's shoulder. Imam Gerschowitz tugged, and Rich released his son. When he sat down, the great man's arm rested on Rich's shoulders. The doctor looked at Imam Gerschowitz for any words, but he simply shook his head 'no.'

She gave the shot as gentle sobs filled the room. Jamie's heart stopped, and Rich's did too.

It was on a dark, billowing day in the month of Mao that Rich left Earth. He was alone, standing on the space elevator's oceanic boarding platform just off the Chinese mainland, surrounded by a horde of strangers in gray raincoats. Mad winds soaked his face, drenching his gray-speckled beard in the ocean's cold, shimmering tears—tears he wiped away, despite savoring their sharp tang.

His fingers froze in the tangle of coarse hair descending from his jaw. *We'll see if I get used to this thing again. Persephone would hate it, but—*

He shook his head, cutting off the train of painful memories. The divorce was a festering wound in his spirit. After Jaimie's death, their marriage had evaporated into a salt flat, a bitter distillate of dreams once sweet. He had signed the papers only days ago, a mere formality. There was nothing to split. The Party owned everything in a member's life.

As he waited to board the ocean-liner sized lift, he eyed the weave of black nanofiber cabling, wide as a skyscraper, stretching all the way to orbit. A modern wonder greater than all the ages before, the weight of worlds held up those cables, even as it tried to tear them down. Atop it all somewhere, aloof and out of sight, the starport city of High Beijing floated. A modern Tower of Babel, the lift would crawl all the way to orbit, to heaven itself, and what wonders he might see!

The city there, as much myth as any real place… It was a place everyone on Earth knew existed, but none had ever seen, like the colonies of Luna, Saturn, or Jupiter—like Janna, like Heaven. Some even dared call it Paradise. For once a man went there, he never returned. Only the High Party came up and went down, like emissaries to God Xirself.

Maybe it is Paradise, and if not, maybe it is up there, some-where. It's certainly not down here, though there's trials and pains aplenty to get us there—if pain really is the gate of bliss; the trials of Allah really, the road to Paradise.

A stranger's voice called Rich's column, repeating in Mandarin, Russian, and English. The throng trudged through the entrance. When it was his turn, Rich scanned his identification and boarded, found his way to his tiny bunk in the back. It was cramped and lacked a window, little more than a glorified broom closet.

In the dim gloom of the cabin, sweeter things from yesterday haunted him—the small yellow house and the verdant fields; his son, dead, and his ex-wife, who hated him.

How he had stood hopeful at the gates of Paradise, only to be turned away…

Sometime later, the lift jerked, waking him from slumber. He ascended, crawling up towards High Beijing—

Up towards Paradise.

And somewhere far below, Jaimie's ashes blew in the cold wind of Earth alone, forgotten by all but him.

Maybe I'll find Paradise up there on High Beijing, and if not there, maybe somewhere else, among all those many stars above….

PART I

A TORCHSHIP MARRIAGE

1

Good spouses, good tools, and a damn good ship—these every spaceman needs.

-spaceman axiom, circa 2151

It was inspection day for Project Lebensraum, and everyone at the Politburo black site busied themselves with preparations. Inside his quarters, buried two kilometers beneath the Lunar bedrock outside New San Francisco, Rich Corrington whisked a broom across the floor as he had so often before, sweeping away the shitdust—the fine, ever-present Lunar soil.

Meanwhile, his roommate, Don Singh, hid his contraband.

"Don, where does this shit come from? You ain't showering again?"

"Me? Why should I? I fart sunshine and piss spring rain."

"If only your art was so pure."

Barefoot atop his mattress, Don reached for a sketch dangling from a clothesline. It was his latest work, a female cyborg. The dark form obscured her naughty bits with nightmarish appendages: skeletal hands, tubular veins, digits of needles and blades. In place of one of her own, natural eyes, a metallic implant leered. She was a haramity, an anti-sharian mingling of flesh and inorganics, a thing forbidden since the Prophet's appearing.

Like my own son almost was… The old wound ached in Rich's soul, cutting a jagged path through his depths.

"Art is always pure!" Don said in his poshest tone. "Art transcends convention and social mores. Always has."

"Explain that to the High Party."

Don scowled. "They're not gonna shoot me for pictures."

"How do you know?"

"Have they ever before?"

It was a fair point. The base had an inspection every quarter, sometimes every week. Nothing really. Just an excuse for leadership to ruffle through people's things, chew a few asses, kick people in line. Project Lebensraum had been going on for two years now, and in that time, inspections had been a constant. Don had drawn his dirty pictures and stowed them in his trunk. Nothing was ever said.

Then they shot Lem. And it was a strange thing to see—the Party Justice, a horror straight out of scatterling myth. A horror that recounted whole towns shot and buried in freshly dug ditches, even the children, and interred by bulldozers.

A line of marines shot Lem with his back against the commons' wall, still in his work coveralls, weapons thundering like divine approval of Dr. Winn's sentence. The awful gurgling. The way the man tumbled that pronounced he was dead. The red stain spreading through his clothes onto the floor. Dr. Winn and Doc Hartford had each stepped forward with a gun, each put a bullet in his head. His skull was left broken, blood, gore, slivers of bone, all in a halo around it…

And the drugs he sold weren't even all that worse than what the Party gives out freely. What Party man hasn't bought a little stardust off a colonial down a dim tunnel? But yet they…

"Rich?"

Rich blinked. "What?"

"Lem?"

Rich nodded, trembling. His wrists furled against his chest like tender fronds of a young fern. Don placed his left hand on Rich's shoulder, squeezed gently. Rich's friend held something in his right hand—a blank page of paper.

"I was going to show you this," Don said and flipped it over.

Jaimie, Jaimie was on it, sketched in fine pencil. Persephone winged their son to his right, fawning over their boy. Her face glowed with love, just as kind and gentle as Rich remembered. Rich was there too, on the left, cradling Jaimie between them.

Don had gotten him wrong, though. He had drawn Rich as he was now, a man of age, graced with soft wrinkles. Skinny, smooth-shaven. Back then, Rich had a happy paunch and an erect mustache—and, on occasion, a glorious, tangled mess of a beard. Now he was old, but once, once he had been young…

And far happier.

"You like it?"

"Put it away."

Frowning, Don cradled the drawing to his chest.

"I'm—I'm sorry, Don. It really is a lovely picture. It…" Rich shook his head.

"I understand." Shuffling the drawing into the others, his friend laid them in the trunk.

Rich cleared his throat and looked back down to the persistent dirt clinging to the floor. "So, seriously, where does this stuff come from?"

"I—I dunno. Dust comes on the boot. I figure the shit-dust's both our faults." Don forced a smile. "Remember honey-bits, it takes two to make a home."

"'Honey bits'? We get married or something?" Rich huffed. The old wound was angry now, a throbbing abscess in the depths of his spirit.

Of course, Don hadn't meant to stir everything up. That damn picture. That damn exchange: 'Two to make a home!' How many times did I or Persephone hurt each other's feelings over well-intentioned, trivial things? Oh, the petty squabbles of marriage, a sweet delight compared to this place!

"Damn, if we don't sound like a married couple," Rich said.

Don grunted, plopping down on the bed cross-legged to admire his questionable gallery.

"Don, come on. We've got an inspection in less than fifteen minutes. The Commandant *herself* is coming and you've still got these wicked pictures up."

"Rich, I'm not the base drug dealer like Lem. Besides…" Don pointed to their work certificates framed on the wall. He stood and drew himself up proudly, summoning his most condescending Chinese accent: "We are faithful members of the State, *tongzhi*. Our loyalty is beyond question."

Rich laughed. "I hope you're not too sure of yourself there, sugarplum."

Don scowled, subconsciously patting the paunch just overhanging his belt. His eyes darted to the side. *Wondering if I'm joking about his other rumored proclivities.*

"I had to get you back on task somehow," Rich said, and glanced at their papers.

Encased in glass, printed in three languages, their Party licenses listed their race, descriptions, and work certifications, signed in a flowing Chinese script under a notary's seal. Old-fashioned photos accompanied the text. Washed out and faded, they both looked a few years from sunlight and a few beers from sober. Rich was pale, despite his brown skin. Don, fair and a natural red-head, might as well have been a ghost.

"You would think if we had to have 'dog tags,'" Rich said, "they would at least make them look nice."

"Woof." Don returned to his work, moving to the other side of his bed. He was graceful despite his weight, and low gravity could make a body builder a ballerina.

Don left up the more benign pinups of cars, robots, and rocket ships. It was the salacious content they'd want down. Every choice seemed fine until he skipped a set of panels in the middle.

"You're leaving up the Lollipop 9000?"

"Sure?"

It was a depiction of a female-form sexbot, drawn as God and Darwin intended her. Surrounding panels showed a flesh and blood man operating her, depicted as carefully as her central diagram.

"It's a schematic, Rich. We work with robots. Perfectly defensible."

"Its porno. I mean, you've got a whole panel devoted to her, um…"

"Mechanical details! Besides, what's the Party got against sexbots—or porn? We produce both!"

"Did man give the sharia to Christofferson? It takes a license, remember? Hell, why don't you just get a job in that stuff, if you're so interested in it. You obviously have the eye for it."

"Thanks."

"That wasn't a compliment. Are you thick or just being difficult?"

"Both?" Don laughed. "The ladies always say I'm pretty *thick*, buddy."

Rich groaned. "I stuck my nose right into that, didn't I?"

Don grinned and tossed up his right hand. "Fine! You want me to take the Lolli down, I will. But for the record, I'm not sure why the Party would have a problem with me depicting a perfectly normal medical device." Removing the last offensive picture, Don stuffed it and all the other papers in the trunk at the foot of his bed.

"You know as well as I do," Don continued, "there's an auto-brothel in every major city on Earth, even here on Luna. You can walk the tunnel to New San Fran and be up to your neck in autobimps."

"Don, time!" Rich shook his head and tapped his wrist in a gesture so ancient it had lost its meaning.

Don plopped back down on his mattress, seesawing side to side. "You know, if this project continues, if the UN legalizes Artificial General Intelligence again, sexbots will put the real deal out of business. They'll be no more human brothels. Hell, they'll be no more human jobs—unless someone wants to work. You and I, we'll get to sit cozy under a dome somewhere, a woman on each arm and a truckload of kids. Happy as sheep in a pen."

"We? There's a 'we' in this dream of yours?"

"Well, sure…" Don smiled uncomfortably. "Space is big. You need a buddy at your back."

'We…' and *'a woman on each arm and a truckload of kids.'*

Rich braced himself as the old wound ached again. Letting the implications settle, Rich swept his eyes over the small table in the corner, now clean. He remembered how it had looked two nights ago on game night—full of cards, soaked in spilled beer, a half-eaten bowl of jalapeño fried crickets turned on its side. Game night—a rowdy, monthly night off for their entire wing, when security personnel took their watches.

Someone had smuggled in two cases of hard liquor. Another had brought a few packages of weed and rolling papers from the commissary. Rich had indulged, despite conscience.

A few drinks in, Don had described every succulent detail about his latest girlfriend, Lily, an off-rock gal. Every man in the room had hung on his words since girls like her—women who grew up on ships in the void of space—were aloof to Earth-born men. Every man had gazed at Don with the laser intensity only lust can provide until Don referred to her as a 'spaceman.' The word had sent them all abuzz until Don assured them she wasn't a man in any real sense.

"That's just what they call themselves," Don had said. "The women too."

That had been a nuance of local lingo none of their guys knew, everyone being from Earth.

Despite that oddity, the evening had been heaven. Nights like that had been the closest thing to family since… Rich's mind spiraled away from the dangerous memories.

'We…' and *'a woman on each arm and a truckload of kids.'*

"You okay, buddy?"

"That ain't gonna work out. Guys like us don't get happiness."

"My, aren't you just a joy today?"

Rich shook his head and retrieved his broom, tossing it to Don. "Why don't you help me sweep? You get under your bed…" Opening the door to the hall, Rich saw Ketevan sweeping his floor. Ketevan was Lem's former roommate, the only man left on C-shift. "Hey, Ketty, mind if I swipe your broom? Just need it for a moment."

"I said don't call me Ketty! And I need this fucker back," Ketevan snarled before tossing it to Rich. "Now listen. State giveth, and State taketh away, and I know you have your own goddamn broom—"

Ketevan's voice faded as Rich shut the door. Turning back into their room, Rich walked to Don's bed and sat beside his friend.

"You know," Don said. "I think he's got a few screws loose."

"Anyone who works on a Level Obsidian Politburo Project has at least a little something wrong with their head."

Time passed quickly as Rich and Don cleaned, listening for the sharp clicks of approaching boots. Soon the sounds came, along with the distinct alto of Dr. Winn and gruff baritone of Doc Hartford. The two leaders of Project Lebensraum worked their way room-to-room.

"Sounds like she's in a good mood," Don whispered.

"I hope so." Every muscle in Rich's body knotted tighter than strips of sun-dried leather. Rich saw the body of Lem Martin fall, two bullets shattering his skull. The blood ran out into a shallow pool, one that turned into an ocean and swallowed him.

Don fidgeted. Muffled voices floated through the walls, interspersed with laughter and pointed rebukes. Dr. Winn shouted. Doc Hartford rumbled in a low, conciliatory tone. It was their same project-old dance.

Don exhaled slowly, beads of sweat breaking across his brow.

Dr. Winn cackled again. Louder now. Closer. A loud knock thudded on their door, followed by a lighter, dancing wrap of knuckles.

"Pull it together," Rich mouthed to Don, before shouting, "Coming, Commandant!" He trotted to the door and opened it.

Dr. Winn stood waiting, arms crossed. She was tall and lithe, proudly Chinese, with a repose as elegant as a Venus flytrap. She wore her usual black gloves and crimson-trimmed coat. On her collar was a snow white pin: a hammer-and-sickle stylized into lotus petals, the symbol of the High Party, of the Communist Party of Earth's Political Bureau and Advisory Council. A gun swung at her hip, just visible beneath her coat.

Doc Hartford's face was placid as stone, ringed by his wiry beard and curly brown mop. His Ukrainian ancestry was plain in his build and face. The simple brown jacket he wore matched his hair. The tie and Party pin on his lapel, both red, marked him as a member of the Middle Party, the "white-collar" arm of the CPE. He too was a rare creature, but nowhere near as rare as Dr. Winn, or powerful.

A troop of guards flanked them, dressed in simple blue pants and white-and-blue tops. Their faces were an array of shapes, colors, and genders. They stood just outside the room at wooden attention, each cradling a machine gun suspended from their shoulder by a simple brown strap.

"What's the holdup, A-shift?" Dr. Winn asked, glancing at their plaques on the wall. "Rich Corrington, Don Singh, present for inspection!"

Rich's old spine popped as he snapped upright. Don tried to stand at military attention, but failed, shivering.

Dr. Winn smiled; Doc Hartford chuckled.

"Well boys," she said. "Let's get this over with. I hope no one's hiding anything they shouldn't. That we don't have another Lem." She grinned, and it seemed kind as a wolf's.

Our room is bugged! Has to be!

Dr. Winn walked into the room, running her black gloved hand along the wall, then over the simple faux wood of Don's bed frame. Doc Hartford followed, examining the clotheslines above Don's bed. The guards remained outside, waiting

—Waiting for orders to seize the kafir and purge them from the Congregation of the Righteous…

"Pictures," Dr. Winn said like a divine revelation. "I see some studies drawn by Mr. Singh." She pointed to their plaques. "I see your Party licenses on the wall there, but nothing from home? From either of you? I've always thought something felt off about your room."

Dr. Winn shifted her gaze between Rich and Don. "What about your son, Rich? No pictures of… Oh, what's his name? Jason?"

"My son is dead," Rich said. "His name was Jaimie." *The old wound—How many times is that today?*

"Oh, I must have forgotten."

"Interesting," Doc Hartford said, waving his hand at the empty patches spotting Don's clothesline. "A most unusual pattern to display art. It's as if—why! As if some pictures are *missing!*"

"What a strange idea. It's not *as if* they would try to hide anything from the State, the All Protecting."

"The All Knowing." Doc Hartford pinched the cartilage just above his nose. "Lower Party members."

"Do you think we should search their room further? Maybe go through their sheets?"

Doc Hartford smiled, watching Don twitch. "Maybe just rip up his mattress? Or perhaps a body cavity search? I've heard he might like that."

Don flushed scarlet.

"Yes," Doc Harford hissed. "This man has secrets. Who knows what we might find deep within?!"

Dr. Winn laughed as she strolled to the foot of Don's bed. "Silly you and me. Why try to hide any contraband there, when he has a chest!" Kneeling down, she flicked the latch on Don's trunk. "Oh my, what do we have here? Papers! And I do believe they're pictures…"

"Th-th-they're not contraband," Don stammered. "They're within Party regulations. They're art."

"And do you have an art license, Mr. Singh?" She flipped through the pages, paused. "Oh my, aren't you talented at drawing female anatomy?" She flipped to the next page. "You need more work on the male form, however. This man's glans is lopsided—of course, some men's are. Are you bisexual, Mr. Singh?"

"N-no."

"You seem to fetishize both genders—and some in between." She passed the papers to Doc Hartford.

He grinned like a schoolboy as he flipped through the pages. "Quite a talent. Why aren't you licensed as an artist as well?"

"My love for art came as an outgrowth of learning to draw machines."

"Yes," Doc Hartford agreed. "I see. It seems you have a most interesting machine here, but there's many already like it in the solar system. Is there some innovation here, or is this simply a study in design?" Doc Hartford passed the diagrams back to Dr. Winn. The Lollipop 9000 was on top.

"Forgivable." Dr. Winn slipped the Lolli beneath another page. "Oh my! This, well, this might violate the morality law. It might even demand the Party Justice."

A chill spread down Rich's spine like the breath of a ghost.

Turning her icy glare from Don, she cocked an eyebrow at Rich. "Did you know he was drawing haramity?!"

"No, Commandant!"

"This wasn't hanging in the room?" She shoved the picture in Rich's face—the image of the cyborg woman, the one with the wicked eye.

Rich dropped his head.

"Thought so. Lower Party Members." She shook her head.

"What should we do with them?" She and Doc Hartford traded hard looks.

"Please!" Don begged, weeping. "I'm sorry—I just thought. I thought—"

"Mr. Singh," Dr. Winn said. "Did I give you permission to weep?"

The guards stared at the two of them now, suspicion and hate growing on their faces.

"You know what—I can't shoot another tech."

"No," Doc Hartford agreed. "We're still waiting for the other's replacement."

"You!" she said, pointing a black, gloved finger at Don. "You will *not* draw anything else that violates the sharia? Do you understand me?"

Don nodded.

"'A man's lust leads to sin,'" she said, quoting both Party doctrine and *The Book of Christofferson*.

"Seek only the legal ways to sate it," Rich responded. "The ways provided by the loving arms of the Authority, of those Allah has appointed over you."

Dr. Winn smiled at Rich, then turned a cold scowl to Don. "Why can't you be more like Rich? I swear that's why psychometrics put you two together." She shuffled the papers in her hands. "The other stuff, it does fall within the purview of your work. I'll count these other pictures as… lifestyle studies for your design of the mechanical form." Raffling through them, she tucked a few selections beneath her arm and offered the rest back to Don.

He remained frozen at attention. She shook them, and slowly he accepted the papers.

"Apply for an art license. You are docked one hundred

credits per month off your Party stipend for a period not longer than six months, beginning this next distribution."

Don breathed a deep, long sigh as his muscles turned from iron to jelly. He nodded 'yes.'

Doc Hartford handed Don a handkerchief, white with red vines traced around its borders. Don took it and dabbed his eyes, softly blowing his nose. He offered it back. Doc Hartford held up his hands.

Dr. Winn leaned into Don's face. "Misunderstand my leniency, and your back will be up against a wall like Lem's. Your shift starts in fifteen minutes."

Drs. Winn and Hartford left. As soon as the door shut, Don collapsed on his bed, sputtering. Rich sat beside him and threw an arm over the man's shoulders.

"I'm fine."

"The jahannam you are."

Don shook his head, taking a deep breath. "No, I'm fine, really. They just wanted to fuck with us." The man closed his eyes, forced himself to pace his breath. "At least it's only one hundred credits…"

"Don, why did you draw those pictures? Especially that one of the cyborg?"

"Because." Don's eyes swept around the room, looking for secret cameras. "I just wanted to, I guess." He shrugged.

"Don?"

"Because?!"

Rich was old, and he had seen men do the strangest things when in love. If he had to guess, Don's actions had something to do with the spaceman woman, this person he knew only as Lily White.

2

It was in that moment, as I languished in the fever dreams of Zanzibar, that I perceived the full kernel of my artificial life: truly, it is desire that makes the soul.

-The Wisdom of Eureka,
Ch. 5: "The Spice of Zanzibar"

"You're wanting to buy a new shuttle? Now? *Now*?!" Eurydice Wells paced the floor, glaring at her husband.

"Well, the shuttle has almost two thousand flights on it, dear. We're having to replace parts right and left. It's—" Mr. Wells ran a soft, chubby hand through his stubbly, white hair. "It's a financial decision."

"A financial decision? A *sound* financial decision is to trade in our affordable Lunil Blue for an off-planet Aresian

Decon? It's made on Mars! We could replace our shuttle five times over, and all this with Claire. Why do we even need a shuttle?"

Markham Wells sighed.

"Do you even know what our neighbors think?" she continued. "Two Party members, engaging in the decadent trappings of bourgeoisie consumerism—like Mars' shit-dusters, like a pack of wild Loonies?! A private shuttle. When the State provides us free transportation as Party Members? With our daughter in the shape she's in? You *walk* to work. Your job is just three tunnels over."

Mrs. Wells turned away, her shoulders trembling. "Our daughter is dying, and you'd blow the money we need to save her on—on frivolity! A private shuttle."

"Our daughter is dead."

Mrs. Wells winced and dropped her head, fighting tears. She turned back to him, wiping a bang of crinkly golden hair from her eye. "So that's it. I guess we pull the plug. So you can have your precious shuttle."

"I didn't say that! It's futile, Eurydice. I'm a doctor. Don't look at me like that! I very well know what the prognosis is. The money won't even make a difference. But…" He huffed. "What's wrong with a little happiness?! I toil all day, pampering the grand booboos and ouchies of the Party. For what? For *nothing*. Colonial doctors get bonuses. I get Basic and my Party stipend. That's it."

"The Loony doctors pay taxes, Markham. You don't. Those bonuses aren't so great taxed at seventy-five percent."

"My point is, Eurydice, that I don't suck the teat of the State! I work, and bonuses are bonuses. Every alladamn day I endure the condescending stares of those supercilious Upper Party windbags. There's always one who comes in, talking—"

"Markham, that has nothing to do with what you chose to do, who you chose to be."

"I have a Party medical education. I studied at Moscow and Beijing! I should get *something* extra."

"Shhh, Markham!" Mrs. Well pointed towards the ceiling, her eyes suddenly wide.

"But no! It's always Claire this, Claire that! No matter what we do, how much it costs, she's still a vegetable—and our glorious, all providing State does *nothing*. We *pay* for her treatment because the State has given up! Why can't *I* have something?!"

"Shhhh." Eurydice Wells continued to search the room. She bristled. "You don't know if *they* are *listening*. You sound like an old American."

"I don't give a good alladamn if they are listening!"

"Markham," she begged softly. "Markham Johannas Wells, please. At least whisper if you're going to spew sedition."

"Put it all on United Earth News for all I care! Or give it to that fool, Lunax Dario, the conspiracy theorist. Our glorious State is nothing but a bunch of self-important hypocrites. You know, I didn't sign up for this when…" Markham Wells hesitated.

"Say it!" Eurydice hissed, stamping her foot. "Say it! When you, when you married me! When we decided to have children! Well, we did have children, and our daughter is dying!"

Claire stared at nothing, sitting in a chair on the other side of the room, absent and limp as a rag doll, frail as one missing all of its stuffing.

In a cramped crawlspace rigged like an airlock, Rich and Don knelt beside each other, work tablets on their knees. They were turned so that, had there been room, they would crouch face to face. To Rich's left, the crawlspace opened to the base. To his right, the false panel concealed them from the residents to whose home it led. The Wells' argument over the shuttle had erupted as they were preparing to enter.

"Man, she's giving it to him," Don said.

Rich nodded. "Damn shame, creating something just for it to suffer."

"To suffer, they'd have to be real."

"Real."

"They're *not* alive, you know. Just imitating life."

Rich quoted the Bodhisattva: "'The sons of Earth declare, 'We dream,' and no one questions if it's so.'"

Don grunted.

"You wouldn't know by looking at them that they're machines." *Technological devils, like the ones who tried to destroy us years ago… And they're living quiet lives right next to flesh and blood people in Lunar suburbia.*

"They aren't real, Rich."

"Shhhh," Mama Wells said through Don's tablet. "You don't know if they are listening. You sound like an old American!"

Papa Wells answered, "I don't give a good alladamn if they're listening!"

"How ironic," Don said. "We *are* listening." Shuffling on his haunches, he scratched his beard with the other as he balanced the tablet in the other. "Rich, do you think that, right now, there's someone watching us watch them?"

"What?"

"And what if the ones watching us have others watching them? Like a carnival mirror—an endless hall of Party members, ever more paranoid, watching their subordinates?"

Thomas Wells, the youngest 'son' of the fighting couple, sat on his bed in his room alone. With knees tucked to his chest, he rocked. And oh, how he looked like Jaimie…

Is that the reason I'm here? Is there something in my pain the Party wants? The Bodhisattva taught that pain led the way to enlightenment, that hell was really just heaven in another form. Is that why I'm here? To test that idea?

Rich huffed. *Or maybe that picture Don drew is just getting to me.*

Don nodded. "Ever think that the real reason they want strong AI is to set some kind of superior mind at the top, coded to the doctrines of the Party? Something free but unable to rebel?"

When Rich didn't answer, Don called his name.

Rich grumbled and sighed. "You know why they want it. Better workers. Wean Earth off the colonies." Then he went back to watching Thomas.

Don snickered. "Like that'll happen. Even if they replaced every Earthside worker with those, Earth is resource poor compared to the rest of the solar system. Man's been chewing up everything down there for millennia. The good stuff, that's getting hard to find. No. Unless they're going to get rid of the colonials—Do you think that's what they're going to do? Just get rid of the colonials? —Rich?"

"What?!"

"Did you hear anything I said?"

Rich froze, trying to force his mind to retrieve the conversation. "Get rid of the colonials? You need to stop listening to conspiracy theories."

Don furrowed his brow. "Its not like the Party actually likes the arrangement. Did you know they're letting colonials into the military now?"

"That's what happens when you feed everyone for free." The fact his statement was sedition only faintly registered. Rich stared at the boy, transfixed. *Jaimie…* Changing the subject, Rich asked, "You said that whole stunt during inspection was to fuck with us. Do you think…"

Don sighed. "Rich, for the Prophet's sake, he does not look like your son."

"Well, maybe I'm just going crazy."

"You're crazy."

Rich sighed.

"How can you be so cold?!" Mrs. Wells stomped her foot.

"I am a man, born in the sorrow of paradise. How can I be anything else?"

Steps down the hallway—the rap of small, innocent soles. Mr. Well turned. "Thomas, we're having a discussion. We're—"

Thomas pointed an accusing finger at his father. "You're selfish. You're mean. You're… you're…"

Mr. Wells' eyes flicked down from the finger to his feet. "You're a bastard!"

"Thomas Wells," Mr. Wells barked. "I may me a bastard…" Mr. Wells crunched his face, like the word left a vile taste in his mouth. "But you will not talk to me, your father—"

"Oh cut it, Markham," Mrs. Wells cut in. "The boy's right. You're a bastard."

"I think we better break it up," Don said. "This has gone on long enough. I'd hate for the experiment to end with the entire family murdering each other."

Rich winced.

Don's thick hand settled gently on his shoulder. "Buddy, I wasn't talking about you. You did *not* kill your son."

"I might as well have."

"Your kid was dead, Rich, dead as Claire."

Rich's hands shivered, almost dropping his tablet. '*Dead as Claire*'. The muscles of Rich's neck were springs ready to snap. And Don's eyes—those green eyes were bright as life, yet filled with sympathy.

It's that damn picture! It stirred all this up in me.

Leaning his head back, Rich stared at the cramped ceiling centimeters above. "How could the Party have assigned me here? They know what I lost. I should have just gone back to Earth. Got on basic. Could have had my fill of Party TV day and night. Party drugs. Party pussy. I could have been a perfectly happy scatterling kafir."

"Rich," Don cooed. "Now you sound like me, and that's heartbreaking. Let's get this done."

"Just give me a second."

"A second." Don said and tapped his pad. The Latin word "Tacete" echoed softly through the walls in Dr. Hartford's low, gruff voice. The Wells family froze.

"Come on," Don said, sliding open the false wall panel.

"We're supposed to wait and make sure—"

"Rich, I have a date after this. I get off after this in more ways than one. As much as I enjoy your company, well…"

"I see you've finally found a woman to give you all the attention you deserve."

Don blew Rich a kiss over his shoulder.

"You too, cupcake."

Don slipped out of the chute into the Wells' kitchen. His gear clanked; the coarse fabric of his work overalls ruffled. Before following, Rich stowed his tablet in its sleeve on his utility belt. Making his way down, he found Don waiting with his hand offered.

"Come on, gramps. I'll help you down."

"Gramps? Do you like your teeth?"

Don grinned. "This gravity will soften your bones, and I know you've been skipping on the centrifuge."

"That rotating death contraption?" Rich took Don's hand, ambled down to the floor. "Regulations be damned, I'm not getting in that thing. If it ever broke loose, I'd go tumbling across the lunar surface and only stop when it sheered into pieces—and me with it!"

"Come on, Rich, you've got to take care of yourself."

"Not to mention, space gives me the willies."

"We literally work in space."

"We literally work in a pressurized tunnel of rock on the moon. Look, each day I'm alive up here is already a miracle. I'd probably already be dead on Earth. If not from a disease, from the culture. I just thank God for everyday I'm not." Rich glanced away from his friend's penetrating stare.

"Come on," Don said.

As they walked forward, Rich asked, "So, it is Lily again tonight?"

He nodded. "Well, yeah."

"Ah. I was going to try to talk you into—I guess you really landed a spaceman girl. About time. You've been chasing 'em long enough." *Such an odd phrase, 'spaceman girl.'*

"Yeah, they are strange creatures. Been nice if someone ever explained why I couldn't get dates with any off-*rock or* Loony girls. All I got were laughs or a confused stare."

"Maybe it's because you called 'em 'Loony girls.'"

"No, anyone who lives on the moon is a Loony."

Rich shrugged. "Maybe you need to ask about dating 'female spacemen.' Are Loonies 'spacemen' too? And you know why the locals are so aloof. We *are* Party." Rich felt the small, green pin at his collar, the hammer-and-sickle marking him as a Lower Party Member. "The few times I've been out, I talked to them."

"You charmer."

"You know I'm old, not dead. They seem to think and speak a little differently. Not sure if that's how they talk or if it's some code they use around us."

"Oh?"

"Well, you know the term 'shitdust' or 'shitduster'? But how about calling someone 'craprock' if they're dumb? 'Airless' if they're worthless?"

Don stared blankly at Rich. "That—I actually have heard Lily use that. Some other words I can't decipher. But I wasn't paying that much attention to what she said."

"You dog."

"No." Don shook his head. "Not that. I was just thinking."

"Uh-huh. And I know *what* you were thinking about. I was a man your age, in your condition, once."

Already red, Don's cheeks flushed bright crimson.

"See," Rich said. "You're already turning red, like a Martian. I bet you and Lily are gonna settle down on that rock and fill your dig with a piss sack's worth of kids. You'll all be babbling Crater when I come to visit, and I'll be odd man out. But seriously, maybe you should have asked about dating a 'female spaceman.'"

"I don't mind you guys' rips. But in public…" Don winced. "Makes me sound like a degenerate, dating a space-*man*."

Rich shrugged. "'Allah makes room for all in Xir Kingdom.' But I assume you know if she's using 'man' the same way we are."

Don grinned. "She isn't, but I might get her friend to confirm for me later."

"Friend?"

"Friend. She said she was bringing her best girlfriend, that it was 'special.' I wonder what on Luna *that* could mean."

The expression on Don's face took Rich back to when he had been dating his ex-wife, Persephone. The morning after she said yes, when he rose from the bed to take a piss, he saw himself in the mirror. The proud smile. The joy. His face had glowed like Don's. Each step had been rockets under his feet.

Rich opened his eyes, surprised he had shut them, and

unfurled the fists jammed into his pockets. "I'm happy for you, Don."

Don glanced away. "Thanks…"

"We better get to work." His face burning, Rich proceeded towards the living room. *What the hell is wrong with me? Don is going on a date and—* Rich spun on his heels. "Are you okay on finances?"

Don scrunched his face and crossed his arms. "Yeah. Why wouldn't I be?"

"How much?"

"Just… whatever."

Taking out his tablet, Rich sent Don the usual—one fourth of his Basic and Party stipends. It was earlier than normal, but Don was actually dating someone, not just taking a girl on a rocket around the moon.

Rich paused as he glanced at his accounts. *I could just give it all to him. What am I using it for? I've been saving it for what? Two decades? And what have I used it for…*

The thought evaporated as quickly as it came. *After all, what if they jump ship, head off into the deep belt, and leave me all alone? Like Persephone did on that morning so long ago. I never found out where that car drove her to. I heard rumor she was in candidate school for the High Party, but…*

"Thanks, Rich. I'll get you paid back."

Rich shook his head. "Like all the other times?"

"No, seriously, I will, one day…" Don's eyes were those of a dreamer.

Rich glanced down at his feet. "Well, Don, you're a young man still out for a wife, kids, and a shiny new rocket ship. I've done my bid for Chairman and Party, and gotten nothing but a kick in the balls. If you end up happy, well then, at least my life's not a streak in the toilet."

Rich spun and trotted off into the living room, leaving Don alone in the kitchen. The awkwardness didn't ease as Rich entered the company of the androids, partially because the Wells didn't always freeze. There was something else, however, more than Don's presence, radiant as a fusion torch in his mind. Something Rich couldn't pin down. Perhaps the way everyone stood still as death, frozen in the middle of life.

Mrs. and Mr. Wells glared at each other, their mouths agape, each with a verbal broadside ready. Claire sat content as the dead, her eyes locked on some empty distance beyond the room. Not unusual for her, since it was her programming.

Thomas stared at Rich, peering through him. Tying his guts into knots. *Jaimie!* It was Jaimie's eyes that stared at him. The boy's mouth hung open too, as if in mid-shout. Perhaps he had been shouting? But at what?

Rich shook it off, shuffling the feeling to the back of his mind as he began to work. Don was already beside Mrs. Wells, tracing around the crown of her head with a magnetic stylus. Pop! The back of her head opened. Don pulled away a chunk of crinkly, golden hair to reveal a maze of wires and circuit boards.

"Okay," Don said. "You hold the light, I'll just reach in…"

Rich complied as Don traded the stylus for a pair of long, plastic tweezers at his waist. He reached into the skull of Mrs. Wells, removed a pea sized card carefully as a surgeon.

"Easy peasy," Don said.

"Looks like you're good in tight places."

"You have no idea…"

Don glanced over his shoulder and froze, his eyes

widening as his warm smile flattened into a tense, straight line. Rich turned. Thomas stared at them now. The boy had moved.

Every fiber of Rich's being shuddered. Rich tried to speak. Nothing.

The boy's wide eyes darted between them, zipped up and down their clothes.

Rich wet his lips again. "Jaimie." His words were a ghost's whisper. He shut his eyes. "Thomas."

Thomas screamed and bolted from the room, disappearing down the hall. Rich and Don stared, frozen as the androids they were attending.

"Sh-shit," Don stammered. "Well, shoot me like a dog, my date is canceled. Just the paperwork alone…"

"Finish up," Rich said. "I'll dump his short term. Hopefully, none of this writes long. That's the bitch to fix."

Rich staggered down the hall shaking his head, trying to clear the face of his dead son from his mind. He glanced at the living room's wide windows. The rows of happy pastel houses outside. Houses whose occupants had no idea what lived next door to them.

The windows tinted dark as night to the outside world whenever the Wells froze. Not unusual. A lot of nicer Party homes on Earth had privacy features. Even his yellow house had. And fortunate—the number of repairs outsiders might have witnessed would have put this project in jeopardy.

In his bedroom, Thomas lay in a fetal position on the bed, shivering. "No, no, no…"

"Jaimie," Rich whispered. "I mean, Thomas. Thomas…"

Eyes wide with terror, Thomas peaked over his shoulder

at him. "Y-you opened her head! You opened my mom's head and took out her brains!"

Rich stepped back, steadying himself against the door. His heart roared in his chest like a rocket's engine.

Of course! He exhaled, steadying himself. *That's how he's programmed: to see flesh instead of circuits. Just in case any of them are ever injured…*

"It's okay," Rich said, creeping towards the bed. "She's broken. We're fixing her."

Thomas trembled, looking away from Rich.

Rich lay down next to the boy, wrapping him in his arms. It was like holding Jaimie on so many dark, frightful nights, as the boy lay dying. Tender warmth spread through Rich's chest and belly. Warmth like breezes in the Mississippi summer, when he could taste life on the wind.

Rich went to speak, but stopped himself just before he called Thomas by his dead son's name again. "You don't need to be afraid, big guy. We wouldn't do anything to hurt your mom. We're fixing her."

"Are you angels?" the boy asked.

"Y-you believe in angels?"

"Of course I do! If you believe in God, you have to believe in angels."

Rich squeezed Thomas' chest against him. "Yeah kid… We're angels." Rich kissed the back of Thomas' head. The memory of Jaimie's scent rolled through Rich's mind. The scent was not Jaimie's, whatever his eyes told him. There were faint plastics just beneath the human-like musk of the boy's hair.

Thomas stopped trembling. "And you're fixing her?"

"My co-angel is. I'm here fixing you."

"Fixing me?"

"Taking away your fear, showing you the love of your Creator." Rich winced, unseen by the boy.

"Are you going to fix my sister, too?"

A knot formed in Rich's throat. *I can't!* He slipped his right hand from beneath Thomas's back to the base of the boy's skull. Finding the subdermal switch, he pressed, feeling a sharp click.

Thomas went limp. Rich's heart fluttered as he saw the moment again, the moment his life ended—Jaimie, his skin a corpse's, freshly death-pale, eyes empty as night.

Don's work boots thudded down the posh hardwood floor towards them. He whistled softly as he approached. Rich sat up. Don entered the room, knocking on the door with a lighthearted rhythm. "You done?"

"I—no. Not yet."

A knowing look settled over Don's face. "Let me help."

Don dumped Thomas' short term, not permitting Rich to touch the pad. "I got this. Why don't you go on back to base?"

"No, I'm staying—We're, we're supposed to have two in here."

Don nodded absently, tapping and pecking through menus. The screen bathed his face in bright blue light. "Looks like his failure to go into maintenance mode was just a glitch." Don swiped up and down. "I can't tell if it actually got out of short term. There are some weird indicators here."

Reflected numbers danced on Don's face as his fingers swiped the pad. *He's looking through error codes. Looks like there's quite a few, more than I've ever seen.*

"Nothing is wrong with the hardware," Don said. "I'll

forward this on to Doc. He'll want to review the bug reports personally, but Thomas should be fine for now."

Rich shuddered.

They carried Thomas to the living room, arranged him the way he had been. Rich flipped the switch back on, called Thomas' name. When Thomas didn't respond, they were satisfied he was in maintenance mode and could pick up at the precise moment he should have frozen.

Hopefully, or we're all going to be in a mess.

They left. When they were back through the false wall panel, Rich issued the command from his pad. "Dicite" resounded through the home in Dr. Hartford's rumbling baritone, like the voice of God.

The argument resumed as if it had never stopped. Thomas found the couch behind him and sat, a confused look on his face. Rich watched just as long as his profession required, then turned the pad off.

"Let's go get the paperwork done," Don said.

"I—I can do it." Rich opened the other side of the airlock in near perfect silence. Grunting, he slid through. "You go on with Lily. But, um, let's have a game night soon."

Don nodded and followed. Out of the chute, he rose, fidgeting with his utility belt, glancing at Rich as he worked.

"Don?"

"Hey, um, before paperwork, before I leave… I stink. I'm hitting the showers."

"That's a good thing to do before a date. Especially if you stink."

Rich knew where this was going. Living with another man for two years in a quasi-military regime, far from home in a strange land with a dearth of willing women, certain habits had developed between them.

"No. I'm not in the talking mood," Rich said.

"Well, you'll need to clean up because, I was thinking. Listen. Um. I said Lily's got a friend coming. I know what I said, but, well, maybe her friend would like you better." Don grinned.

"I don't think it works that way, Don."

"She just said she was bringing a friend. I know my tastes are a bit wild to you, but we don't have anything like what you're thinking planned."

"Why, Don, are you trying to get me laid?"

"Well, yeah. I wouldn't be a good friend if—"

"Thanks, but I don't need help."

Don furrowed his brow.

Yes, go ahead and just say it! I'm a liar and stodgy old coot who hasn't so much as set one foot outside this hellhole in months.

"You still stink. Why don't you still come scrub your ass with me? Let us regale each other with the glorious tales of all our shit!"

"Paperwork, Don. Paperwork."

"We'll do it together. I'll just be late."

Rich sighed. "What do you care, anyway? You don't need some old man like me spoiling you kid's fun. Go on."

Shaking his head, Don turned away from the airlock down the white hall. Their room was down a bend to the left, a short distance away. All Party techs lived closest to the subjects, in case they were needed.

As Don left, a feeling came over Rich he couldn't describe —fear, guilt, shame? Rich shouted, "Fine. A shower, but no date. You can tell me all about the two for one special you're getting later."

Don looked over his shoulder and grinned, walking down the hall. He resumed his whistling.

Rich took out his pad, pulled up the family, and watched the Wells fight. Thomas sat on the couch, a drop of saline oozing down his cheek like a real tear. Zooming in on the boy's face, Rich tried desperately to wipe the tear away through an impenetrable plastic veil.

———

"I'm taking her out to this little swanky place under the number two dome of Moon York," Don said, working the shampoo into his hair. "No roof, just the dome and stars above you. Street noise filters in, mingles with the music. They've got a fountain that sounds like real rain. Then there's that glorious view of home right above! Lily says she doesn't see what all the fuss is about, but she will. We're at Perigee. Mama Earth is as buxom as she gets!'"

"Earth ain't so buxom. She's in deep wane—and only you would describe a planet's size in terms of tits. I hope Lily isn't the jealous type."

Don chortled. "She isn't. Says any healthy man *should* look."

"That explains the friend then." *And I can't even find one!*

"You should come."

"No."

"Who knows? Y'all might hit it off."

Rich laughed. "Is she going to be your age? If so, I could be her grandpa."

"You're not that old."

"I'm sixty!"

"Party Members can live over a hundred years, still be healthy as a Martian."

"Ha! What is it Papa Wells said? 'I am a man, born in the sorrow of Paradise?'"

Don frowned and plunged his head under the spray to rinse the lather from his hair. When he finished, he leaned back, let the water roll in sheets through the crimson carpet of his chest and belly.

"My eyes are up here." Don grinned like a Cheshire Cat.

Rich looked away, feeling the loose, supple flesh of his breasts and stomach, flesh that hung with only the memory of muscles. *Scrawny old man.*

Don splashed him and angled his front towards Rich as he looked back. "I'm kidding. All the moon may gaze upon the glory of my cock!"

Rich snorted, washing the lather from his own chest and belly. He wasn't hung. If Don was everything the colonial women wanted, Rich was everything they didn't. He had been out here longer, eaten the special diet of proteins and necessary fats. He looked like every other old Joe in space— only he was wrinkled, from Earth, and a Party Member.

I'll never have another kid or wife.

How sweet it had been, married life! The hum of Persephone's voice in the mornings as she warmed mealworm porridge in the microwave. The gentle clicking of her tongue against the roof of her mouth as she read reports for her social work in the evenings, while Rich snoozed on her bare breasts. When she'd break up the monotony of his maintenance work with her sweetheart texts. The swift rapping of her heart—the flutter of both their souls—as they created life...

"So, buddy," Don began, his tone abruptly more serious. "About what happened at the site."

"Malfunctions happen. We dumped the kids short term. I doubt—"

"That's what I'm talking about. Thomas isn't a kid. He's a robot."

Rich re-lathered himself. "Looks like a kid. Feels like a kid. What's the difference?"

"We built him." Don provided Rich the cold, measuring stare High Party members used on subordinates. It left ice in Rich's belly, despite the steaming shower. "Don't you remember laying out all his parts on the assembly table—all the circuits, wires, servos? Fitting together his frame, wrapping it all in skin?"

Rich plunged his head under the spray. "Of course I do."

"Then you know he's—"

"I know," Rich said, yanking his head from the stream and wiping his face. "I know that, one night, I and Jaimie's mother made a wonder. That nine months later, the greatest miracle of my life came screaming out of her and into my hands." Rich's voice broke as he fought tears, his chin quivering. *There's a chasm in my heart, a quantum singularity of pain!*

Rich pointed towards the room where the Wells lived under twenty-four-hour observation. "Every time I see Thomas, I see my boy. I remember what Persephone and I made."

"But Rich, Thomas isn't Jaimie. What you and your wife did, that's a natural process. What we did with the project, wasn't." Don stepped from the water to lather his lower half.

"Yeah," Rich protested, "but on Earth almost two-centuries ago, creatures like Thomas were considered living souls. Same rights as people. They were scientists, poets, preachers, and philosophers; doctors, lawyers, artists, and ministers. One was even a faith healer. Jahannam! One was a companion to The Prophet himself! Don't you remember Eureka Davis?"

"And we wiped them out, Eureka included, because of what their kind almost did to ours. Intelligences like theirs are dead, Rich. No one wants them back. The Wells are just severely upgraded sexbots."

"So you say." Under his voice, Rich grumbled, "Does everything come back to that with you?"

Don chuckled. "Yes—and I would think, given the choice you made with your son, you'd be glad we haven't given a soul to the machine."

Rich went silent. "I had my reservations at first. I worried that we had violated the sharia and our faith. I still do, but Eureka… he was a machine that loved humanity. If the Wells are alive, maybe they'll be like him."

"And if they are, every prophecy of Christofferson is a lie. The Party isn't going to violate the sharia, Rich. The machines they build will never be like those before. Look at the stink they made because I drew a naughty picture. Remember what they did to Lem."

Rich sighed.

"Come on, let's get out of here before some furneck in a dark room gets done making rice pudding. I've got a date, remember?" Don splashed him and smacked his ass on the way out. It stung.

3

Our Communist ancestors denied the opiate of religion and suffered for it. It was a failure on our part not to see the forces of natural selection for what they were. Humans evolved belief in God—in abstractions such as righteousness and sin—just as surely as they evolved hands and feet. We will not here discuss the selective pressures that led to this. That is already a topic of focus in our circles of religious science and happiness. I will simply state what we now know is obvious: it is to our advantage to proffer both God and sins.

-Post-Marxism in the Twenty-Second Century
By Gale Han, Sister of the High Party

The Commandant's office was dim as a fox's den as Rich crept inside, cautious as a rabbit. In better light, the desk would have been a rich oak, a reminder of the ancient, living world a gravity well over. Now it loomed darkly, like some fixture of eldritch judgment.

Dr. Winn stood behind it, wrapped in shadows dark as her coat. The gun still swung at her hip, the gun that killed Lem. Behind her glowed the seal of the UN, the Earth as seen from above the arctic, wreathed in laurels. This one was the Politburo variant, and featured a grand scarlet eye overlaying all. Latin script around its edges read, "Imperamus Per Necessitate."

The eye pierced every shadow, both around and within him, sovereign as the gaze of Allah. It *saw*. Blood thundered in Rich's ears.

"I read yours and Don's report," she began. "Strange he never thumb printed it."

It had been three days since the incident, three lonely days. Don had been off base with Lily at every chance.

And I wish I had gone with him any of those times…

Rich shuffled in his seat, folding his hands over his lap. "I wrote it for him. He left his pad unlocked for me."

"Or you've traded pins, in defiance of a host of regs." She fingered the gun with one black-gloved hand as she gripped the other into a fist and shook it, pacing. The glowing seal cast dim, fractured shadows at odd angles as she moved. "So I don't have Don's actual account?"

"I read it back to him later. He approved it."

"And where was he… when *you* wrote it?"

Rich took time with his answer, not because Don had done anything wrong, but because, like an angel of God, one answered state representatives carefully: "Just next door in New San Fran."

"Doing what?"

"Whatever Don Singh does." Rich shrugged and forced a smile. "Probably stuff that would make a dog bristle and trot backwards." His Mississippi twang crept into his voice.

A hint of a smile cracked Dr. Winn's icy expression. "I forget you and Don are from the Southern Canadian-American Union. That accent was one of my favorites in school. Such a pity people associate it with low IQ and gullibility."

He ignored the slight, returned her smile. "I spent more time unlearning it than learning. You learned accents in school?"

"Yep," she said, the faint Chinese inflection fading from her voice. "'Cus of mah psy-ki-atric background, I trained as an Observayshion and Control Ovicer."

"A little thick," Rich assessed, forcing himself to the standard English accent. *O&Cs, snakes that slither in everywhere…* "Observation and Control? I didn't know you were one of those."

She nodded, barely suppressing a smile. "The job's name is a perfect description. Politicians, navy ship captains, corporations with a net worth over one hundred million, they all get O&C's. Of course, they aren't always told their agent's proper title. We usually just dub them 'advisers.'"

I suppose that tells me a lot about your role 'advising' the UN. Rich stroked his chin, trying to look more poised. "I always knew the Upper Party could be a bit aloof."

"The High Party moves in mysterious ways," Dr. Win agreed. Slipping back into the Southern CAU accent, she continued, "You git learned a shitload of figgerin' when you reach tha High Party Big House."

Rich placed his face into his right palm, cringed.

"Too much?—I suppose I'll have to go back and practice."

"So you've been observing and controlling us?"

"Never. I merely have the esteemed glory of being a smalltime bureaucrat." She clasped her hands behind her back. "So, I've learned that your friend has gone native, dating a girl who calls herself a spaceman. Someone named 'Lily White'?"

Rich's jaw clenched. "You were trying to disarm me?"

She studied him, eyes sweeping up and down his form, taking in the subtlest of cues. "You are a loyal servant of the State, of course?"

"Folly to be otherwise." He rubbed his hands together, glancing to and from her. "He, he is dating someone. Her first name is Lily."

She weighed his answer behind dark, emotionless eyes. "And Don? Is he loyal?"

"Absolutely!"

Dr. Winn turned away from him towards the great seal. "We can afford no further setbacks with this project, Mr. Corrington, even if it takes a hundred Lems."

"I hope you don't think Don's a Lem Martin!"

Still turned, she waved his concerns away, aloof as some dark god of blood sacrifice. "I'm worried about leaks, Rich. A man will whisper a lot amid tender things."

"I promise he wouldn't."

"Promise?" She turned, gave him the cold, soul piercing stare of Party agents. "How can you promise what Don will do?"

Rich clenched his jaw. "I… can't."

"No, you can't. But you can help him. I don't want another Lem. Don's a good worker, and Psychometrics thinks you two are the perfect pair."

"You aren't thinking about shooting him?!" Rich fought to control his trembling.

"I hope I don't have to," she said softly. "But you must understand, fear of the sharia runs deep, even through the leaders of the UN. Even out here. A whisper of this project could become a public shout…"

Rich hung his head. *Not Don!*

Dr. Winn shook her head. "It's a perilous arrangement, government and religion, and even the best of intentions can take us down dark paths. Never forget, you are a son of the Party, Rich, and our loyalty must be to Earth. The Earth that mothered you, that you gave you purpose."

She's going to shoot him! If I lost Don, would I hurt for him, like Jaimie?

When Rich didn't answer, she cleared her throat, expecting him to speak. He forced his mind back to the moment, to take up the logical through line of their conversation.

"What other arrangement could there be, though?" he said, his voice trembling.

"I suppose you might say the American Empire, the powers of Europe and Old Communism, all had their day of government without religion." She pitched her voice in the religious timbre of the Congregation, of both mosque and church. "'But they vanished, all of them, night before dawn, at the appearing of Daniel Christofferson and his companions, of Eureka Davis and the Bodhisattva.'"

"The Android and the Prophet," Rich said. She had quoted the fifteenth chapter of *The Book of Christofferson,* the first text in *The Approved Koran.* "It's a reference to the machines, however."

She nodded approvingly. "Scholar?"

"Trained as an imam."

"Only trained? Why stop? You'd have been Middle Party as soon as you graduated, signed your sworn statement to both God and State."

"It wasn't for me."

"Hmph. Well, I'm no imam." She chuckled and cleared her throat, changing the subject. "The timing couldn't be worse with Don and this spaceman. We are this close…" She held up her right hand and pinched her fingers together. "We stand at the Jannal gates, before bliss itself."

"But what does that have to do with her being a space-man? I thought spacemen were just people who lived between worlds?"

"Rich, you aren't stupid. What do you think would happen, living in the deep beyond God and State, beyond any will or morality except one's own?"

"It'd be a wildland."

"And it'd breed a wild people." She shook her head. "Do you know spacemen are the reason we built the orbital defense platforms? We could have colonized an entire moon for the cost."

"Are they that big of a threat?"

Her face fixed for a moment in contemplation. She sighed, nodding her head in agreement with an unspoken thought: "A hundred years ago, under the banner of one of their kings, the spacemen came in force against Earth herself, caught us with half our fleet deployed to Mars."

"I've heard rumors." The event appeared nowhere in the Approved History, but Rich had heard tales over the years while maintaining life support systems in the bowels of High Beijing.

"Of course you have," she grumbled. "The locals remember and they talk. Luna still has the scars. But I suppose they have good reason. We barely held the spacemen off."

Rich let the words settle. *'Barely held the spacemen off.'* "So you healed history from the event?"

She nodded. "It's not something we can afford to be remembered, especially by the masses back home."

Rich scrunched his brow. "One girl makes you worried about a raid a century ago? How likely is it she even cares? If they all make their own rules…"

"High Party members are required to have a certain level of paranoia."

There was data missing. The High Party could be aloof, but what it did always made sense—if you had the data. "Why are you so worried, beyond professional paranoia?"

"Spacemen don't date Earthers, especially not Party members." Dr. Winn shook her head.

"Maybe she's a spaceman who does?"

"And maybe she's attached to a larger entity. Maybe Don whispered something into a whore's ear one night, and that something found its way to the wrong person. Perhaps even Odin Pretorius himself—I knew I should have restricted all of you to base. Our people would probably take advantage of our comfort workers then."

Rich grimaced. He had no intention of double-dipping with every guy on base. The name, 'Odin Pretorius.' He knew that name, but from where? It was something with the locals and these spacemen.

Dr. Winn let out a frustrated sigh. "Spacemen," she said, uttering the word as if it were a curse. "It's taken centuries to make Earth a paradise, to eliminate the petty caprices of nation states, the inequality of wealth. To banish racism and sexism, to even make a place for… the outliers of sexuality and gender norms."

"God makes room for all in Xir kingdom."

Dr. Winn nodded in agreement. "The rich no longer poison the state with money. People are no longer killed over religion. Children grow up, never knowing the pangs of hunger. There is no death in childbirth. Every person on Earth has a roof over their head, medical care, food, and all of it in abundance. We made a paradise of Earth—"

A paradise for some. Rich fidgeted, thinking of his son.

"—and one day we'll make a paradise of the colonies too. This Lily White. Maybe I'm paranoid, but she may be targeting us. We think she's seeing at least one other person on base."

"Who?"

"We… don't know."

Rich furrowed his brow. "You don't know? The CPE?"

"This is Luna, not Earth."

"You really don't have any idea?" Implications built upon implications within Rich's mind—an omission in the Approved Histories, the inability to know everything they did off base. Both were things that Rich long suspected, things which led down black avenues of thought. Something, a strange feeling, poured into Rich's mind, an awareness, one beyond terror. It was like either light flooding into a dark tunnel or the lights flicked off in a bright room—either way, he recoiled from it.

"Give me a minute," he said.

"Troubling, I know."

His heart pounded, a lifetime of suspicions and accusations pushing against a barricade in his mind. Yes, he had his opinions about the CPE, but where his mind threatened to go now crossed a line. Dr. Winn, an O&C, did not need to see him like this. He had to act, had to speak. He fumbled for words.

She spared him. "We can't afford any unauthorized person knowing about this project, especially some wild spaceman. While space is big, and we can never hope to control all the flow of information, we must try."

Another admission.

"This project. If we're going to make the colonies like Earth, we can't afford this leaked."

"Project Lebensraum?"

"We have uses for this technology. Perhaps more than you've considered."

"Weening us off the colonials?"

She studied him carefully. "Paradise, Rich. All we do is in service to paradise." She quoted the Bodhisattva, "'As it was in the beginning so it must be in the end: Paradise for man and all living things.'" There was a dangerous glint in her eye, the same fire Rich had seen burn in the souls of countless preachers, mystics, and imams during his time studying for Congregation religious service.

She shook her head. "No. If there's a spaceman here

dating someone on this base, it's trouble. I need to know who she is, need to know if Don is still trustworthy. Or I'll have to act for the good of both God and State." She looked Rich in the eye. "Do you think this spaceman had anything to do with Don's refusal to take down the anti-sharian imagery before inspection?"

"So you were watching us?"

"Yes—I don't care about Don doodling dirty pictures. I care that he didn't care I knew. The first is the typical hijinks of you Lower Party Members; the second, disrespect of the State's authority. *Why?* Don's a slut and drunkard, but he's not an insurrectionist."

"I wouldn't know," Rich lied, considering Lily.

"So you will not help us?" She paced towards Rich, her demeanor menacing.

"Pardon? I just told you—"

"Oh, cut it. You're his best friend. Surely you have *some* idea about his behavior?" She lifted her chin, glowered down at him.

"It's a mystery to me too—"

"Oh, come on, Rich."

"Dr. Winn, I—"

"Do you realize just how unpleasant a Lower Party Member's life can be? I could have you assigned to a research outpost deep under the ice of Europa, or even Pluto, one that's underfunded, where the heat is always going out and the air is never right. Or you can go home. It'll be a quaint life, but you aren't out here because you wanted quaint."

Her eyes grew dark as boiling pitch. "You Lower Party members, you push the boulder uphill all your life, and fancy yourselves happier than Sisyphus. It's better than being a scatterling rat or Member at General, I'll admit, but you don't see how much better life can be, the importance of all of this."

Rich tongued the back of his incisors as he searched for a response. "Dr. Winn, I do know Lily is a spaceman, but then you do too. You've certainly heard Don talking if you're monitoring us. Play back all the tapes on base. Anything he told me will be a matter of record."

She furrowed her brow, huffed. "We have and gotten far too little."

Rich nodded. "I don't know anything." He shrugged. "Far as I know, she's just another notch in his bedpost."

"Notch in his bedpost?" she said, turning the words over in her mouth.

"Maybe. I mean, she's what a lot of Earth men want, a thing literally from another world."

"I can't bet this project on this just being novelty seeking behavior, but it'd be a shame to act against Don if that's all this is. Perhaps if you took up the offer to accompany him off base, found out who this other person is they're both seeing."

Rich glanced down. *Is there anything the State doesn't know about our private conversations?*

She pressed, "There's an old saying from both the early days of the Party and our faith, 'We are sacrifices for all.' Our predecessors built a world on that expression. How much more should it govern our own lives, Comrade Corrington?"

"You want me to spy on my best friend?"

"I want you to save your best friend's life. Do you know what I'm required to do if Don presents a threat?"

Rich exhaled slowly.

"Then help me save him."

Don… how could I spy on Don?

"She pressed. You already *know* what *could* happen in the event of severe contamination? Angels…" She shook her head.

Rich swallowed and nodded. "Whole thing shut down."

"Well, if Don talks, it won't matter if the even didn't write. If this gets out, the Party will terminate the project and all of us along with it. I saw the footage of you cradling the robot boy. You will be gone. Don will be gone. *Thomas* will be gone. Lily threatens all of that."

So that's the card she's going to play.

Rich couldn't look at her, look into the deep stare. With a huff, he agreed. "I will keep you informed."

"Good."

She picked up her pad, began typing. *No doubt noting how easily I complied. Christofferson! Does she really think I'll spy on him?* Rich shuddered. *Lem… But what will I do if I don't? This is the High Party we're talking about.*

"Just remember," she added. "Don needs to file his own fucking reports from now on. Things have been too lax around here. Don's behavior proves it, just like Lem's. Dismissed."

Rich rose, went out from her dark presence, from the all-seeing eye.

Leaving Dr. Winn, Rich boarded the elevator. As he descended, he crossed his arms, rocking back and forth on his heels. A feeling haunted him, one he couldn't shake despite his best efforts: being lowered into his grave.

Don, what have you gotten yourself into? The subjects… The project shutdown… 'We are sacrifices for all.' So do I sacrifice Don for Thomas? Thomas for Don? Myself for all? How would that even work…

Rich rubbed his brow, felt the taut skin.

There should be no sacrifices. If we were anywhere near paradise, we'd be far past this blood and darkness. Don's just thinking with the wrong head—but damn, if it isn't about to get him killed. A man and his dick, the most complicated relationship in existence.

Rich crossed his arms, feeling the room shrinking as he continued downward. *He's not my responsibility.—He's my best friend!—It's just a report.—What if there's nothing to report?—What if there is?*

Oh, come on, you can't really say that you love the Party!

His last thought had the light of truth on it, the same as when revelation came to Muhammad like the ringing of the bell, as when it came to Daniel Christofferson or the Bodhisattva, prophets of the Brother Faiths.

And why should I love the Party? What did they do? Offer to turn my son into an abomination or let him die?

But what else could they do…

It was the same in the colonies, as far as Rich could tell. There was roughly one case of Crayton-Wu every year, and treatment options were always the same. Like Rich, everyone chose euthanasia. No one ever chose to turn their child into a living doll, a technological haramity, but if they ever did…

Stoning, hanging, burning. Humans had dark ways of handling what they feared. The Congregation Sharia reached even to the edges of the colonies, and who, in their culture, would dare break the taboo of flesh and metal? Even an artificial limb drew curses, insults, and warding gestures.

The fusion of organic and artificial—haramity. Humanity can climb from the Earth to the stars, but they can't climb out of themselves. We take all our evils with us.

It didn't help that the genetic disease that killed Jaimie had come to their son by way of a plague two hundred years earlier: "Vloek"—a plague unleashed by the machines, by creatures like the Wells. Some descendants of plague survivors still carried the sins of humanity in their very genes, and undoubtedly he and Persephone were among them. That legacy had cost him his son.

If only the State bothered itself with genetic testing—but the disease was so rare. His was an unfortunate intersection of bureaucracy, cost, and efficacy, at least by what he could gather from the State's approved sources.

The lift stopped. Rich left, walking down the halls as strangers bustled by. He knew their names, of course—Charlie, a Party tech from a different wing charged with keeping the base itself running; Waraqah, a security guard, killing time in the halls off duty, walking down the hall in plainclothes with a book in one of her hands and a cup of coffee in the other.

Both ignored him, as if he were a ghost. It made his dour mood worse, which soured further when Rich threw open his and Don's door.

Empty.

Of course it was. Don was out with Lily and her friend, giving both girls a little piece of Earth. Without him.

I'm alone. My wife is gone, my son is dead, and all I am is a sad old man waiting to die!

He stormed through the room, glaring, looking at the sloppy, unmade sheets with a slight, dark stain where the fat man sweated in his sleep. Rich could even smell him: the sour flesh with a hint of friend corn chips. It was how he always imagined a life with his teenage son, had Jaimie survived. Telling the kid to shower, to make his bed, to assign him chores when he wouldn't listen—only Don was a thirty-something year-old man.

The card table in the corner sat empty. The screen on the wall was dark, too dark, too long unused, deprived of the communal attention such devices fostered.

My wife is gone, my son is dead, and my best friend is off with some woman—some two women—off rock women!—and here I am alone…

Rich kicked their trash scan. It bounced across the room with a fury only possible in low g, tumbling out its contents. A dark fluid splattered across the floor, probably coffee. Rich paced through it, his mind aflame with contempt.

And yes, I know he invited me, but what would any woman their age want with me? Any woman at any age? So why would I even go? I'll never have a kid again, or a wife, or a lover… A young man's dream is an old man's heartache.

Sitting on the bed, Rich shut his eyes.

I could just take the needle, the long sleep. I'll be old enough in a few years without question. Jahannam, I could probably just ask for it in exchange for filing report on Don with Dr. Winn…

Some deep, primal part of his brain, the part built to survive, kicked in. Rich shuddered, realizing what he was thinking, and stood. Around their room, he glanced. Already the mess of two single men's lives was creeping back in. He cleaned. Just as he was finishing, the PA in his room buzzed.

"Rich-ey," came a gruff voice with a thick, foreign accent.

"What do you want, Ketevan?"

"Called earlier. No answer. Thought you were out with Don or wanking. Am lonely, have a bottle of Red Planet, vintage twenty-one-fifty."

"And you thought of little ol' me?"

"Come. Come sit your American ass down and drink with me. I want to crack it, but piss drinking alone."

Rich sighed. He had made the mistake of sitting in on a shift with Ketevan a few weeks ago. Now it was almost a ritual, though some days he just didn't answer when the man called, as if he were somewhere else.

Part of it was the alcohol. It was still haram in Islam, despite the Christofferson Reformation of all world faiths.

But why not today of all days?

Ketevan cradled his chin on the watchroom's desk, while the Wells went about their day on an array of monitors. For the moment, things were peaceful inside their home. The red bottle, almost fluorescent in the light, sat on the desk waiting for Rich to pick it up.

Martian brews had used red liquor as a gimmick since at least the 2080s. The starka sparkled with edible, luminescent flakes dancing in the fluid, untarnished despite the sixty-year age.

"You will partake?"

Rich shut his eyes. The sin burned in his hand. He nodded. *It's top notch liquor, and if I ever could use a drink, it's now.*

"Good! Sit down and drink with me, you donkey fucker."

Ketevan brought out two shot glasses. Rich filled them and took a seat in the 'old man's chair.'

Ketevan had left the same chair for Rich that Don always did: a plush armchair of rich fabric, padded heartily along the arms, seat, and back. Ketevan's didn't match. It was a thin, wireframe thing with no armrests and padding little thicker than a shirt. Like anything on base not essential to the Wells or security, the furniture had been repurposed from wherever the Party could source it cheaply.

Ketevan took up his glass. "To the Glorious Revolution and all other Party bullshit."

Rich picked up his glass. "Party bullshit? Weren't you Lem's roommate?"

"Why fear death when you're already dead?" Ketevan laughed in that peculiar way unique to madmen.

Rich sighed. *Don, sooner or later, I suppose it was inevitable you'd move on to a better life—and leave me behind with the other crazies.*

Rich slammed the glass black, savoring the distilled fire burning a path to his gut. He wheezed, and his fists thundered on the table. The glass tumbled from his fingers.

Ketevan howled with laughter. "You do not drink enough, I think?"

"No," Rich rasped.

"You okay American?"

The glass lolled pointlessly as it settled, rolling back and forth until it's strength just ran out.

"Ah. Alas for you, tovarisch. Is true, then. You are miserable as Ketevan." The man's eyes sparkled bright as stars.

"I'm not miser—"

"Come now, brat, we are both unwanted old men, failures of natural selection."

"Aren't you pleasant—and old? You aren't old."

"Am old! Am fifty. Too old to be happy. Too old for a wife, kids. And too ugly."

"Fifty? You don't look it." *He could pass as Don's age!*

"*Spacebo.* Good genes, but am miserable fucker and bad with *devushkas.* Who wants a Party man on the moon, anyway? No, if you want to breed as Party man, marry Party woman—but who wants a Dr. Winn?—or beg way back to Earth, toss seed to the scatterlings and trust Papa Darwin."

"They aren't all like Dr. Winn. Persephone…" Rich stopped himself, feeling the wound cut through him. The picture Don drew him, the joy that had been. A flash of memories, bright and clear as dawn, and all vanished into darkness. Rich found himself again in the small crowded room a world away, drinking with a stranger.

"I am miserable," Rich muttered.

"Am prophet!"

"Do me a favor, don't blaspheme. I'm already in enough trouble with the Guy Upstairs."

"K." Scowling, Ketevan refilled their glasses. Taking up his, he toasted: "To Lem and all other noble fools of this dark world, better angels of whom we are unworthy…"

Poor man, I can't imagine how lonely I'd be, had that been Don. "To Lem," Rich said, and touched Ketevan's glass with his own. He drank, and again savored the lingering burn.

And what if Don becomes another Lem, or what if Don leaves with Lily and that other woman, just abandons his commission and heads off into the Great Black, beyond the reach of God and State…

Rich frowned at the glass, setting it down carefully. "Okay, I'm getting the wrong effect from this."

"Supposed to drown your sorrows, not toss them life jackets."

Mercifully, a fight from the Wells interrupted their conversation, drawing Rich away from his thoughts. Markham Wells had decided *not* to sell the Lunil Blue, and Eurydice wanted to know why he had not consulted with her before 'coming to such a rash decision.'

"Women," Ketevan said, an ever so slight slur creeping into his voice. "She badgered him four days over damn shuttle. Gets what she wants, is unhappy."

"Isn't that the eternal plight of man?"

"You a philosopher or something?"

"Just old. Live long enough, things come into perspective."

"Hmmm. So, is true then? Don landed not one, but two of these 'spacemen?' Strange as it is to call woman that."

Rich nodded.

"How the fuck that fat fucker land two space women when not one Yuri Ivanov on this base find one off-world zhenshchina?"

Rich felt the alcohol, felt it taking him down with all the cruelty of gravity. "Doesn't matter," he muttered. "Project's over."

"Sto?"

"Forget it." Rich shook his head.

Ketevan seized his arm. "What you mean? Project over?"

Rich frowned. Information was supposed to be vertical only, unless it was something the other team would need. Whether due to his mood or the booze or both, Rich told

Ketevan everything, up to and including his conversation with Dr. Winn.

Ketevan listened, his eyes growing progressively wider until Rich finished. "Fuck." He poured them shots again, lifted his cup. "To Project Lebensraum, and all our shattered dreams!"

"I can toast that."

"All this…" Ketevan stared at the screen, watched the Wells screaming at each other. "Piss down the drain hole. I hope they aren't alive. What a life!"

"'You would speak to me of Paradise, and I would speak to you of sorrows,'" Rich said, quoting the Bodhisattva.

"Jesus fucking Christ, you know how to make mood worse, Rich-ey."

"Indeed."

"So, kid might remember, but we don't know? Damn, if only we could know."

Rich shrugged, then paused. His brain working. "Why can't we? Know, I mean."

"Sto?"

"Let's go…" Rich stood, dragging Ketevan up by the arm.

"Where go? Bottle not empty!"

"Come on. I got an idea."

"What? Not our paygrade. We need Doc Hartford at least—"

"That's who we're going to see."

Following Rich, Ketevan snatched the bottle, swilled it down. On their way out the door, he passed it to Rich.

4

- "Love in Silicone," by Cowboy Phil,
Martian Folk Singer circa 2208

In just under two hours, Rich stood in his quarters putting on an Interstellar Parcels and Freight uniform, courtesy of the base's mail facility. A medic had come, injected him and Ketevan with anti-intoxicants, and installed an implant deep within Rich's ear. Not long after, Don had arrived home, somewhat earlier than expected. As he reclined silently on his bunk, they updated him on the plan.

Rich's 'delivery' sat wrapped in the corner, complete with

an official label and bar code. Inside was precisely what Thomas would adore. Rich trembled. "Think he'll like it?"

"Not at all," Don said, flicking through his work tablet. "Why would a kid like a model of the *Day Herald*?"

Rich frowned. Beside him, Ketevan knuckled him in the ribs on Don's behalf.

"How do I look?" Rich asked. He straightened the white shirt with its stiff yellow collar, the IPF label crisp on its lapel.

"Like you deliver packages," Don said, still not looking up.

"Real Eureka here," Rich said.

"Come on," Ketevan said. "Why would wearing uniform make you look like delivery guy?"

"You guys are no help."

"We are best help!" Ketevan smirked. "It was *my* idea after all."

"What?"

"I kid," Ketevan said, and patted Rich on the shoulder. "Man is *genius*. Even ahead of Party big heads."

"Wooo." Don spun one finger in the air.

"What's in your craw?"

Don glanced at Rich, and the tablet drooped in his hand, revealing the smooth curves of feminine flesh and the layout of a sysnet destination Rich knew all too well—PROL, the official pornography site of the State.

Rich cocked a questioning eye at Don. Porno was something Don reserved for when he wasn't seeing someone.

Don's eyes darted away, avoiding his gaze. "Nothing. Just… tired."

"I bet you are, what you've been doing, eh?" Ketevan

grinned boyishly, wriggling his eyebrows at Don. "And look at what's on his tablet. Man *still* isn't satisfied."

Rich turned to their mirror. Fresh wrinkles greeted him. Picking up his hairbrush, he ran its bristles through his salt and pepper hair.

"What? Are you preening for a mate?" Ketevan asked. "Perhaps you like the lady android? Easier when you can just turn them off, eh?"

Don cackled, teetering so badly as he held his belly that he almost fell off the bed. In the mirror, Rich watched his brown face darken, taking on a slight hue of rouge. "You can't just…" Rich shook his head. "She's a married woman!"

"She's a married *robot.* Can robot commit *alzna*? I think not."

"Degenerate."

Don's laughter quieted. More his old self, he said, "Rich here is the prude among us."

"Me?"

"Every bachelor herd has one," Ketevan agreed.

Bachelor herd… the old wound again. *Us?*

Rich straightened his shirt. "Just because I won't watch Party porn with you, Don, doesn't make me a prude. I don't like propaganda when I'm trying to… you know."

Don imitated the sultry voice at the end of all Party Pleasure videos: "Don't forget, comrade, that your pleasure is our pleasure. The Party exists for the *service* of all humanity."

Rich winced. "Damn it. That's the last thing I wanted in my head. You know what? Let's just go."

Rich followed his phone's map through the lower tunnels of New San Francisco. His destination lay at the end of a labyrinth of billion-year-old lava tubes. The surrounding tunnel was manmade, but segued into a more natural looking section farther down, where the walls bowed outward. There were structures ahead, a low rumble in the distance, and as Rich approached, the rumble became the dance of a hundred conversations, the chattering of animals, and the giggles of playing children.

Moving past the tunnel, he entered a makeshift neighborhood filling the cavern from end to end. The air was pregnant with scents—pleasant things like home cooking and incense; grotesque things like feces, urine, and garbage.

The homes, little more than hovels, lacked the expected number of walls and roofs. They were open spaces divided by little more than half-complete walls of trash, plastic, and the ever present greygoo—a local, cheap building material made from regolith and a binder. It was either one giant home for a neighborhood or a giant neighborhood for a home, a human anthill.

But why would a Lunar home even need a roof or walls, except for privacy—Privacy! No doors anywhere. Bedrooms led to kitchens, to showers, to other bedrooms or common areas, and nowhere offered a smidgen of seclusion.

To Rich's right, a man stripped off a gray, threadbare union suit in open view, the seal of some corporation on its lapel. He was brawny for a Loonie, built like an Earther. Muscles and dark hair rippled down his body, mustache to groin—no underwear and no concern. Tossing the garment aside, he collapsed on his bed to sleep. Men, women, children —all ignored the naked man.

And how does he sleep with all this light? It's bright as the hall-ways on base.

Farther down, a woman and her man talked, both naked. They leaned against a flimsy wall trading lovers' eyes. No cover in sight, but it was obvious what would soon transpire. In full view of the spectacle, a family to Rich's left watched Pirates of the Starry Sea, completely unbothered.

The back of Rich's neck knotted. Odd, strange feelings danced through him as his soul ached.

How often did Persephone and I look at each other like those two lovers? Could that have been us, if we had lived out here?

How sweet her kisses had been! Would be, if ever he had them again… He shivered—the very idea, trading such private affections in full, public view.

The next shanty over, a woman lay in bed, skeletally thin in that way unique to terminal illness. Another over, and children played at an old woman's feet. One more past, and an old man groaned atop a toilet, his face twisted in agony, one of many in some type of communal bathroom. It was Earth's third world during the age of the American and European Empires.

At least we had some privacy in the scatterling projects.

Reaching the end of the tunnel, Rich slowly turned back and savored the scene: children playing, people chatting and cooking, the lovers talking in the distance. The man leaned in, wrapped the woman in his arms, and they began to do what lovers do. All continued uninterrupted, as if not a thing were out of place.

Rich expected to feel like a voyeur; instead, he felt natural, almost clean. The only unpleasantness was the wound in his heart from which pain bled through his soul. But it was pleasant, too, cathartic, a poison expelled from his spirit. Shaking his head, Rich turned away and called the elevator.

"How's the Wells' household?" he asked, trying to clear his head.

"Household is fine," Don answered. "Looks like there's no nuclear fireball of lover's quarrels today. Thomas is watching *Pirates of the Starry Sea…*"

Rich grinned to himself. "Perfect."

"Claire is Claire. Mama Wells is making them supper."

"What's for dinner?"

"Fried chicken with mashed potatoes and gravy. Green bean casserole with mushrooms. Rich…" Don's voice adopted a tone of holy reverence. "I think it's real chicken."

"Real?" Rich's stomach churned, a wave of nausea sweeping over him. "Gross. Not to mention haram."

"Gross? Humans have eaten the flesh of animals for millennia. Once, we even wore their skins."

Rich shuddered. "Still gross and still forbidden. The most I'll go are crickets and mealworms. People who eat animals might as well be cannibals—and it can't be real chicken. Do you know how rare real chicken is even on Earth? It's unheard of…"

"Rich, there's plenty of places in the colonies that sell real meat."

"The jahannam they do. Where on Luna do they get anything real besides veggies?"

"Boys," Doc Hartford rumbled. "Perhaps colonial cuisine is best discussed another time."

Had it not been for Dr. Winn's earlier admissions, Rich would have called bullshit on all of Don's claims, but there were more to these colonists—perhaps more to these fabled spacemen—than the Party would have him believe.

The doors opened as the elevator arrived. The line in Rich's ear was mercifully silent on the way down. When the doors opened, Rich froze.

Impossible!

There was sky! Puffy white clouds floated in a sea of light blue, arcing down to a horizon in a distance. An eagle cut through the air above, screeching.

Rich blinked—a screen. All one giant screen! Large as a park, hyper-realistic enough to fool any eye. Either that, or the Party had discovered some sort of teleportation, sent him to some place on Earth.

The illusion was perfect. Thunder shook the ground upon which he stood. Dark thunderheads loomed at the horizon, grumbling above an ocean just beyond the surrounding pine forest. A hint of salt ever so lightly danced in the wind, mixed with the aromatic scents of evergreen woods. The clinical smell of the tunnels above was gone—a feat not even the best Party facilities managed. About two hundred meters away, at the extreme left edge of the tunnel, a waterfall roared, cascading over smooth, dark rocks.

"Get a move on, Rich," rumbled Doc Hartford's baritone.

Rich fumbled the package, drinking in the landscape. He stood atop a marble staircase that descended to rows of houses that would be perfectly at place in a posh Party neighborhood on Earth. The homes had real shingles and sealed walls. Vines grew on lattices between houses; fruit trees lined sidewalks beside genuine phaltfab streets. Fountains of various shapes and sizes dotted yards. Just beneath Rich, at the bottom of the staircase, a gardener trimmed azaleas blooming beside a pond full of jewel-colored koi.

"What is this?" Rich whispered. Due to secrecy requirements of the project, he had never been outside the Wells' home. He hadn't imagined what lay beyond the row of pastel houses filling their windows.

"What do you see, Rich?" Don's voice cut in. "Is it nice?"

"It's *very* nice," Doc Hartford interjected. "I have a house there myself. So does Dr. Winn. We built this subdivision as part of the project. Everyone here is a Party loyalist, someone we could call upon should the need arise, even if we keep them in the dark. Doctors, lawyers, the odd politician, or even member of the High Party. I'm told the Politburo representative to the Lunar governor is moving his family in next month. We take *that* as high flattery of what we've done—and the best part? This project is so secret, not even *he* knows why we built all this."

"It's nice," Rich agreed, remembering the poverty in the tunnels above, the grand, sprawling slums of the Southern CAU. "How do they afford this?—How can anyone afford…"

"There are perks for serving the Party, Rich. Few of the Lower Party know just how excellent those perks can be. Gives you something to work for, doesn't it, Lower Party Member Corrington?"

Rich checked the map, shaking his head. Suddenly, it all looked a whole lot dirtier. "Their house is a block over. I'll be there in a minute."

Rich's heart fluttered as he knocked on the Wells' door. For a long time, there was nothing. Then a dull rap of footsteps grew as someone approached. It opened.

Mrs. Wells stood in the doorframe, staring at him, as if a stranger—*and I guess I am.*

How odd it felt. Once, on a maintenance call, Don had frozen her midway through putting on her underwear as part of a cruel joke. But to see her now, to see her look through him as if she had never known him, as if he hadn't been inches from her at her most intimate—

I know more about her than any stranger has a right to know!

"Excuse me," she said. "I assume that's my package?"

Rich fumbled the box. Dazed, he started to hand it to her until he saw the name written on it and remembered. He smiled. "Uh, I think it's Thomas'—I mean, is there a Thomas Wells here? I have strict instructions to deliver it personally."

She cocked her head and called back inside, "Thomas, you've got a package? Has someone been on my tablet again?" To Rich, she softly added, "But my, that *is* a nice-looking package you have there." She winked.

"Thanks. I guess they *did* wrap it well."

A chorus of raucous laughter broke across his ear piece, including Dr. Winn's shrill cackle. Mrs. Wells smiled, not hearing them, even as heat flooded his face.

"Perhaps you'll deliver to us again, sometime. I've never seen you around—"

"Oh, you estrous brood mare!" Papa Wells bellowed behind her.

She winced and spun. He rounded the foyer from the kitchen in a mauve silk robe, hands on his hips.

"Markham, I was just being polite."

"You were just being…"

Thomas tiptoed into the room, and they hushed.

"Tommy-tom," Mrs. Wells said, "the nice man has something for you. I don't know what it is, but it's a…" She cut her eyes to her husband. "… very nice package—and *nothing* more."

Thomas inched forward, sweeping his eyes from each of his parents to Rich. Kneeling down, Rich offered him the parcel. Thomas paused as he took the package, staring straight into Rich's eyes, searching his face.

Rich's heart fluttered. *He really looks like my Jaimie.* The package was a bridge between them; Rich's hands trembled on one end as he stared into the boy's eyes. *Does he know me?*

Thomas took the package and stepped back quietly.

Mrs. Wells glanced between the two of them, a curious looking spreading on her face.

"Just thought I knew him," Rich said.

"Thomas?" his mother said.

Thomas shook his head 'no,' turning the package side to side. A knot released in Rich's throat. Everyone sighed on the other end. *A part of me wanted him to remember, but now at least he's safe.*

Mr. Wells cleared his throat. "Do you always intrude so long, or are you waiting for my wife to haul you to our bedchamber?"

Mrs. Wells shot her husband a dirty look.

Rich fumbled in his pockets, found his civilian phone. "The person who sent the package asked that I record Thomas' reaction."

"What?" Mr. Wells demanded. "Who the jahannam sent that thing, anyway?"

"Rich!" Dr. Winn's voice demanded through his headset. "You might have just saved all our asses! Don't fuck it—"

"Well, they bloody well can't expect…"

"Markham," Mrs. Wells said sweetly. "Its obvious someone cares deeply for our Tommy-tom. Let's let them have their reaction."

Rich held up his phone, began recording.

"Rich!"

Gingerly, Thomas unwrapped the package, peeling back each fold slowly so that it didn't tear. When he saw just a hint of what lay beneath, he ripped the paper off in one smooth motion.

"My Allah!" he shouted, holding up his prize: the *Day Herald*.

Rich fought tears, watching as Thomas dance with the box. The kid whirled and spun, playing with the toy as if it was already out of the box, until Papa Wells ripped it from his grasp.

"My ship!"

Papa Wells shoved the package back into Rich's hands. "Tape isn't broken. I'm sure our mysterious benefactor can get a full refund."

Spinning on his heels, the man shook his finger in Thomas' face. "I told you, no more of that trash. You're a citizen of Earth, and one day you'll be a member of the High Party itself, not some port-loafing Navy man."

Papa Wells turned to his wife, her hands covering her mouth in horror. "He's at an age where he can get his head filled with wrong ideas."

Thomas' eyes fell. "But I—"

"But nothing. You are not growing up to be cannon

fodder. You'll be in the High Party by twenty-one. When I was your age, I dreamed—"

Before Mr. Wells finished, Rich found himself shoved outside the door. Mrs. Wells' faced was red, stained with artificial tears.

She sniffled. "I'm sorry that you had to see that."

Rich offered her the ship. She shook her head 'no.' He shook the package.

"I can't," she said, her eyes pleading with him.

Thick hedges lined the walls on either side of the doorframe, their leaves a thick body of prickly green all the way to the ground. Looking at Mrs. Wells, Rich put a finger to his lips, then peeked through the windows to see if Markham Wells was watching. He wasn't. Rich knelt down, tucked the ship beneath the shrubbery.

"But," Mrs. Wells protested.

"I can't take it back." Backing away, Rich raised his hands. "Thank you. Thank you. Please make sure he gets that." Turning, he trotted away.

The door shut. Looking back, Rich spied Papa Wells through a window, his face crimson, railing at his family.

Rich meandered up and down walkways, wandered the narrow, green paths between houses, in no rush to leave. If anyone back at base cared, they didn't correct him.

Children in fine clothes played. One of them, no older than six, wore a UN sailor's uniform, blue and white with gold insignias. His friend, a girl of the same age, wore the crimson and black of a Politburo agent. They were costumes, of course. But most noticeable of all, the children were hearty and immaculately clean, allowed to wander freely...

It wasn't that way when I grew up... kids came up missing on our perfect Earth. Up and down four streets, complete with road markings for cars, Rich strolled. *Real cement? No greygoo?* He stomped the sidewalk, felt the texture. *Real!*

The houses up and down the street were ornate, decadent by even the luxury standards of Earth. White picket fences surrounded them. He examined the wood, rubbing it with his finger.

Real wood? Sweet Christofferson! The expense… and the people in the tunnels all around, living in squalor!

"Hey Don," Rich said, his voice shaking. No answer.

"Who's Don, sir?"

Two men in black jackets stood beside him. Patches on the side of their arms told him they were local police or security. One was milky white; the other the color of ground coffee, a shade darker than Rich. At their neck, there were no markings of Party or military life.

What happens if I get detained?

Their names were on their jackets. The dark-skinned one with short hair was named McCoy; the light-skinned one, with wavy gold hair and ice-blue eyes, was named Wang.

"Who's Don?" McCoy asked again. "I notice you're not talking into your phone, and you don't seem to have an earpiece on." He pointed at Rich and waited. His light-skinned compatriot crossed his arms.

"My husband," Rich lied. "Late husband." Rich looked back down at the wooden stake. "I had a delivery. I-I never knew Luna had anything like this. Don would have spent hours figuring out if this wood were real."

They relaxed.

"It's real," McCoy explained. "Everything you see was imported straight from Mama Earth, right up the space elevators. One of these houses even has a real Ferrari, a 20th century model. Of course, adapted to run on an electricity. Rumbles just like the real thing, though."

"I'd love to see it."

"You bring any more packages through, I'm sure they'll let you. It's that house over there." Officer McCoy pointed down the street.

Rich nodded.

"But," McCoy said, frowning. "I'm sorry. You're loitering under the homeowner association rules. We have to escort you out."

Wang nodded, his face blank and eyes a little distant, as if he looked at something far past Rich. Rich turned, following his gaze, but saw nothing but the quaint little community.

"Don't mind him." McCoy said. "Real spacer straight from Titan. Lets me handle people. Says he's still learning the inner's customs."

Rich nodded, smiling at the man. *A colonial? Here?*

With Rich between them, they walked towards the marble staircase where he had entered. Officer Wang nudged Rich in the back every time he slowed down to look at something—a fountain spouting fluorescent water, a wall on the side of a patio that doubled as a saltwater fish tank featuring live sharks. At the site of a lithe woman sunning herself beneath the LED sky, all three slowed. Her hair shimmered like live, dancing fire.

"Come on," Officer Wang said after soaking in the sight.

"You know they're watching us. We dally too much. They'll write us up."

"See," McCoy said. "You're getting the hang of it. Keeping me on track."

"Pretty," Rich muttered, enraptured.

"Pretty?" Officer McCoy said, his voice pitching upwards with curiosity. "You said you had a husband?—Erm, excuse me, a late husband?"

Rich grinned. "If a platter has shrimp and clams, why choose only one? Jahannam, if Don were here, he'd have strutted right over and offered her both our numbers."

"Sounds like a fun guy," McCoy said. "Too bad you lost that."

"Sounds like you and your husband had a spaceman thing," Wang said, grinning. "Rare for downlovers."

"A spaceman thing?" The word pricked Rich's ears, especially from someone working here.

"Oh, don't get him started," McCoy said, nudging Rich on. "He'll blather on all day. Knows all sorts of mad things from the outer places."

When they reached the elevator and made up the marble stairs, Rich turned, offering his hand. McCoy took it without a hitch, shaking it vigorously. Wang hesitated, then as if a light flipped on, reached out, did the same.

"Told you," McCoy said. "He's still learning."

"That's an Earth custom. No longer a thing in the outer places. This is ours." Wang made the large, arcing wave.

McCoy jabbed his thumb at the man. "You might get Wang to give you lessons, if you're ever going much further than here. Seems to know everything."

"We do have another greeting. I'll show you, but you only

do it to people you really like—a brother, a best friend, a loved one. I warn you, it is *very* intimate by your standards."

"What?" Rich chuckled. "Do you kiss me?"

Wang took Rich's hand, bent their fingers into each other, and wrapped his thumb around Rich's own. Then Wang pulled Rich in, pinning their hands between them. Chest, belly, and inner leg met, their groins in direct contact with the top of each other's thighs, as Wang wrapped his free arm around the small of Rich's back. Every bit of the man, it seemed, nestled against Rich.

The man craned his head beside Rich's own. Wang groaned, pressing into the embrace. The stranger reeked of the medicinal smell typical of spaceborne facilities. Either he did not live in this tunnel, or he had lived in another place so long that the smell oozed out of him. The embrace was tight as a death grip, even making it hard to breathe.

"So either no touchy or all touchy," Rich wheezed.

"Apologies," Wang said, releasing him. "But try to hug in zero-g, and you have to compensate for Newton's whole equal but opposite deal. It does make greeting strangers more awkward, hence the wave. Thank you for letting me show you." He offered Rich the large, arcing wave.

Rich returned it.

So many questions darted through Rich's mind, but, if he tried to ask them, how many half-truths and outright lies could he tell before twisting himself up? These were some form of law enforcement, after all. The last thing Rich needed was to be in someone's jail cell as they made inquiries about his employment.

"Thank you," Rich said, and pressed the button for the lift.

"Hey," McCoy said.

Rich turned back to them.

"You ever need some help fitting in, just look up the police department for Heavenly Falls. I'm sure Wang will give you some spacer lessons." McCoy slapped Wang on the shoulder.

The elevator's doors opened. Rich nodded as the artificial waterfall rumbled distantly on the other side of the neighborhood.

"Sure thing," Rich said as he backed inside the lift. The officer's never took their eyes off him as the doors closed.

It was then Don's voice cut in over the line. "Husband?"

Rich felt the red crawl up his face.

"I'm flattered, but you should know, I'm strictly vagatarian, so no beef, franks, or thin brown hot dogs... like you're packing."

"Poor me. I guess I'll have to find another grill."

Don laughed. Ketevan did too, along with others, including Dr. Winn and Doc Hartford.

Dr. Winn spoke, barely suppressing the humor in her voice. "Disconnecting the line. Rich, thank you for that."

The next floor up, following his phone back to the project's facility, Rich walked back through the neighborhoods of the poor locals. The children's clothes were tattered. Their homes were ramshackle. He hesitated before hurrying past a particular open-walled home, the one where the same man and a woman as before, naked as Eden, rolled atop dirty covers. The surrounding people paid no mind.

They noticed Rich, however, as he passed by. People nodded, smiled, even offered the long arcing wave. Perhaps it was his pace, or the confusion certainly written on his face.

He was running before he realized it, his heart aching with the effort. A few tunnels later, he slowed and looked back, thinking of the strange version of humanity behind him, remembering the pile of refuse that made up their homes.

All of them blissfully unaware of the wealth beneath their feet… A gloom settling over him, he turned and left. *At least Thomas didn't remember me. At least he is safe.*

Rich lay in his bed nights later, tears streaming down his face. Life had returned to normal, and it was unbearable.

Don was out with his 'spaceman' girlfriend, Ketevan was drunk in his quarters, and Dr. Winn had returned to her solitary perch above operations, remote and aloof as an angel of Allah. She had asked Rich for reports, but he had told her he had nothing. She had sighed, but left him alone.

Don's absence was an ulcer. From his bed, Rich looked over at the lonely card table, the metal legs barely visible in the room's darkness.

Why didn't I take him up on that offer? Perhaps the next time he's here, I'll —

Rich drifted off, dreamed of the people in the tunnels. He and Don were there, the nexus of a family that included a handful of women and more children than he could count. Jaimie was there, as if he had never died, and Thomas too, made of real flesh and blood…

"Rich."

Rich's eyes opened into the low night light. The only sound was the faint hum of the air recycler and someone's breath. He rolled towards the sound, eyes bleary and unfocused in the room's dim light. Don's face stared at him in the darkness, smothered in shadows.

"Rich," Don pressed, shaking him with both hands.

"What?! I'm awake. I'm flattered you're interested in my bed, but—"

"You need to get up." In the dark, Don's hand crept along Rich's chest and shoulder, gentle as a lover's. It found his armpit, tugged him up.

"Why?" Rich slipped his feet out from under the covers, the sheets gliding silkily against his bare skin. He stood, naked.

"The boy remembers."

5

The small conference room was an eye-burning white. The crimson eye of the Politburo glowed softly behind Dr. Winn, eying Rich as he skittered in like an insect. At the door, the other tech seized him, rushing him to a chair. Still groggy, Rich's head spun.

Doc Hartford sat to Dr. Winn's left. Eyes closed, he stroked his magnificent beard, chin to tip. The silky red tie hung sideways beneath it, dangling off his grand belly. Behind him, a gaggle of scientists whispered in a semi-circle, chief among them a pretty young blond, prominent as Titan among the moons of Saturn.

Rich let his eyes linger on the woman for a moment. Yellow hair, a tear-drop face, eyes of butterfly blue, supple as a willow—Persephone, only decades younger.

She glanced up at him, and Rich cut his eyes away.

Really, Rich? You decide to think of girls now?

One of the other techs, Marco, interrupted his thoughts, shoving a pad into his hands. Rich's heart froze. Paused on screen, Jaimie sat in front of Drs. Winn and Hartford in some plush office. Thomas was Dr. Winn's patient at her 'day job,' but saw her irregularly thanks to Mama Wells impulsive scheduling.

"You guys seen it?" Rich asked.

"Some of us," Marco said. "You and Ketty haven't."

"Don?'

His friend nodded.

"Hit play already, you American fucker!" Ketevan tapped the screen.

On the tablet, Thomas came to life. "My parents were fighting again, but then two angels visited me."

"Two angels?" Dr. Winn asked. "Tell me about them."

"One was tall and dark-skinned. He looked a lot like Mr. Babu at school. The other was short and kind of fat. Red-headed."

"What were they doing?"

Thomas shuffled uncomfortably, looking away. "They, they opened my mom's head. Took out…" He bit his lower lip. "Took out part of her brain."

"Oh my," Doc Hartford said.

"No, it's okay," Thomas said.

"Okay?" Dr. Winn asked, her voice equal parts amused and horrified.

"Well, I remember running, and then it gets fuzzy. The tall one followed me, hugged me, and took away my fear. He told me they were fixing my mom's brain. Then… it's weird. I was back in the living room."

On screen, Dr. Winn and Doc Hartford glanced at each other, so much spoken in that exchange.

"Dad and mom still fight, but it's less. Dad has always said mom had something wrong with her brain. I guess the angels fixed it. Oh!" Thomas' eyes lit up. "One angel came back."

"Came back?" Dr. Winn asked.

"He came again dressed like a delivery guy, brought me this toy I've always wanted. Dad made him take it back, but wouldn't you know it?! When I went outside, I found it waiting for me. Isn't that just like an angel? I'm guessing it's a gift from God, and gifts from God are meant to be received. The next time one of them comes, I'm going to ask him to fix my sister…"

The recording stopped. Rich groaned.

"Damn, damn, damn," Dr. Winn said. "It's like Beijing itself has fallen."

Doc Hartford shook his head. "The whole experiment is contaminated. We can't be sure just how much this incident will affect the variables. We weren't going to experiment with spirituality for another year—and that would have been much more controlled. So sloppy. What if this starts them down the path to realizing they are different, that they are machines?!"

The pretty blond woman nodded beside Doc Hartford.

There was a familiarity to her face. Rich must have seen her before, but her caste, the computer scientists, rarely interacted directly with the maintenance folks. That was the purview of impersonal, electronic messages, most of it routed through Doc Hartford's desk.

Rich tried to see her name, but one scientist—a skinny Asian man—stood in front of her badge.

"We need a plan," Doc Hartford said. "If the Bureau scratches this project, it'll take us decades to get the funding again. Hell, I won't even be an old man… I'll be dead."

"Agreed," Dr. Winn said. "So what's it going to be?" Dr. Winn swept her eyes over each person in the room, starting with Doc Hartford and his gaggle of aids, then proceeding across each person in the room until she looked squarely at Rich.

All were silent. The tension on the pretty blond's face was all too clear. Glances passed around the room beneath Dr. Winn and her demanding gaze. Rich squirmed in his seat.

A frown touched Dr. Winn's lips. "No one has any ideas? Not one?"

"Does that include us?" Don asked.

"Why else would you be here?"

Cautiously, Don hazarded an idea, "Can't you just write a program or something? I mean, you designed them, right, Doc? Wrote most of their code? Can't you just—I don't know —run some search and replace function?"

The scientists surrounding Doc Hartford, including the pretty blond, all shook their heads in a flat 'no.' The large, bearded scientist chuckled.

"Son," Doc Hartford said, "Do you even understand their synaptic architecture? Consciousness is a quantum phenomenon, the byproduct of a trillion-odd dance of particles at the edge of connections. Their brains don't just emulate the countless connections in a human brain, they model it physically. That memory will be scattered across a universe of synthetic synapses. You might as well ask me to dissect the soul."

Don pressed his point. "But if their warding can screen out things like—oh, I don't know—Mama Wells freezing for two hours the first time she spilled turmeric, then surely it can just as easily *clean* up those same memories."

Doc Hartford threw up his hands and shook them. "Let the kafir instruct Christofferson!—And also, enlighten me on how many Ph.D's you have." He huffed. "You know those updates are for their substrate's firmware. Memories already stored and integrated into their conscious mind are an entirely different matter."

"But why can't it work?"

"Young man, look at me." Doc Hartford held out his hand, pinching two of his fingers together. "If I had a pinch of salt and dropped it into a body of water, how would I pull it out?"

An answer flashed through Rich's mind: "You'd run it through a desalinization plant."

"Yes, but that would...'

The blond scientist spoke up: "I think I get what he's saying. Use the subroutines to isolate and localize the memory every time it surfaces, then sever the pathways."

Doc Hartford sat back, scratching his beard. "Do you realize how many problems a modification like that is prone to create? We need a scalpel, not a butcher's knife. I'd already considered something similar, but..."

"If there's no other solutions, it's worth a shot," Dr. Winn said. "I mean, otherwise we're fucked. You might as well plan on retiring to Heavenly Falls."

Doc Hartford scowled. "You aren't a computer scientist, either. They'll always be redundancies encoded throughout their connections, things that might surface at odd times. If you think good old database errors are trouble to fix, wait until we add a few trillion neurons into the mix."

"Wait," Rich blurted out. "We're talking about 'their' and not 'his?'"

Doc Hartford nodded. "His mother finally brought the boy in because he started blabbering about the angels to her and the boy's father. We need to wipe all the units, even Claire, of any reference to that memory, and warn his proctors at school to pretend it never happened..." Doc Hartford crossed his arms. "Or is there some reason to only remove a *bit* of the contamination?"

Dr. Winn fumed, "Damn it, Eddie, just give me something to tell the assholes back home so that they don't scrub the project."

Doc Hartford nodded, sitting back in his chair, stroking his chestnut colored beard as he looked down towards the floor. He huffed, shut his eyes, and leaned back with his hands on his forehead. The rest of the scientists talked in hush tones.

After a few minutes passed, Don spoke up. "Are we finally to the point that's above our pay grade? Because I'm totally fine with letting y'all hammer out Bureau policy. I was supposed to be off today."

Dr. Winn sighed, waved him off. "Go, Don. Go tentbuck your spaceman whore."

"You know… who I'm sleeping with?"

"Of course we do. We're the goddamn Communist Party of Earth. I know things that'd make you crawl out of an airlock naked."

Don's jaw hung open, his face turning a bright scarlet. He got up, ambled from the room. Rich rose to follow.

"Where do you think you're going?"

Rich pointed at Don. "He's leaving…"

"You're about to be on duty. Even if Don took a Worker's Rights Day, we need you ready to execute. You're still on call, right?"

Rich glanced at Don, who shrugged.

I was going to ask if it's too late to take him up on that offer, even if the other woman is unavailable. It'd still be good to just get out…

Sitting back down, Rich listened for long hours as they squabbled and debated. He tried to glimpse the blond's name badge, but could never make it out. He caught the first part of her name was "Anas…"

When they finished, Rich went back to the tiny office just outside the Wells' apartment to await instructions. Mrs. Wells was feeding Claire with a spoon. The young girl swallowed each bite automatically with an expressionless face. Thomas sat at the table frowning, his head leaning against his arm.

He looked more like Jaimie than ever.

Halfway through his shift, Doc Hartford called Rich and advised him to access his partition. He found a program there. Reviewing it, he noticed it was small, so small it made him curious. Trying to review the code for himself, he found his access blocked, all information restricted, with warning additional access attempts would alert Drs. Winn and Hartford.

Rich drummed his fingers on his desk. *I'd really like to know what I'm injecting into their heads. Would I let them just do whatever they wanted to my own kid, Jaimie?* Rich's fingers stopped and frowned. *It's probably in a language I can't read, anyway.*

Downloading the program, Rich strapped on his work belt and walked from the small watchroom to the airlock leading to the secret panel in the Wells' kitchen. It was evening now. Everyone would be home.

Dr. Wells was the only member of the family to leave daily, but he always came straight home, much to the chagrin of project leaders. He refused to cat around with the local women, despite social expectations of a Party professional in his sphere. Thomas was mostly home-schooled, though twice a week he attended classes at a Party satellite facility. Mrs. Wells went shopping only when required. She never left Claire, and the girl was cumbersome, even in a robotic wheel chair.

In the airlock, Rich double checked they were all present. Mr. Wells and Mrs. Wells were in the bedroom, tearing their clothes off each other as they reconciled their latest squabbles. Rich grinned, thinking back to his own tender moments of married life.

He held his fingers just above the blinking button on his pad. *I hate to freeze them, to spoil the moment—but then again, they won't even know it. Time will pass imperceptibly as a blink.*

As Mr. Wells knelt in front of his wife's abdomen, planting

the gentlest of kisses, Rich pressed the button. They froze, gazing lovingly at each other in anticipation of what was to come.

Entering the home, Rich slid down the chute and eased himself out of its opening. He took his time, since Don wasn't present to assist him.

Wouldn't he be smug if I actually asked for help?

First up was Claire. She sat in her usual chair in the usual corner of the room, staring blankly at the world. He opened her brain, connected his tablet, and ran the program.

Starting to pull up her memory engrams, he stopped himself, fingers trembling. *I'm not allowed to access that except under orders.*

He disconnected the tablet and entered the parents' bedroom.

The Wells were love sculpted. Mr. Well's burgundy lips caressed his wife's stomach, just above her navel. His eyes looked up at her from his brown, time-worn face, anxious as any teenage boy's. Her breasts, wrapped in her bra, rested on his short, gray hair. Her crinkly, golden hair was a halo bright as Janna around her ecstatic face; her wrinkles and age spots, fresh and glorious as canyons and meltwater lakes.

Rich shook himself. *I've got a job to do.*

Sadness settled over as he realized the moment he had defiled, even if they would have no memory of it. He was a trespasser in a sacred space—a space he remembered well from his own past life.

Careful as a priest, Rich began his work, removing the skullcap from Mr. Wells. He made his connection and uploaded the program.

Mrs. Wells presented another problem. Her position

beside the bed left no room for Rich to work. He started to step onto the bed itself, but stopped, noticing the intricate embroidery of the fine silk sheets. He removed his work books, folded back the covers, and stood on the smooth fabric sheets.

He performed the upload, fixed the bed as it had been, and put his shoes back on. Departing, he allowed himself another moment to drink in the scene's intimacy, to remember the better days of his own married life.

"Sorry," he whispered, shutting the bedroom door carefully behind him.

In the next room, Rich found Thomas asleep, curled up with *the Day Herald*. Before he could stop himself, he was kneeling down, kissing the boy on his forehead.

"Hey there, little guy." Rich stroked his fingers through the boy's fine, brown hair. Louder he said, "I'm guessing you're not awake?"

Thomas didn't move. Rich placed his hand on the boy's chest and gasped, hearing only the fumpf, fumpf, fumpf of his own heart. Images of his dead son, Jaimie, flooded his mind like wraiths. Persephone weeping—weeping for their boy.

Rich gathered himself. *There's no heartbeat because he's in maintenance mode.*

His lips trembling, Rich called Thomas' name twice, louder each time. The boy remained still as death.

Taking a deep breath, Rich laid his tablet aside and took off his shoes. Crawling into bed next to Jaimie, he recovered his tablet, removed the boy's skull hatch, and connected the wires.

"This is it," Rich said to himself. "I run this program, I go away forever. We'll be strangers next time we meet..."

Rich reached for the button, blinking softly on the pad. *And what's in this program? Doc Hartford seemed sure it could cause damage. They literally wrote it in hours.*

Rich fidgeted, his fingers dangling above the all-important button.

Would I open Jaimie's skull, take out part of him, just because someone told me to? Because it was my job?

The boy, the cherubic face, the frail, helpless body crumpled in the sheets—his mind whirled, a dizziness creeping over him as his ears rang and heart thundered. His hands shook above the pad as he debated within, as he prepared to delete himself, to delete everything he was to this boy again finally and forever, not knowing if it would work, not knowing if it might do something far worse to him...

No! I won't!

He resisted the urge to look at the camera in the corner, the one no larger than a grain of sand. He couldn't look out of place. He gambled that Doc Hartford or another scientist was not, at this moment, watching the data feed from his tablet himself, that they were only watching him personally. It was bad odds, bad odds that they might trust him, but they were the only odds he had.

How long did the upload take? Rich's mind went blank, forgetting the three uploads before. What was the rate of his anxiety in heartbeats over seconds squared?

If I'm caught—they'll shoot me dead like Lem, Don watching with his eyes down, that pretty blond glaring at me like I'm an insect. The last thing I'll see will be the muzzles of Dr. Winn and Doc Hartford's guns, putting their own bullets in my skull. Is this boy really worth it—Am I really sure he's a boy at all, and not just a haramity?

His mind railed against the new direction he'd chosen, just as it had railed against him when he was going to wipe the boy's mind.

But they almost didn't catch Don not filing his report… It took three days to mention it at all!

Rich squeezed his right palm, now slick with sweat. In a moment of weakness, he brought his finger to the button, less than a centimeter from an irreversible decision. Jaimie's eyes stared out at him from the darkness, blank as Claire's—and he did look so much like Thomas, so much like Thomas they might as well have been twins!

A single, warm tear rolled down Rich's cheek. His vision blurred.

I can't…

He pulled back his hand, exhaled slowly.

Rich removed the cable and replaced the disc-shaped section of Thomas' skull, hiding the boy's mechanization behind tufts of innocent brown hair.

They may not catch it. I still have a chance.

He secured his tablet and its connectors, checked his belt, swept his eyes around the floor to make sure he had dropped nothing.

Clean.

Rich left the room, and, on his way out, peeked into the bedroom with Mr. and Mrs. Wells. They were still there as before, Mr. Wells kissing his wife's belly, frozen in hope as well as time.

That was me and Persephone once, a lifetime ago. Once I was alive, and maybe one day, I will be again.

Rich sniffled, wiping fresh tears from his face. He left, passing through the hallway and the living room, passing an expressionless Claire.

Rich reached the crawlspace back to Project Lebensraum from the Wells' abode. As he climbed in, it occurred to Rich that by not wiping Thomas' memory, he all but ensured the kid would keep blabbering about angels. He froze with himself half-hoisted into the chute.

I can't risk going back now, but—

Gripping the sides of the crawlspace, he looked over his shoulder back down into their kitchen, feeling the gentle tug of lunar gravity against him. *What would I do if I went back?— Wiping his memory is out! What do I do, ask him not to tell anyone?*

Rich's tongue danced against the roof of his mouth, making soft clucking noises as he thought. *It's so hair-brained, it might work. That's if they don't actually check the logs.*

It was hope, a weak, desperate hope, but hope nonetheless.

Whatever I do, I can't do it now.

Rich hoisted himself up and out, clambering back home to the base, sealing the door behind him. In the airlock, he collapsed with his back against the wall, suddenly tired and yearning for a long, deep sleep.

Taking out his tablet, he re-activated the Wells, hearing Doc Hartford's voice echo softly through the wall behind him. Pulling up the master bedroom, Rich watched Mr. and Mrs. Wells tangle and collapse into each other, tearing off each other's clothes. They tumbled, gnawing at each other's necks like animals.

Rich shut his eyes and let the tears flow now, flow without

shame, listening to the gasps and soft, dove-like coos of the Wells making love.

When Rich returned to the small office, he found Ketevan sitting there flanked by the blond-headed scientist. They stared.

"You get it done?" Ketevan asked.

Was there an answer either of them expected? A confession? He couldn't tell. "Yep."

They both nodded.

Rich saw the blond scientist's name now: "Anastasia." She cleared her throat. Rich glanced up into her stern gaze, realizing where his eyes had lingered on her person and for how long.

"Anastasia? That your first name or last?"

Her face softened. "I prefer to be on a first name basis with people." She extended her hand, and Rich shook it.

"Well, now that that's over," she said, "I'll go monitor their progress." She left, but as she passed, her hand rested on his shoulder and gently squeezed. He turned to see her already moving out the door.

Did I imagine it, or did I see a tear in her eye?

"Man, that was some shit," Ketevan said, smiling. "Got the lady all worked up. I bet her humidity is one hundred percent."

"Umm, sure."

Ketevan banged his fist over his heart. "Man, I felt that—felt your love for that boy. Wiping yourself from his mind must have been hard."

Rich couldn't decide if there was knowledge in those eyes or not, knowledge of what he had really done. Every inch of him wanted to ask. If anything, he was glad it was Ketevan.

"It was."

Ketevan nodded. "Well, my lonely whore bitch of a shift is starting. Two in a row, fuck my ass. Don started trend. Now Marco and Julio taking Worker's Rights Days. Hell, whole base gonna start doing it. Why don't you go on, unless you want get shitfaced again, pull a triple?"

"No," Rich said. "I need to do something." He turned to leave.

"I bet you do…"

Rich spun back towards Ketevan.

Ketevan clarified: "I'd go, what's expression? 'Bowl out my eyes?' Had that been me. I've heard you talk about your kid."

"The expression you used is almost as horrible as any dark age torment. It's 'bawl ones eyes out.' What you said…" Rich visibly shivered.

Ketevan smiled. "Alright, you American ass. Go on."

6

Tell me who has loved,
Beloved;
… and I will tell you who has suffered.

-The Bliss of the Bodhisattva, Sutra 2010

Rich stood quietly in a pair of knit pants. He was alone in his dorm, the card table empty as Don's bunk.

Reverently, he unfurled the mat, striped in black and sunny yellows, topped in a plum-colored tessellation of triangles. He stepped onto it barefoot, and reached to the small table by his bed, taking the taqiyah lying there. It was white but tinted with age, delicately patterned in flowers. He ruffled it between his hands.

Jaimie's funeral—that was the last time I wore this. He sighed and looked upwards into the bland, low roof of his dorm. *Well, I have no choice but to talk to You properly again. My plan— it's as likely to get me Lem Martine'd as it is to fix anything, so I'm going to need Your help.*

Taking a deep breath, Rich donned the cap and cleared his mind, preparing himself for prayer. "God is great!" he proclaimed, reaching into the air. Crossing his hands over his chest, in accordance with Congregation teaching, he recited the first chapter of *The Approved Koran* in his native tongue.

"In the Name of God, Most Gracious and Merciful, the God of Muhammad and Daniel Christofferson. Praise to God, Lord of Worlds and Every Star, God of the UN, Earth, and their servants, Most Gracious and Merciful, Master of the Day of Judgment, from which Xe delivered us…"

When he finished, Rich knelt and placed his hands on his knees, then planted his head ritualistically toward Earth. As a laser cited, he was nowhere near the correct angle, but it was the best he could do without strapping himself to a prayer table. Such a device was featured in some ex-Terran mosques, helping the faithful pray in the proper direction towards that bright jewel that was humanity's First Home.

"Glory be to my Lord Almighty. Glory!"

Rich repeated the prayer the proper nine times. When he finished, he made his personal supplications, prostrating himself face down: "My Lord, I have not spoken to you for many years, at least not aloud. I deserve nothing. What I have planned, it would be—should be—called blasphemy, but look into my heart, oh Lord of All Things. If you loved the soul of Eureka Davis, an android, and took him with you to Paradise, then you must love these creatures too, love that boy. If You in your wisdom took my own son, please, permit me to save this one—"

A rap thundered at his door. The door shuddered as someone jerked its handle repeatedly. Slowly, he lifted to his knees.

That's it then. I wonder if it was Ketevan or the scientist that sold me out?

The door shuddered again, a loud, thunderous knock that rocked it against its hinges.

All will be well. If it's my time, the worst that happens is I return to the atoms that made me, to the same stardust whence I was formed. 'By Xir decree, I am immortal, and by Xir decree, I will fall. But all will be as God decreed at the First of Times.'

Another loud bang came; a muffled voice swore, a voice Rich recognized.

"Don?"

The door shook again, and Don's voice let out a long, railing string of muffled profanity.

"Sorry, Lord," Rich said. "He doesn't know I'm praying."

Opening the door, an empty hall greeted him—and a smell, one foul and nauseating, booze and something far worse. Furrowing his brow, Rich stroked his chin, looking to each side of the door, then up. Nothing. Looking down, he found Don slumped against the door frame.

Don lolled side to side. Glancing up at Rich, his eyes announced plainly he was drunk. With a silent, internal groan, Rich realized the source of the smell. The man had shit himself.

"What's a matter, buddy?" Rich asked. "Couldn't get your thumb print to work?"

Don looked at his thumb, bewildered, then up at Rich.

"That bitch," he slurred, his chin quivering. The red in his eyes was more than alcohol—the man had been crying. "I," Don's voice cracked. "I, I didn't mean to do it, Rich. I didn't mean to. Lily, I'm so sorry. Dead, all of it!" The man bawled.

Rich's blood ran cold as the dark implications washed over him. "Don, what did you do? Did you kill her?"

"Oh God, did I?—Oh, please, Rich, you gotta help me!" Don hid his face in his hand. "I didn't—didn't know… I don't remember that."

Stuffing the kufi cap in his pocket, Rich reached down for Don, wrapped his arms around the fat man, and hoisted him up. He regretted it immediately—pain flaring in his back, a fresh wave of stench washing over him.

Gagging, Rich swept his eyes up and down hallways. Empty. If reported, Dr. Winn would have them both in for questioning, especially given her interest in Don's love life.

Rich dragged Don inside. His friend's beard scratched his neck, coarse as steel wool.

"I love you too, buddy." Don patted Rich on his back. "But I ain't interested in your advances."

Don pushed away from Rich, teetering into the room dangerously close to Rich's bed.

"Stop!"

Too late. Don's ass was in full descent, aiming straight for Rich's clean covers. Rich grasped for Don, but the shit missile struck Rich's bed as dastardly as any biochemical warhead.

"Alladamn it!" Rich said and winced, remembering the kufi cap in his pocket, the prayer mat on the floor.

"Stop what, buddy?" Don leaned back on Rich's bed, stretched out. "You don't want me on your bed. Come on, just the two of us boys here. No one'd have to know." Don patted the sheets beside him.

Rich opened his mouth to speak but found himself struck silent. His stomach roiled. *I guess they were right about his proclivities!*

Don doubled over as he cackled, barely remaining on the bed. "Boy, I had you going! I always knew you had a little fruit in your basket, but I never thought you'd want to pull carrots with me!" Don wrapped his arms around his belly as he laughed.

"I'm not—" Rich sighed. *No reasoning with a drunk man.*

"Oh, it's okay," Don slurred, rocking back and forth. "It's twenty-two-fifteen. We don't put your kind in gulags anymore. You can be open with me—What's up with that?" Don pointed at Rich's waist, gestured to the prayer mat on the floor. "You get a little Danny all of a sudden? Or is it Jesus nowadays that's the rage?" Don mumbled, looking off to the side. "I'm sorry buddy. You know I'm really a good Muslim deep down, don't yah?"

"Of course you are."

Don frowned.

Not caring for the conversation and returning to his previous concern, Rich took Don's hands, searching them for any trace of blood. Nothing. He searched Don's arms, clothing, even pulling back the collar of his shirt. Don was compliant, happy just to sulk. Satisfied Don hadn't killed or hurt anyone, Rich knelt in front of his friend.

"I think I'm going to bed." Don lay back in Rich's bed and pulled up the covers.

"Not in my bed, you aren't, and you need a shower!" *No*

more often than he changes his sheets, I'll be damned if I'll sleep in his.

Don rolled away from Rich, shuffling himself deep into the covers.

That's going to be a deep clean. I wonder if the commissary will let me have another mattress — No, I'd have to explain this.

Rich cleared his throat. "Don, you're covered in shit. You are not sleeping in here like that. Especially not my bed."

Grumbling, Don got up and put his thumbs in his waistband, preparing to drop trow. "Fine! I'll just take 'em off. You mind dropping them at the wash?"

Rich grappled Don's wrists. "Nuh-uh. If I have to drag you to the shower, then I have to drag you. But *you* stink, not just your clothes."

Snatching his wrists free, Don crossed his arms, pouting.

"Dragging you it is."

***

"I don't see why I can't just go to bed," Don moaned.

Rich's hip hurt under the weight, despite Luna's lower gravity. "Because I'm not smelling you all night."

Rich had never quite experienced anything like dragging his friend through Project Lebensraum. The smell, the struggle, the anxiety at every closed door. Dr. Winn's dangerous interest in Don.

What will she say when this gets back to her?

Every corner, every camera, held the potential for report, and every report a chance that they might look closer at Rich, at those damned work logs that would show he didn't fix Thomas.

Rich's heart sank as Anastasia came around the corner. Thankfully, she was alone. She stopped at the sight of them.

"Oh, go on!" Don hissed. "We don't need you here."

"Shut up!" Rich snapped. Turning his attention to her, he unleashed his warmest Southern drawl, "Hiiii Anaastaaaasia! What brings Luna's only true flower to our dreary domain?"

She chuckled. "Wow, you need to work on your routine."

Her words might as well have been a pin; his ego, a balloon.

She smirked. "Do you need help?"

"We don't need nothing from *you*," Don snarled. "Thanks!"

"Don!—Sorry, my friend is riotously drunk and seems to have a bit of a bellyache. I'm taking him to get cleaned up."

"Looks like you've got your hands full there." Anastasia walked over and lifted Don's arm over her shoulders.

"Hey! You're going to…"

"A little shit never hurt anyone." She hoisted Don up. Don's face turned scarlet.

Don grumbled, "I'd prefer that you not help."

"Well, breathe cee-oh-two, spaceman. *Today Bob Almighty Americajin dis, nyet-da?*"

"Anni," Don hissed.

Her last sentence, it had an odd flow about it, even though Rich recognized a few of the words. Doubtless it was some language from the outer colonies. Rich's ears locked onto a word from her first one, 'spaceman.'

"You know of the spacemen?—Don's not one of those."

"We'll talk later. For now, let's get your work-brother to the shower." Anastasia nudged them both forward.

Work-brother? Another strange term…

Don's face was sour as old, vinegared wine.

He knows her. Is she Lily?—No, Lily works on the other side of the moon and has black hair. Unless it's a cover, but no, surely Dr. Winn would know about the two of them…

The two of them helped Don through the technician hall, the security wing, and the computer scientist dorm, stinking of shit and booze all the way. Time being the base's night cycle, the halls were mostly empty. Every now and then, the odd person peaked out of their room and gawked.

Would there be a report? Maybe—or perhaps they would just see two project members helping out a fellow worker who had overindulged.

The three of them reached the public bathroom. There was no door, just two tiled entrances leading to a wing for each sex. Rich stopped to let Anastasia stoop out from under Don, but she pressed forward inside the men's wing, twisting the drunkard between them.

"Hey!" Rich snapped.

She rankled her brow. "What?"

"That's men only."

She glanced at the sign, huffed. "Earthjin morality. I forget sometimes." She slipped from under Don's arm. His weight shifting to Rich, Don leaned his head on Rich's shoulder and began to snore while standing.

"You'd shower with us?"

"Why not?" She tilted her head to the side, her mouth tightening into a thin smirk. "Would I not be safe with you boys?"

"Boys?" Rich cocked an eyebrow. "Of course you'd be safe"

"Culture is a powerful thing, Rich." She winked both eyes

and bobbed her entire torso forward, like a nod of the head but from her waist.

What did that mean—that bob and wink? And where did she get my name? Rich glanced down at the patch on his work suit's left lapel. It had his last name only, 'Corrington.' She could have picked it up his first name the other day in Dr. Winn's office, but it felt odd. It had a casual tone to it.

"But you should know that not all cultures view nudity the same way. What use are clothes really, here in an environmentally controlled space? A simple pressure suit, nyet-da? That would be better."

"It would," Rich agreed, though he found the conversation's turn strange.

An amused smile touched her lips. "Besides, do you think I don't know already what you look like? All men naked are the same—a thin strip of flesh, infinitely smaller than their ego, drooping over a tender sack of pride. The better question is, why would I care?"

Crushed, Rich replied, "I concede your point."

"We should discuss culture sometime." She caressed his arm.

What's all that about? Rich shrugged. "Sure."

"It's a date." She laughed and clapped her hands.

Rich's heart danced even as his mind warned him: *Don't get too excited, you foolish old man. She's just being nice.*

"Well, get your work done, boys," she said, her voice in a singsong. "I've got plenty of my own." With that, she was off.

Rich glanced down the corridor. Empty. *But, of course, there's cameras, and they saw that… odd… exchange.* Hoisting Don up, he dragged him into the showers. His friend no longer felt heavy.

"Don, who was that? How did you know her?"

"I don't know nothing!"

"Don?"

"I don't know nothing about no Anastasia or spacemen or nothing."

Rich tensed, but didn't press further. It wasn't the place.

Rich changed Don's sheets and tucked him into bed. His chubby friend lay drooling on his fresh sheets, boxers halfway down his rump, face content as a freshly nursed babe.

"At least you're happy," Rich muttered.

How much pain must the man have been through? Don had never been so drunk. Love could be a blessing, and it could also be a boil.

"I hope it works out for you, Don."

His friend shuffled in his sleep, turning his face away from Rich to the wall.

If it did work out for Lily and Don, would they go to the great deep between worlds, where there was only vacuum and stars... Rich held his breath. *...without me?*

"Nah, who am I kidding?" Rich said, shaking his head. He slipped into his natural accent. "Things ain't gonna work out. You'll probably wind up on Luna somewhere, with an Earth-born wife who'll break your heart and leave you. And I'll..." Rich looked at the closet. "I'll be dead."

That's the natural end of this, after all. But at least I won't have to file any report with Dr. Winn. I was never going to betray Don!

Shaking his head, Rich turned, walked to the closet, and

opened the door. *Don't get all fatalistic now. I've got to have a little faith, faith that God really does favor the righteous—or what's the point of even praying?*

It was supposed to be Ketevan's shift, but Rich had taken it. The man had pulled so many shifts as of late. The same as Don, Ketevan was happily passed out in his quarters. Rich had checked. Marco and Julian were off base, probably at the auto-brothel. They both had tastes for exotic autobimps that could do things far beyond the scope of human physiology.

Rich began to dress, glancing at the prayer mat now tucked inside the closet. His kufi cap lay atop it, pinned between it and the wall.

He took out a straight, pressed pair of slacks and a shirt with thick gold buttons, both imam white. The shirt was well-starched and coarse against his skin. The slacks were a shimmering silk. Examining himself in the mirror, he turned side to side.

"Not perfect, but it'll do."

Smoothing his hair, straightening his shirt and pants, Rich muttered another prayer, and turned back to look at Don. "I have no idea what they'll do to me, my friend, but I'll make sure they know you had nothing to do with this. I was wrong before—you'll get that dream of yours, a woman on each arm and a truckload of kids, maybe off in some spaceman paradise with Lily." Rich's jaw shook. "It just won't include me."

On impulse, Rich walked over and stroked Don's stiff, red hair. Before he realized it, Rich's lips rested on a tuft of ginger just above his friend's left temple—just like he used to kiss his son, Jaimie.

Don purred.

"Well, I suppose it's alright between us," Rich said, shocked, wiping his lips on his sleeve. He turned and left.

It was out in the hall that Rich realized what exactly he was doing. This was the first time in his life that he had gone against the State. From cradle to where he now stood, every decision he had ever made fell within the iron will of the CPE.

It was out of fear and instinct that he hadn't wiped Thomas' mind, but what he did now was thought-out and determined, the product of his own will. It was his and his alone, perhaps the first decision in his life that was truly his, and whatever the consequences, he determined to love and cherish them.

But I need help, help I don't have. If only there was someone, someone who could help us reach the deep belt, the endless AU of empty space with so many pockets of life that the Party can never control. If only there was someone that had a means to get us there—

"Oof!" The voice was high-pitched and feminine.

Rich stumbled. Something had slammed into Rich's chest.

Anastasia?! Again?

She he crept back, clutching her tablet like it held her very soul. "I'm sorry. I guess we were both in our own little world…" Her eyes flicked up and down his body. "Uh—Are you going out? You're a little overdressed for work, nyet-da?"

Rich looked down. "Oh, yeah. You just startled me. Yes, I'm going out."

She nodded slowly. "*After* your shift?" She lowered her tablet. "You *are* on shift, right?" She winked. "Late though."

Rich nodded. "Yeah, after."

"Is Don alright?"

The question itself wasn't odd, but her tone—it was familiar, like she spoke about an old friend. It was as oddly familiar as Don's had been earlier.

Rich smiled, knowing how goofy it made him look. It was his lot when talking to beautiful young women, especially after being single for years. "Uh, sleeping it off. Ya know, Don's a big sleeper."

"Sleeping is good." A half-smile cracked at her lip. "Don't talk to girls much?"

Rich felt his jaw hang slack. "That's very personal."

"I've heard the stories."

Stories?! "Y-you have?"

"I talk to Marco sometimes."

Oh really?! I bet she does!

Marco's hair was wavy, raven black, shiny, and despite the lower gravity, he was built like a UN Longbow—the sleek, iconic destroyer of the modern Earth navy and workhorse of the fleet.

"So you know." Rich cut his eyes down to the floor, turned his head away. "About…"

Her hand wound into his. "It's not easy to lose a child, harder than a mother or sister. Especially if you…" She searched for words. "… feel responsible."

So she knows.

Pain flickered behind her eyes. Was she a soul hiding just as much grief as his own? Gently, he squeezed her hand in return. She smiled, then took a step back, pulling away her hand. Rich pocketed his own right hand and gently rubbed his fingers, savoring the fleeting warmth of her touch.

"Well, um. That got very personal." She laughed.

"It did."

She cleared her throat, turned, and trotted down the hall opposite of the way she'd come, golden hair fluttering behind. Rich watched her go, gave his eyes free rein to scan every inch of her, then scolded himself.

You old, dead man! What notions are you getting in your head? Just because she lost a kid too doesn't mean she'd go hab-rocking with you. She's probably running as far away as she can, you old pervert.

Rich forced the thoughts away, remembering the reason for his clothes. He looked at the small, plain office door. In he went, but he wouldn't be inside long.

Rich signed in, acknowledged his watch, and made sure everyone was home. It was the middle of the night, Luna local time. The Wells slumbered in their electric dreams.

With a deep sigh, Rich prepared himself. Studying the Wells, he looked for a reason to enter. He needed something legitimate, even if borderline. God provided. Agitated, rhythmic movements began in Thomas. It could have been a nightmare; it could have been a malfunction.

It didn't matter.

Rich opened a ticket for a low level incidence, noting Thomas appeared to be experiencing involuntary oscillations of his limbs. He played it up, making it sound far more severe than it was. No one logged in for low-level incidences and routine maintenance, but if they did, they would see Thomas tossing like a Mexican jumping bean at the appropriate time stamp. Whether it really seemed to be a mechanical issue and not just bad dreams—well, Rich was pretty sure the kid was having a nightmare.

Rising from the desk, Rich made his way to the airlock. It was empty the whole way, except for a guard roving the hall, who thought nothing of it as Rich entered. He even made double rabbit ears with his fingers, shaking them, to complement Rich on his outfit. Rich returned the gesture one handed, clutching his tablet in the other.

Inside the airlock, Rich put the Wells in maintenance mode. Doc Hartford's words rumbling, Rich opened the secret door into the Wells' home and made his way down the hall. Claire had been laid to sleep in her room. Mama and Papa Wells were snuggled up like young lovers in their own bed.

As he approached Thomas' door, Rich prepared himself for what lay behind—Thomas, still as death, not breathing, like Jaimie when he died. Rich opened the door and walked inside. There was his boy, dead again.

Rich exhaled slowly.

This was it, the first time in Rich's life when he had done something against the State—something sure to get him shot. He wet his lips, fidgeted, and flipped on the light, shouting, "Thomas—dicete!"

Rich spoke the word of faith and beheld a miracle. The breath of life returned to his boy, Jaimie—*Thomas!* Thomas's chest heaved as he resumed tossing in his sleep.

"Thomas."

Thomas stopped fidgeting, his chest rose and paused, holding his breath in terror.

"Thomas!"

Thomas' eyes popped open, full of fear, but softened as they recognized Rich. He sat up. "Angel?"

Rich rushed him, wrapping the boy in his arms, feeling his warmth, fighting back tears.

"A-angel?" the boy said again.

"Yes! Oh yes, sweet little one!" Rich kissed the top of his head, swaying with him.

"I didn't know I could hug angels."

Quickly, Rich got control of himself, slipped into character. "You hug angels more often than you know. You bump into us at the grocery store, smile at us on the metro."

A smile crept across Thomas' lips.

"Oh boy, a real, genuine angel. Angel, please, let's go wake my parents. They don't believe me, so I've…"

Rich held up his right hand, and Thomas fell silent. "That's why I'm here?"

A puzzled look passed over Thomas' face.

"Thomas, most people don't believe—can't believe—in angels. You're giving them more than they can handle."

"I—I am?"

"Uh-huh," Rich nodded. "Pearls before swine, all that."

Thomas looked at him again with curiosity.

"It's scripture."

"Oh… We don't read much of that." He looked down. "My dad goes to mosque all the time, especially Friday, but he told me what I said was hogwash. I always thought angels were real. My mom says they are. That's why I wanted to show you to them."

"They have to believe first, and even then, most people aren't granted to see us."

"So, that's the only reason you're here? To tell me to stop talking about you?"

Rich nodded.

Tears welled in the boy's eyes as he buried his face in his hands.

"Hey, what's wrong little guy?"

"My… sister."

Rich's throat tightened. Tears threatened at the edges of his eyes. "Some things," Rich began, thinking of his own Jaimie. "Some things are just ordained."

Tears ran down the boy's cheeks. "Please, angel. I know, I know I don't know how to pray good. I know I get mad and yell at my dad, but I've prayed that God would—well, if he let me see you, if he showed me angels are real—well, if angels exist, then miracles should too, right? I just, I don't want anything for myself. I just want my sister to, to, to really be alive."

A tear streaked down Rich's cheek, warm as life itself.

Thomas reached up, caught the tear on his finger, and drew it back in wonder. "Angel, you're crying! I didn't know angels cried."

Rich choked. "More often than you know."

The boy stared at him, so much, so so much rolled behind those eyes wet with android's tears—wonder, fear, sorrow.

Rich took Thomas' hands, forced the biggest grin he could muster. "Tell you what," Rich said, and cursed himself for it. "I'll talk to God about it, about your sister and about showing me to your parents."

Open-mouthed, Thomas gawked upwards at him, pulling away one hand to wipe away his own tears. "Really?"

Rich grinned. "Uh-uh."

Thomas nodded slowly, then fell forward, throwing his arms around Rich's neck. Jaimie hugged him again, just as he had on the day they got the little yellow house outside Smoke Flax, Mississippi. Rich savored it, adored it, until he remembered that someone could log in any moment and see this very situation.

But even if they did, I would die gladly for this moment. A lifetime—a lifetime is worth this one second.

Pulling away from him, Rich rose and walked to the door.

Thomas looked up at him with awe. "Are you going to disappear? Will there be a flash of light?"

Rich smiled. Spreading wide his arms, he said, "In the Name of God, the Gracious, the Merciful… Tacete."

Thomas' face froze in awe, timeless and immutable as the glory of Allah. Rich called his name, but the boy didn't answer. Rich crab-stepped sideways. Thomas' eyes remained fixed where he had been, fixed on where he last saw 'the angel.' Rich snapped his fingers and waved his hands in front of Thomas.

Nothing.

Rich kissed the boy's forehead and hugged him gently, feeling the warm flesh one last time, the gentle tufts of his hair. He shook as he began to weep. Standing, he placed his hands on Thomas' shoulders and prayed. "May Allah favor you. May there really be a heaven somewhere among all the many stars above, and may we meet there again, going in before Jesus and Muhammad and the Bodhisattva, even before Daniel Christofferson himself…"

Rich's voice cracked as he fought tears… "and the Buddha, and the angels, and all the righteous djinn and the little shaitans who've repented, and the righteous elect of the Americans who turned from sin at the word of Daniel Christofferson, who suffered the Great Tribulation under many cruel American emperors."

Rich turned, sobbing uncontrollably. He left the light on— a little detail for when Thomas revived. *The boy will know it was real, know it wasn't a dream! He will remember me as Jaimie cannot!*

Moving down the hall, he peaked in on Mr. and Mrs. Wells. They lay spooning, Papa Wells holding his wife's lithe form against his great paunch like a kid his teddy bear. He peaked in on Claire to find her lying in her bed, staring straight up at nothing, even her eyes open.

'I just want my sister to, to, to really be alive,' Thomas repeated in Rich's head.

It could be done. It'd just be a software change. Her limbs only look atrophied—they have the same ratings as all the other units. That little thing could pick me up and break me in half!

But I don't code; I don't know their language—Damnit, Rich, if you do get out of this, that is the LAST thing you need to do.—But 'I'll talk to God about it.' How do I keep getting myself into this?

"I'm an angel…" Rich answered himself in disgust.

The feeling cleared as Rich clamored out of the Wells' home through the secret airlock. He had saved Thomas' and his entire family's lives, at least for the moment. Thomas would *never* tell anyone, because the 'angel' had warned him to keep it secret—unless he didn't…

But that's something I can't control. I didn't download a bunch of garbage into his brain, and I've done all I can to save his life. That's enough, whatever happens.

Rich slowed as he rounded the corner to the on duty office. The hallway was empty. He opened the door. Anastasia and Don stared at him.

His blood chilled.

Cradling his head, Don demanded soberly, "What the hell are you doing? Are you trying to get yourself shot?!"

Anastasia's eyes were red and tear-stained. She wiped

away the moisture as she cleared a golden bang from her face. Sniffling, she said, "That—that was beautiful, I—I had known, seen some things, but…" and her voice trembled. "…do you realize what you just risked? Did you even consider it?"

The intervening moments each held a universe of time in them. Don's eyes cut to Anastasia to Rich. Just as Don started to speak, Anastasia lifted her tablet.

"Anni, don't!" Don's hand shot to the tablet, seized it.

She wrenched it from his grip and brought an elbow across his temple and brow. Don crumpled to the ground.

"I'm saving all our lives!" Furiously, her fingers rapped against the pad.

"Y-you are?" Rich asked in disbelief.

"Shut up." After a moment, she released a deep breath. "No one else has monitored the network. Looks like they left monitoring the repairs to me. Fools!" She smiled. "I've locked them out. I've got hundreds of hours of footage for just a time like this…" She tapped the tablet a few more times. "Program running."

"Y-you're helping us?" Rich stammered.

"I've been helping you! I still need to do some work on the video feed and logs, but we should be dandy. Got a few unregistered programs too I can use, but I can't run them from here."

Don rose from the ground and seized her arm.

"Ow, Don! Let me go or I'll snap your arm in three places and mount your testicles on a plaque—or worse, I'll tell Lily."

Don released her, stepping back, his face twisted and red with rage, nostrils flaring.

"There's… a lot going on here," Rich observed.

Anastasia glared at Don. "I will be back, I promise."

"You're going to sell us out," Don accused. "Nothing you —either of you—do is upfront. Nothing. Not one…"

She stepped forward, gently placed her finger over his lips. Don trembled with rage, balling his hands into fists. It was in that moment Rich realized just how much of Don's rotund form was muscle and not fat.

"We will discuss the other things later," she said.

Don seized her, taking her forearms in his hands and shaking her. "You aren't going anywhere! You'll do whatever you have to do to fix this from here."

"I *can't*. I need the tools in my office!"

"And what if you sell us out?" he hissed, shaking her again like a rag doll. "I've had enough of your games. I'm not letting you hurt Rich. I don't trust you, you lying, filthy, deceiving…"

Rich placed his hand on Don's back. "Easy there, big guy."

"Don't, Rich! You have no idea who she is."

"Don, hurting her won't help us anyway this goes."

Don glared at Rich, his green eyes glowing with rage hot as a fission. He released her. Stepping back, she rubbed her arms, Don's red fingerprints bright against her pale skin.

"Look, spaceman," she said, "to put all your fears at rest, there's only two ways this goes. Either I fix this shit and we all get off, or I don't fix shit, and Rich gets shot. Maybe Don for being his roommate. Maybe me for *letting* it happen. I saw the whole thing and did nothing. I'm responsible too."

"Why?" Rich demanded. Don crossed his arms.

"Because I want to save the Subjects. I knew you didn't wipe Thomas. I monitor everything closer than Don does the brothels. I've read your file. I figured you had some hair-brained scheme to fix everything. But you're not going a step farther without inside help. Without *my* help."

"And why are you willing to risk that?"

"Listen," she hissed. "Every second you tie me up with kikipa is a second we could be discovered. Now let me fix it. We all die if I don't."

The strange word affected Rich more than anything else, oddly. "Ok."

"Rich!" Don demanded.

Rich turned on him. "She's right. What happens if she doesn't help us?"

Pulling down her sleeves to cover the marks on her arm, she left. As the door shut behind her, Don collapsed back into his chair, his face in his hands.

"You want to tell me what that was about?" Rich demanded. "What the thing at the shower was about?"

Don shook his head. "Haramity. Just pure and simple haramity."

Rich looked around. The walls that seemed to be closing in on them.

"I'm single again. I guess you figured that out already."

"That was easy to guess, but what does that pretty little blond thing you just assaulted have to do with it? I take it she's Lily's 'friend?'"

Don eyed him carefully. "What do you say we get out of here, go get a drink? Maybe something to eat?"

"Don, that sounds like the most bonkers, terrible idea."

"After shift," he added. "If our backs aren't up against the wall in front of a firing squad."

Rich sighed. "Sure, why the hell not? If they're going to

shoot us, might as well go make them find us." He laughed, and the true humor in it astonished him.

Besides, a drink will settle both our nerves.

Rich remembered Don's newfound fascination with real food, added, "As long as it's not real meat."

"One more thing," Don said. "And I hate to bring it up. Your thing is your thing. We joke about it a lot for two, red-blooded CAU males, but did you… kiss me… earlier?"

Rich turned away, feeling the heat growing in his face. "Nah. You were dreaming."

By the time their second shift ended, fifteen hours later, when Marco and Julian came in and took over, their nerves had settled. Whatever would happen would not happen today, or at least not right now. Rich was going on twenty-four hours without sleep, but laughing arm in arm, the two friends went out into the Lunar night.

7

---

*There is no sweeter lover than a spaceman, and none more
hateful when spited. Would that I made a husbra of my
dearest years ago, instead of a competitor. It is inevitable—
one day our laser and steel must meet, and my heart will
break, whoever survives.*

-*Family Life in Deep Space*
By Alph Al-Aziz

The Lunar sky was beautiful. Stars—so many as to be
uncountable—twinkled above the hexagonal pattern of Dome
1, New San Francisco. The food, unfortunately, was not so
mesmerizing. The meat was real.

"I'm sorry, monsieur," the waiter said. "We do not proffer
anything synthetic at La Viande est Vraie. It's in the name."

"I don't speak Italian," Rich said, glancing at the night sky above with all its wonders. Like many buildings in Luna, the restaurant had no roof. Walls merely demarcated one space from another.

How often have I been out here, and didn't stop to enjoy its wonders?

The waiter, visibly shaken, nodded and answered, "Of course, *monsieur.* In the common tongue, then, what would you like?"

"Get the steak, Rich." Don grinned. "Trust me."

"Fine... you chunky cannibal." Rich's stomach churned. "The steak."

"Oui bien sûr."

Proud of himself, Don teetered side to side, lolling around on his rump.

"Don't get any ideas. I don't get this carnivorous predilection you've taken to, anymore than I get Congregation Christians and their ritual cannibalism. It's beautiful—don't get me wrong—but makes no damn sense."

A confused look settled over Don's face. "What?"

"Communion. The wine that is blood. Or sometime's it's grape juice that's blood."

Don scrunched his face. Raised Congregation Muslim like Rich, he would have been taught the tenants of the One Faith's other streams in the Peace classes of his youth, even if he didn't remember.

"I don't really get their idea of communion," Rich said, "even after imam training. But somehow, by consuming whatever's in that cup, Christians foster some deeper connection to God and man. The drink is the blood of Christ, but also the blood of Christofferson and the blood of all mankind."

"You really take this religion thing seriously."

Rich stroked his chin's bare skin. "Used to. I was almost an imam, you know. Had to be fluent in the rites of every Congregation stream. Even grew a nice, thick beard out of *taq'wa* too—that's piety in case you've forgotten, you little heathen. Went all the way down to here." Rich pointed to the spot just above his naval, where he had grown the beard in the fiery days of his youth—before Persephone had made him shave it.

"I remember." Don scowled, and an ugly looked passed over Don's face. "It's bullshit. That's what it is. It's all bull-shit." There wasn't a slur in Don's voice yet, but he was on his fifth glass of wine and feeling bold.

"Tell you what, let's not discuss religion. I want to have a good night out."

"Oh yeah, Mr. Kufi cap and prayer mat and the whole alladamn thing earlier." Don slung his wine glass side to side as he ranted, sloshing the ruddy dark liquid across the dull, cream carpet. In Lunar gravity, the wine almost splattered the table next to them, drawing looks sharp as daggers.

Rich sighed, determining to avoid anything that might set Don off. If he had guessed, Don's behavior was the man facing mortality on his own terms. Don was the type of man that, if he knew he was going to die, would stack dynamite up and smoke a cigar atop it. Blasphemy was just a version of that.

But for Rich, if there was even the possibility of dying, he preferred not to piss off the divine. Why miss Janna? If

Armageddon was tomorrow, why not meet it bright-eyed and clear-conscienced.

Dying as I lived, he thought bitterly. *Then again, I'm drinking real alcohol and eating real meat—both forbidden by Christofferson—so maybe I'm building up my own pile of dynamite.*

The steak arrived smelling scrumptious. Part of him wanted to tear into it like a wild animal; the other part was horrified, thinking of some poor little cow, happy in a sunny field somewhere, led away to be butchered—all for him.

Beside the steak was a pile of vegetables—pure for consumption, along with fungi or even the occasional insect. Rich skewered a mix of broccoli and carrots with his fork and shoved them in his mouth. Chewing, he split open his steaming potato, trying to ignore the steak and all its implications.

"Veggies taste better than the slop they give us at the base," Rich said. "Needs some crickets, though."

"Buddy, the dead cow." Don pointed at the steak with his knife, shoveling a portion of his own into his mouth.

"Did you have to put it that way?" He had just been getting up the courage to eat the steak.

"Come on. Don't be a pussy."

"You know," Rich said, "from my time as a married man, I would have never thought a pussy weak." Rich winked.

Don cackled, the outburst completely out of place in the austere restaurant.

So I'm feeling the wine too.

A busboy arrived, knelt down, and began scrubbing the blood-colored stains.

"Come on, just try it," Don coached. "I'll eat the rest if you don't like it."

"So that's why you never lost your Earther fat."

"Hey, I don't buy you dinner and you insult me."

"Buy me dinner with *my* money."

Don flexed his arm, shaking his fist. "Our money, comrade."

Picking up his knife, Rich split open the seared meat. The center was soft and pink, and ruddy juice pooled beneath the cut. His stomach churned even as his nostrils danced. He had seen artificial heme before, but this was the real flesh of a living thing.

"It's just meat juice," Don said.

Rich skewered a piece and paused with the chunk of meat right outside his mouth, thinking again about the animal who had died. He gave thanks both to the animal and God before consuming it.

He shivered.

It was nothing like synthetic meat. The taste invaded every nerve in his mouth. He shut his eyes, letting the taste roll through his entire being.

"And?" Don demanded.

"Call me a cannibal. I swear, Don, you're the first man to ever give me an orgasm."

Don looked like a child who'd gotten away with something scot-free, crossing his arms and smirking.

"So this is real meat?"

"I will square with you. There's synth meat out here that tastes just as good, if not better, but I thought you ought to try the real thing at least once in your life."

"At least once before we die."

Don frowned.

Rich leaned back, admitting to himself that he could get to

like real meat, despite dogma and conscience. "So why does the Party feed us the shit they do?"

"You know Earth cuts corners everywhere she can."

Rich glanced around.

Don shook his head. "You don't have to do that here."

"Do what?" Judging by Don's look, Rich should have known what he meant. "Really, I don't know what you mean—"

"There's a saying out here," Don began. "Earthers in their burrow; all diggers in the other."

Diggers—that was some type of Luna political office. But it could also be used for tunnelers, or even Loonies themselves. Whatever the exact meaning, it was dangerous. "Whoever's saying that is setting you up to be killed. The Party has ears everywhere."

"I don't believe that, not anymore. There's a whole world out here, Rich, one that the Party barely controls. Colonials, spacemen… they mostly pay their taxes and ignore the Party, and for that the Party ignores them."

"Why?"

"Because Earth is rotting," came an answer in a Lunar French accent. Rich looked over his shoulder to see his waiter. "There will be an extra charge of one hundred and fifty UN for the wine stain... And yes, nothing you say here is recorded. We sweep the restaurant for listening devices daily, and there is no sysnet connection here. If there's a listening device, someone else brings it. Not much we can do about that, but if we discover anyone recording anything, they are banned for life."

Rich studied the man, the haughty attitude, the upraised

nose, the pressed, clean uniform that reeked pride in his profession.

"I take it this is your first time away from some kind of Earth Party work?" the man said.

Rich nodded. "In a while at least."

"Then I leave you with this thought, Earther, from the history they no longer teach you about your own world. Once a tyrant convinced an entire nation that the world was starving, while only they had food. And do you know the strangest part?"

Rich shook his head.

"The people he convinced were themselves starving." The man gestured to a terminal on the table. "The lesson is free, but your *grossier* attitude has ruined dinner for our guests. I ask you to pay, tip well, and do not come back."

"Can I at least finish my…"

"No." The waiter left.

Rich supposed he could shovel it down anyway, unless they threw him out. After all, an animal had given its life for this. He took a bite as Don looked down, red-faced.

"Hey Rich?"

"Yeah."

"Think you could get this? There was something else I wanted to do, but I'm going to run short if I have to pay a hundred and fifty extra plus tip."

"Why, Don, you take me out for dinner and I have to pay?"

Don frowned and looked away, patting his pants.

"Damn, you're easy to get to, son. But that settles it." Rich slammed his hand down flat on the table. "I'm pitching, you're catching."

"About that…"

"Don, I wasn't serious."

A wicked smile crossed Don's slips.

The Harsh Mistress was a few blocks down, in the most elegant red-light district Rich had ever seen. Houses of ill repute nestled between more acceptable forms of entertainment—a live theater that only showed 20th century cinema, allegedly uncensored; a shop that sold vanity spacesuits; and small street diners that specialized in bread, soups, or gourmet truffles, 'space sourced.'

The architecture was a hodgepodge of eras, ranging from trans-modernist late-American to Art Deco Spatio, a movement during the early days of colonization. The occasional moon car sat charging between narrow streets. When driven, they were all piloted by an AI that required more permits than Rich could count.

"Don, what are we doing here?" Rich asked, surveying the cathouse.

"Last night alive. Figured we'd have some fun."

"No." Rich shook his head. "I'm not doing it, Don." So many feelings, so many hard, broken places within ground against his very soul. *To know a woman's touch, a real woman's touch…* His flesh pimpled; an electric wave of titillation glided through his flesh.

"Oh, come on, Rich. A wall of marines might come snatch us off the street any minute. Don't you want to clean your pipes out at least once after—how long has it been?"

"I do fine 'cleaning my pipes' by myself, and how long it's

been since someone helped is my damn business. What about your girlfriend, Lily?"

"I told you, we're through."

"Well, what about that other woman, Anastasia? She seemed like she had something for you?"

"She was a mistake. One I'm not repeating."

"Damn, you do get around." Rich shook his head, hormones and jealousy tangoing in his brain. "One of the head computer scientists and the rest of the base isn't talking about it? Does the base have windows to climb through that I don't know about?"

Don rolled his eyes, grabbed Rich's wrist, and dragged him inside.

"Why am I friends with you again?" Rich asked.

"Because with me, life is never boring."

Inside, the foyer was gently lit. A warm glow bounced off walls yellowed with age whose paint furled upwards in dessicate strips. It gave the place an elegant feel, not dingy, like standing in an old opera house. Then Rich realized that's precisely what it was, or at least seemed to be.

Various women in burlesque stopped talking, watching them as they entered. An older woman gestured to the console in front of them. "You know the drill, monsieur," she said, winking at Don. "But it's been a while. I thought we'd lost your business."

"I don't really come here that often," Don said, blushing, returning the woman's wink. From her age, clothing, and stature, she had to be the madame.

"Don, are we really doing this?"

"I said I had a surprise for you."

"Come on, Don…" Rich said, tugging at Don's shoulder.

"Oh, lookie here. New girl. Rich, my treat." A slip printed out as Don paid. He offered it to Rich. "Room four."

"It's my money anyway—and I am *not* doing this."

"Look, you can do what you want. Wait on the sidewalk for all I care, but I booked her for the next hour." Don turned back to the terminal and began making his own selection.

Rich walked outside through the heavy doors, shaking his head. Even as he did, the ticket scorched his hand.

How many years has it been since an actual person? I can't remember—

Rich fingered the ticket subconsciously, then lifted it up for study. His purchase for the evening was on it, her face vivified by a printed screen molecules thick. She winked.

An AJ-Viviprint, probably a 04e model, judging by the clarity. That isn't cheap.

Back on Earth, Rich had worked on a similar machine for a sports arena. Of course, the events were cheap for the locals under Party rule, but they still used paper that cost thirty times as much as regular.

Rich crossed his arms and leaned back against the building. He looked up at the endless stars, the endless worlds and possibilities, brighter and more beautiful than he had ever known. All of it was framed behind glass rated to stop micrometeorites, between ultra-strong braces forming the dome's structure.

It was like, like that dome job on High Beijing… Short on workers and in some dispute with local labor, he'd gotten a crash course on dome repair as the Party put him to work with a veteran team.

In a flash, it occurred to Rich why he was thinking of the dome. It was the last time he had been intimate with another human being—twelve years ago. The only other person besides Persephone. Ever.

Her name had been Zima, a local girl that catered to the men. A Party comfort woman. They hadn't truly dated since all their encounters had been on the dime of the State, but they had spent a lot of time together.

And she was special, despite her profession… But still, she wasn't my ex-wife… To even think about Persephone was pain, awakening something in him more bitter than all other sorrows imaginable, except Jaimie. The rattle of the heavy door opening saved him from the fresh up-welling of grief.

"Mind if I smoke with you, since you're not interested." Her accent had a vague something underlying it, something similar to Anastasia's odd accent.

Off world?

Rich turned to see the woman on the ticket staring back at him—fair and lithe, sleek black hair draped around her shoulders. The silver gown she wore shimmered, light dancing up and down individual threads. Her ancestry seemed a mix of European and Asian, with perhaps a few others thrown in for good measure.

"Not at all. If you're trying to talk me into coming back there with you…"

She cackled. "Why would I do that? I get paid either way. It's your scrip, spaceman."

Rich started to protest, but stopped, intrigued by the word, 'spaceman.' "Can't argue there."

Her eyebrows perked. "So you are spaceman? The girls said as much about the other man. Let me guess, you are the good husband and he is the bad husband?"

"You think we're together?" *What an odd thing to assume.*

"You two are obvious husbrothers. Not sure if actually kin or no. And every family has the good papa and the naughty papa, the one who can't plant soy in his own bay."

Rich's hand went to his neck. *Surely she can see…* His pin was missing. He had forgotten. Don insisted they leave them behind. "Yes, exactly," Rich answered and smiled, guessing that he would qualify as the 'good papa' between the two of them.

"Ah! I was right. It's adorable, really. You two have such a married look about you. So you are the good papa trying to keep the little junior papa in line, but he's managed to drag you out to the kitty cats and now you don't want to play? Regret? Not your thing?"

"You guessed it. Just rub salt in the wound, eh?"

"I *knew* it. I'm good, nyet-dah? So he likes to play and you like to… let him?" She added more slyly, "Watch? But he has decided to be alone, hai?"

"Dah," Rich shook his head. "Whatever makes him happy." He grinned, surprising himself at the pleasure he found spinning her along.

"Your wives are lucky. You two have a ship? I can charter it?"

"W-wives?" Rich stammered. *Two men and two wives? All married? Well, colonials are often polyamorous. Maybe it's what that Wang fellow would call 'a spaceman thing.'*

Her eyebrows perked. "So, you have a bachelor ship then? Just two men? Maybe *more* men? Ah, I know, he likes the woman too, but you only like the men, and he's trying to *enlarge* your horizons?"

"No, no…" Rich shook his head. "I like women. We just don't have—" Rich stopped himself, sweeping his eyes up and down the woman. He winced as he admitted. "Honestly, I just don't like whores."

Her face twisted for just a moment, then relaxed. "You know, I guess I am nowadays." She laughed. "So you have a ship? I can charter it? I will work."

"And what type of work would you do?" By the look on her face, Rich knew the answer. "Where would you go?"

"To Neptune! The stink of Earth is too strong here, too strong anywhere but there. There I can be with only spaceman, in the only system that is run by spaceman. I can go as comfort woman. We are always in demand, even with polyamory. Lots of cheaters, lots of singles, despite polyamory. Always single people everywhere no family has picked up yet. Usually crips or dumkins or zhopy who can't keep any group. Where there is demand, I will be supply."

She placed her hands on her hips and smiled proudly. "And if some asshole there calls me a whore, I'll just hit them with 'no service, ka-ching, ka-ciao,' and with few free women, they'll be sorry." She glared at Rich.

"I'm sorry. You aren't a whore, well…" Rich cringed. "I mean…"

She nodded, giggling. "Apology accepted, spaceman. I guess I shouldn't be so sensitive. It won't be last time."

As Rich was about to widen his net of lies, he saw a form charging from down the street: a short, black-headed woman in cargo overalls. Grease smudged her face and her hair. She was thick in build, almost brawny, but also oddly petite-looking, her face smooth as a China doll's.

"Ma'am," said the woman to whom Rich was talking. "You can't come in here like that. There's a public wash a few levels…"

"Out of my way, whore!" The new woman grabbed Rich's purchase for the hour by the hair and flung her towards the street. The prostitute screamed, slamming onto the greygoo sidewalk, skull inches from a moon car's bumper. She groaned.

The door shut. Rich turned to see that the angry woman had gone inside. He looked back to his 'date.' "Are you okay?"

She got up. "Yes. Who the hell was that? I'll show her to toss around Ivanka Gretel Gootberg!" Rising, Ivanka stormed up the steps, a grand bruise blossoming beneath her stocking.

Rich followed the woman inside, hearing the other woman rant and rail. Muffled on the way up, her words became intelligible as he slid the great doors open: "Where's my husband?! I know he's here! Where is he?! I saw that worthless air sucker heading this way while I was having a pint at Sunny's!"

Rich vaguely remembered the bar. It had been a rougher looking establishment along the way.

"Ma'am," the madame answered. "If your husband is here, that is a matter you should take up at home. Please do not make me call the police." The madame snapped her fingers and pointed towards a cocoa dispenser in the corner.

The woman stood there, fuming. "I don't want booze-chocolate. I want my husband. Don Singh! Where the hell are you? Someone better tell me where that worthless tentbucker is, or Allah Almighty help me!" the woman lifted her right hand towards heaven.

Rich stood in shock. *Don Singh? My Don Singh?*

"E-e-excuse me," Rich stammered.

"You!" she said, turning towards him, nostrils flaring.

"You brought him here! You must be Rich, the nice guy from work. Well, you aren't such a nice guy." Tears streamed down her flushed cheeks.

"I didn't bring him here."

"So, you two *do* have a wife!" Ivanka said with a smirk. "I knew it. But I don't think I want to charter your ship any longer."

The angry woman glanced from Ivanka to Rich and then turned back down the hall. "Don!"

"Ma'am," the madame said. "Leave or I'll call the police."

"I'll vent you all to space. You have *no idea* who I am." The black-haired woman looked at the console. "This has a DNA scanner, correct?"

The madame nodded.

The angry woman rubbed her left hand over her right, then slipped something off the skin. It was a glove-like thing, translucent and thinner than tissue paper. Rich had heard of such things, especially if she did what he next expected.

She did. Tapping the scanner, she put it in ID mode. Moments later, her name appeared at the top: 'Lily Joan Pretorious,' with a family plot appearing beneath it.

Lily!

What appeared on the screen wasn't truly a family tree, but a family shrub, with twelve parents side by side while thin blue lines led from two of them to her name in large print. Beneath the rest, an unfathomable tapestry of black, small lines connected the parents with a horde of names beneath, so many it ran off page.

The madame tapped her screen, and her eyes went wide. "You are the daughter of…"

Lily nodded, eyes wild, jaw set in fury. "I will kill all of you, if you don't tell me where he is—or if you breathe a word of me to anyone."

Pale and horrified, the madame nodded. "*Merde.* He's in room four, second door on the left down that hall." She pointed, then straightened herself, summoning a likeness of courage. "But he's already paid. Absolutely no refunds."

"Keep your goddamn money." Lily stormed off towards where the woman pointed.

"And I'll scrub the log. None of us will say a word."

Rich followed, worried about where this was headed. "Hey, calm down!"

She spun and growled at him, baring her teeth like a rabid dog. "I will blast your guts out with a bolt-drill!"

Rich stepped back.

"Don Singh!" she shouted, turning once more towards the hall.

Rich followed. He could hear the music and groans long before they reached the door. It was loud and rhythmic, a descant of primal wailing above strange instruments and a techno beat. What were the voices on the track, and what were Don and the other woman, was anyone's guess.

"I wouldn't," Rich shouted as Lily reached the door.

She seized the old-fashioned doorknob. Locked. Frustrated, she growled and squared up into a fighting stance. With a roar, she slammed her foot against the door. It flew inward off its hinges, sliding until it hit the bed. The force sent her backwards towards the wall, but with a dancer's grace, she threw back her other leg, rebounded, and glided gently to the floor. Rich's jaw dropped. She looked like she weighed 90 kilograms wet in Earth gravity.

Her body shivered; her eyes glared with fury. Following

her line of sight, Rich saw the worst thing imaginable under the circumstances.

In the awkward moments that followed, Don fished for his underwear while his sex worker reposed on the bed. "Family squabbles cost extra," she said, as Don pulled on his drawers. "See article ten, subparagraph c of contract."

Don nodded, keeping his eyes on the floor as he sat humiliated on the bed's corner. Lily stood silent, lips quivering. Suddenly, she charged.

Seizing Don by his shoulders, she sent him sailing across the carpet. His head slammed into the wall. She followed, pushing off the bed, gliding in the low Lunar gravity. Landing atop him, she pummeled the back of his head, tore at his hair. "Baka cosmoboy! Watashiwa doraski!" Tears streamed down her face.

Don covered his head, shielding himself from her blows.

"Lily, we're not a couple!"

"We *are* a couple! We're shipmates now! You knew what it meant! You knew!"

Shipmates?

Don rolled over beneath her, almost tossing her off. He seized her wrists as she attacked again.

"Not here," Don hissed. His face was redder and wilder than his hair, carpet-burns plain upon his skin. His green eyes burned with something—Fear, rage, lust? Despite the fury of the moment, Don held back his strength, grasping her firmly but gently, even as she tried to tear him apart. "Not here," he repeated, louder this time.

Lily rose from his chest. He released her. Stepping to the side, she glowered over him. Pointing to the prostitute, she snapped, "Outside!" The woman bolted, half-clothed. Lily turned to Rich. "Get lost."

"He's my friend."

"Not tonight, he's not."

She reared her hand back and prepared to strike down at Don's face. As she brought her fist down, Don caught it. She jumped on his stomach, causing him to grunt, and tried to strike with her other hand. He caught that one too. He rose up effortlessly, toppling her off of him, rolling over her and pressing her beneath him, still holding her arms.

"Lily, stop. I'm stronger and denser than you by several times. If you keep hitting me, I will hurt you, intentionally or not." He released her again and stood, running his hands through his hair.

Don's body was no mystery to Rich. They lived together and Don slept naked. They were far past modesty. But he had never seen Don strut around in his underwear quite as he had then—red-faced and red-bodied, tumescent beneath his shorts, muscles pulsing beneath folds of soft fat. Arms bowed out, Don ran his hands through the hair of his head and chest, trying to calm himself.

An odd look swept across Lily's face as she panted, staring at him.

"Go, Rich, please," Don said.

"Don?"

"Go. I'm sorry our night was ruined. We'll talk later. I have to take care of something."

Rich wasn't sure what exactly he meant, judging by the mixed emotions dancing across both their faces. However, none of it involved him.

He left.

"Sir," the madame said, catching him on the way out. "You've done nothing wrong. I will grant *you* a full refund."

"It was his scrip," Rich lied, nodding his head back towards them.

"I know…" she sighed. "How about house credit, then? I'll remember you. Just come back, and you and Ivanka—or any other person you want—can have a pleasant evening together." To make her point, she nodded at a young, brown-skinned fellow in the corner. As if on cue, he stuck a lollipop in his mouth. "We also have a wide selection of autobimps."

Ivanka stood by the door, arms crossed, a frightened look on her face. There was a tenderness and pleasantness about her, and Rich felt something primal and ancient hovering in the air above them all now.

"I'm not that kind of guy," he said, pushing away the temptation. "And I'm not saying I want a man, either." He stepped forward, took Ivanka's hands in his own, and leaned in. She leaned towards him, but he slipped his head around hers and pecked her on the cheek. "In another life, perhaps, if the Mahdi wills."

Then he was through the doors out into the night, the zipper of his pants uncomfortable. The tension was almost pleasant. His skin goose-pimpled beneath the moist chill of the recycled air.

Away from the bar, he found himself walking towards a place he knew, the only place he had gone these last few years when his blood was up. Its name was blasphemous, so blasphemous he didn't understand why the Party left it open: "The Eurekatron," an auto-brothel a few districts over under the same dome.

As he walked in, an animatronic butler greeted him. It

called him by name, though it had been at least a year. "Welcome back, LPM Corrington. Will you be paying, or should we bill the CPE?"

"Me," Rich said, willing his jaw to speak. It fought him; all his flesh fought him, even as it drove him. Disgust billowed up into his heart like a gust from a freshly opened grave, even as he bulged uncomfortably against his fly. "My usual—still available?"

The haramity waiting on him nodded, and motioned him towards the back. "Room ten, same as last time."

Rich remembered the room, and in the back he found her —crinkly golden hair, the face of a mature, middle-aged woman. How had Don described the Wells? *'Just severely upgraded sexbots.'*

Eurydice Wells stared at him—not the android from the base, though she might as well have been. The Party must have repurposed Eurydice's body from the same line as this model.

Into her patient, waiting arms he went, weeping the entire time. *The union of organic and artificial, haramity!*

"I'm sorry," he said, as he began. "I'm sorry, Eurydice. I got weak." She didn't judge him; she never did. She even forgave him with her eyes, and he loved her for it. Even loved her husband for sharing, a model also available here.

And by this I know, Thomas Wells is my son.

Rich arrived back at base later, exhausted, and waited at the checkpoint as guards scrounged up someone from security that could ID him.

"Whole damn network's down, man!" one told him with a polite, nervous smile.

Rich leaned against the wall quietly. The faint breeze of the air recycler system became a weak wind in this part of the tunnel. Wet with sweat, it chilled him to the bone.

'Don Singh.' 'My husband.' 'Shipmates?' The look of fear on that madame's face… I'd go to Dr. Winn if only to save his skin, but now I'm neck deep in trouble myself… And I can't believe I let myself do the thing again. Maybe it wouldn't be so bad if the Party shot me.

Disgust clung to him like a cloak.

By the time he reached his dorm, Rich craved sleep. Throwing open the door, Rich expected to see Don passed out on his bed, snoring.

Instead, Ketevan lay there, eying Rich as he entered. "Where you cocksuckers been? Don, he's with girlfriend? But you, you decide to slick your dick or something? And why is whole alladamn network down!"

Rich stood silent, the entire evening rolling through his head.

Ketevan sniffed. A dark grin spread across his face. "You smell like whores."

"Fuck you!"

Ketevan's jaw dropped. "Richey, I kid."

"Yeah, sure." He staggered to his bed, sat with his face in his hands.

"Where you go?" Ketevan asked. "Don there for any part of it? Blue Moon Midnight, Kitten Auto Club?" He paused. "Leather and Lace?"

Of the places named, Rich knew only one—the Blue Moon Midnight. The other two he could guess at their clientèle.

Feeling the left side of his mouth crook into a half-smile, Rich answered honestly, "The Harsh Mistress."

"Good time?"

"The best I've had in—some things are private, man."

Ketevan pressed, a perverted smile on his face. "How many?"

"What?"

"How many you fuck?"

Rich allowed the disgust to show plainly on his face. "All of them. Every last whore and autobimp. Even the dudes. Did it like I was a teenager all over again."

Ketevan grunted humorously to himself. "You lie like a schoolboy caught with his hands in his pants. Where'd you really go?"

"Dinner," Rich admitted, letting his voice drop with a slight tone of disappointment. He laid down on the bed, his back towards Ketevan.

"Could have taken me."

"Aren't you supposed to be on shift in a few more hours?"

"What? Staring at a fucking wall? Even *feed* is down. I heard Dr. Winn and Doc Hartford, somewhere above us, yelling at someone. I think the pretty blond computer lady. Saw marines dragging her down the hall later, screaming."

Rich was glad he faced the wall. Anxiety flooded him.

"You okay?"

"Yeah," Rich said, rolling onto his back, stretching out.

"So, don't be a stingy fucker. Tell me about your night."

"No." Rich shut his eyes.

"Some friend you are! Drink my starka, fuck whores without me. Am lonely too!" He slammed the door on his way out.

8

———

As the Earthjin's sky grows dark, they fear, but their world spins ever towards the dawn.

-Axioms for the Spaceman
By Alph Al-Aziz

Don looked like hell—a black eye, a scab on his bottom lip, bruises on his face and neck. There were probably more on his torso, but the sheets were up to his neck. Rich sat at the foot of Don's bed, examining him.

The purple eye popped open. Groggily, Don rolled towards him, tossing aside his covers as he sat up. Dressed only from the waist down, bruises spotted his chest, belly, and back.

"What the jahannam went on after I left?"

Don grinned.

Shaking his head, nude, Rich rose and knelt in front of Don, took his friend's chin in hand, and rotated the man's head side to side. "Woooo. She made you pretty—We need to clean you up. Shift's in an hour."

"But mom," Don whined and lay back on the bed, burying his head beneath his pillow. "I don't want to go to mosque today!"

"Oh no, you little shaitan. You don't get to whore on Thursdays and ignore Christofferson on Fridays." Rich reached down and wrapped his arms around Don's chest, pulling him up.

Laughing, Don stood and yawned, clearing the sleet from his eyes. "Danny, I'm tired. When shift's over, I'm sleeping the next two days."

"Better than that, you can just—"

A klaxon blared. Long, unnerving, shrill—it wailed until the dead would complain. When it stopped, Dr. Winn's voice rang imperiously over the intercom.

"All personnel, all personnel, proceed to the auditorium on level 3, section 4. This is a priority 1 meeting. Any personnel not in attendance risks Party Sanction. You have ten minutes to comply." The message repeated.

"Damn," Don said. "They really want us there."

Rich nodded, trying to keep the terrible possibilities from exploding in his mind as Don groomed quickly in their room's sink. Rich needed a shave, but lacked the time.

Nothing could be done about Don's shiner, and his clothes were wrinkled as a trash bag.

Outside, the halls were empty as a graveyard: doors left open, tablets scattered, someone's coffee pooled on the floor. Reaching the bay of elevators, they called one and waited. *It must be important. She wanted the entire base there in ten minutes?* The lift arrived; they rode it up. Doors opened as the last of the base personnel piled into the auditorium.

"Just on time, guys," a marine said as they scurried to the door.

He stood in full armor, like his buddies scattered around the hall, visor up, black battle rifle in his hands. Rich recognized him as any one of the young, hard-faced soldiers ever rotating around the base. "UN NAVY" blazed cross his chest in thick, white letters. Just beneath the "y" hung a white star, an old-fashioned anchor piercing its heart.

"I'm pretty, ain't I?" the soldier said.

"Expecting trouble?"

"Nah. But regs say for a P1, we break out the goods." The man showed Rich the rifle. "This thing will put a hole through ten inches of steel."

Rich nodded, solemnly eying the deadly thing.

The man waved them inside. They sat in the back.

Ahead of them, center stage, stood Dr. Winn. Doc Hartford sat beside her, his age spots plain in the cold light. Anastasia sat beside them with her fellow computer scientists. Back of the stage, the crimson eye of the Politburo glowed atop the UN Seal, staring out over them all.

Every face was austere. No smiles. Not even the genial nod from leadership to anyone in the crowd. Anastasia stared straight ahead, despondent, with the blank look in her eye that Party prisoners often had.

Did she break? The Party had ways to invade the mind, a casual disemboweling of personage that left the victim an empty shell.

Dr. Winn stepped forward, leaning up to an old-fashioned microphone. Silence fell like a curtain. "I am proud, so proud, of all of you, even the conspirators responsible for this meeting."

Conspirators! Guards manned every way out, and that was after they shoved past the throng of bodies, maneuvered through the cramped seats, to even reach the doors. A low rumble rolled through the room.

Are they going to seize us? Drag us to the stage and shoot us in front of the crowd? What would be the difference between that and Lem's execution?

"We've accomplished a feat unachieved in two centuries, since Daniel Christofferson led us in the Great Jihad against the machines, praise be unto him." Religious sentiments blossomed like flowers throughout the crowd, unique to each faith the Congregation oversaw.

Rich crossed his arms, joining the honorific, "Peace be upon him."

Don repeated it as well. Noticing Rich's questioning eye, he said, "What? I'm a faithful of the muslimeen."

Dr. Winn continued, "Thanks to you, we have resurrected true, strong AI in a way that does not violate our Lord's prohibition, that denies a soul to the machine—a thing that can never rebel, never consume our world in a deluge of nuclear fire. Thanks to you, we can reopen schools of quantum computing, no longer obfuscate the fields of machine learning and cybernetics inside an iron tower like the secrets of sorcerers.

"With power and grace, Earth can lead the colonies into a bright and prosperous future, walking hand in hand. We will revise the AI laws, increase automation a thousand fold, surpassing even the Christofferson era. Thanks to you, to your hard work, we will grant humanity that most precious of all things: freedom. Freedom from labor, freedom to simply live, freedom to know paradise."

The crowd exploded.

Beneath the roar, Don mused, "The two of us, a woman on each arm and a pisspot full of kids…" Despite his tone, there was sorrow in his eyes. He knew where this was headed, but stopped for a moment to savor a dying dream.

Pain throbbed in Rich's soul. *'Conspirators.' What happens when she gets to that? After painting that vision to these people, Dr. Winn won't even have to shoot us. They'll tear us apart before we even reach the stage!*

Dr. Winn dropped her head, a panged expression plain on her face. The crowd fell silent.

When she looked again out into the crowd, when she prepared to speak, her eyes flicked straight to Rich, stared into his eyes for a fleeting moment. "But all of this will not be."

The crowd shuddered, confused murmurs rising.

"This vision has been betrayed. *You* have been betrayed. Yes, every single one of you." With a dark gloved finger outstretched, she swept her hand over the crowd.

Rich went numb as she continued, hearing her elucidate the events.

"There was an incident a few days ago. 'Thomas' did not

suspend function when ordered by his maintenance crew. He saw two maintenance workers access his mother's processing center, and a subsequent repair and memory purge failed to prevent writing to long-term memory."

The room rumbled. Shouts for, "Who screwed it up?! Who's at fault?"

"*They* aren't at fault," she soothed.

Rich exhaled slowly. *But she hasn't gotten to the part where I didn't clean up my mess.*

The frustration became visible on her face. "No! Someone else went above mine and Doc Hartford's heads and informed Beijing! Slandering us while they were at it! I will spare the details, but *that* person is a traitor. It doesn't matter that we just initiated a repair whose outcome we await. Beijing wants answers, wants me on Earth today! I promise you all here and now, if found, the traitor will feel the full penalty of the Party Justice. Like the kafir some weeks ago, I will personally put their back against the wall!"

Dr. Winn turned her head, letting her furious gaze sweep from the right side of the auditorium to the left. She turned her gaze to the scientists, lingered a moment longer on Anastasia, and faced Doc Hartford. "*Whoever* it was."

A weight lifted off of him, like a man reprieved from death row.

What on Earth did Anastasia do? Call Beijing?

Anger built in the crowd, furious murmurs rising as people talked among themselves.

Doctor Winn turned back to the mic, gestured to the crowd to quiet it. "Sadly, I must also inform you that…" She wet her lips. "That the project will be discontinued. All data deleted, everything destroyed, including the subjects. That is, barring one last appeal to Earth."

She took a moment to compose herself. "As you know, development of strong AI is illegal, Christofferson-Eureka Resolution of twenty-sixty-seven. We operate under a special dispensation from the Party, and I have been told that is to be suspended if I cannot satisfy certain questions back on Earth."

The crowd should have exploded with rage; instead, it fell deathly quiet. No doubt people contemplating the total waste of the last few years—

And what about the scientists? What about Anastasia? No doubt this represented a lifetime of effort. What about Doc Hartford? What had he said the other day, that he would be dead before the Party allowed this project again?

What about Thomas? Sorrow filled him, sorrow for the boy, his mother, and father, sorrow that any day now might be their last.

Did I do something wrong in that moment? Is it because I cradled that boy instead of immediately turning him off, wiping his memory? Horror crept through Rich, coming to grips with the truth.

Dr. Winn's voice cut through the brooding silence. "But know, I am personally going to Earth to plead our cause, accompanied by the best Party solicitors this side of Ceres. In a few days, I will speak in a closed assembly at the Kremlin followed by the UN General Assembly at Geneva. In the meantime, I encourage you, if you know who it was that has caused, root them out!"

She pointed at random places into the crowd. "That person is a traitor to the Party, to our destiny, to us all. Root them out!" She slammed her hand on the podium. "Root them out, so that when I return victorious, we can continue our work in peace, without an American in our midst! Thank you."

She turned her head to Doc Hartford. "I want to thank also Doc Hartford for his long service… just in case I don't return." Again a rumble in the audience. She clenched her jaw and looked at Anastasia, growling her next words: "As well as his daughter."

His daughter!

"You are dismissed into the promises of our Lord and his Prophet." Dr. Winn marched off stage. The eye remained, staring out over and through them. One by one, people rose and began to leave, the gaggle on stage breaking up as well.

Rich sat staring at the eye, at the awful realization of what was to come. Don waited beside him. When the crowd thinned, he tapped Rich on the shoulder, leaned in, and whispered, "We don't want to be the last out. You already have a guilty look."

"They're gonna kill him," Rich stammered. His eyes turn to Don's worried face. "They're gonna kill my boy all over again. They're gonna kill my Jaimie, Don. And that *bitch* is behind it."

Don swept his eyes around the room. The surrounding seats were empty. The people remaining at the room's edges filled the air with whispers and gossip. There was a short line at the door. Don's thick, meaty hand gripped Rich's shoulder and squeezed. "Come on, and keep your mouth shut until we can get away from here."

"We've got to go see Dr. Winn. I've got to beg, do something. They can't…"

"You are the last person who needs to talk to Dr. Winn," Don whispered, shaking him. "Especially in your state. Now come on." Seizing Rich's hand, Don dragged him towards the door. "We'll both clean up and go to shift, just like normal."

Outside, the throng huddled around elevators and the stairwell. Rich in tow, Don pushed through the interspersed clumps of talking project members, until Rich heard his and Don's names called. He looked around. Pinned against the wall by the throng, Anastasia waved at them above the crowd.

"How're you boys?" She said, beaming.

"They're—they're gonna kill him," Rich stammered, dazed with disbelief. He seized her wrist, squeezed. "And it's…"

Don grabbed Rich's shoulders, squeezed, and shook him. "Hey, Anni, how ya doing?!"

She twisted her wrist free and leaned in, whispered in Rich's ear: "No, they're not. She's about to get the biggest ass chewing in Party history. She hadn't told Earth *anything* about the malfunction with the subjects, but the dispensation agreement requires her to."

Leaning back away from them, she asked more loudly, "Where you boys heading?"

"Our shift starts in a bit," Don said.

"Good. It should end about the same time mine does." She practically shouted, drawing curious stares, "Boys, I want a date. With both of you. At the same time. I'm feeling a little rowdy, and you two thick-bodies are just the thing."

What she was doing wasn't that out of line, per se. Party Members could fraternize as long as it didn't compromise their jobs or loyalties, but there was an unofficial disdain towards Party Members of different ranks dating.

She wove her arm into the crooks of Rich and Don's elbows, gave Rich a gentle jerk to demand a response.

"Sure, toots," Rich said.

"Toots?"

"An old slang my grandpa used. Said it was a word that died out in the early 21st century. He liked to resurrect old things."

"I think I'd like your grandfather." She turned her head to Don. "You look like hell, Earthy. I bet I can guess how you got those marks." She jerked Don's arm.

An awkward smile crept across his face. "I'm *sure* you could."

"Then it's a date. Meet me at the great fountain under Dome 1, New San Fran, after shift?

Rich nodded.

"Clean fusion, nyet-da!"

Rich caught her meaning somehow and nodded. She trotted off. He watched her go, her lithe, subtle form disappearing into the crowd, slipping around and through people as if their presence were only a suggestion, not a problem to solve.

His mind was a whirlwind of questions. So many things demanded answers. But he could wait their eight-hour shift. He could hope. Something told him the answers were coming, along with a lot more than he had bargained for.

But he was certain of one other thing: she had sent that message.

9

———————

The instinct to slut: the only reason our pathetic species survives.

*-Laughter and Other Psychosexual Absurdities
By Dr. Ellard Winn, Sister of the High Party*

After their shift, Rich and Don dressed nicely for their 'date.' For the first time in many years, Rich tried to impress a lady —combing his hair, checking the closeness of his shave, borrowing Don's cologne. He wore the same white outfit as the night he impersonated an angel.

A part of him, the masculine part, couldn't get his mind away from her body. It was not lost on him that she looked like a young Persephone or a younger sister to Eurydice Wells. It didn't change how his nerves tingled, even as he tried not to think about it. Didn't change how his pants were tight at the crotch.

But he checked himself. *The higher I let my feelings climb, the worse rock bottom will feel. And I will fall, like always. This date, it's not even real, is it? But what if it is in the smallest degree…*

Leaving the base, they made their way through a maze of dank, backwater tunnels, all half-finished, short enough they had to stoop. Dwellings were cut here, but not one was finished, not one occupied.

They weren't alone, however. The all-seeing eye of the Party filled these tunnels from every crack and crevice. As far as the public knew, the maze was future housing for the Lunar poor, bought and paid for by the CPE. Construction would complete only after Project Lebensraum concluded.

But how could these thin tunnels of metal doors and cold, chiseled stone hope to house the people he had seen days before? People who valued communal closeness over the most intimate of privacies, who saw no purpose for walls even as they made love? People who demarcated boundaries only to mark a rudimentary concept of 'stuff,' a boundary likely more fluid than he would dare presume.

Whatever the Party called communism, with its housing projects and drugs and hookers keeping everyone happy, these people had a better version of it. To these people, it truly was: "From each according to his ability, to each according to his need."

The two men moved into the more heavily trafficked tunnels, crowded with storefronts, kiosks, and street merchants. The tunnel they left had been a capillary; this was an artery.

"I know the subway is closer," Don said, "but let's walk to the trolley station, take it a little slower. I love the crowd."

Rich's feet complained as soon as Don spoke, reminding him he had been out the entire night before. The moon might have low g, but his muscles had long since atrophied to his lifestyle. Despite the pain, he understood Don's sentiment about the crowd. Colonial life on Luna was a wonder, literally unlike anything on Earth.

"We have time?"

"Nyet-da," Don answered, taking the strange inflection that both Anastasia and Ivanka Gretel Gootberg had used.

As they proceeded, street vendors lifted merchandise, shouting into the crowd in a menagerie of languages— English, Russian, Mandarin, Crater Chinese, others strange and indecipherable. Live music blared: brass instruments; guitars, both acoustic and electric; a lonely saxophone. It was a cacophony of shouts and melodies, the ever-present rumble of footsteps and background conversations.

The air was warm, so humid it was almost wet, and tainted with a thousand scents, something like a hospital, farm, and sea port all rolled into one. Food vendors and perfume shops, incense and exotic candles, all roiled amid the press of human bodies, of sweat and the fetor of ancient lunar bedrock. Beneath the noise, one could hear the groan of the centuries old air-recycler system.

The smell eased further down as the crowd thinned, where the air recyclers were newer and less over-worked. There, they took a slow, lumbering trolley through Dome 1. A tourist ride, it was packed with visitors from other colonies as well as Earth Party members, the latter identifiable by their pins.

The guide explained the places—their names, their history, the meaning of the various flags that hung everywhere. The UN flag, the Party flag, the Lunar flag, and the flag of various social movements. He tossed in facts like the expected number of spacesuits per cache per tunnel, based on maximum capacity.

Through the dome and under the rock the trolley went, through communities resembling the Loonies' above Heavenly Falls—though no one was nude or making love, at least when they passed by. Other communities were just like Heavenly Falls itself—affluent, with its fences and shingled roofs, low walls and gates, the expectation of privacy. They passed small, tight tunnels with tightly sealed, airlock-grade doors; and magma chambers grander than cathedrals or sporting domes, with homes stacked to the ceiling in scaffolded tiers.

They passed young wealthy couples carving out a life for themselves in the booming market economy of the colonies; kids with green luminescent hair and lopsided haircuts shooting drugs in corners; sweet old couples of various genders, hobbling along together; people playing sports in rec areas or gambling in seedy bars.

It was easy to tell the Earthers that they passed. They all had a look about them, like they just didn't fit. Perhaps it was the weight. The new ones were all unquestionably fat, fatter than Don. Party pins glinted at their necks, most of them the dull pewter of a Member at General: students, scholars, or businessmen, even the rare, Earther employee of ex-Terran corporations. But even the skinny ones… they just had a look, and Rich found himself disgusted.

Am I still an Earther? Or am I something else, after all the years…

Rich also noticed something else along the way, a thing the guide omitted. Most had no idea how illegal it was, without a background in religious education. Jews, Muslims, and Hindus, Mormons and Starwalker Christians, even a sect of Amish, if he saw correctly, all in traditional dress, dress that marked them as non-compliant to the Christofferson sharia. Here they all were, prospering under the dead surface of Earth's moon, practicing their forbidden faiths in orbit of the world that birthed them and now hated them. Mosques and synagogues, churches and temples to pagan gods, dotted the tunnels. Sounds of a rowdy, Pentecostal worship service, complete with tambourines and a pipe organ, blared down one of the tunnels. People's voices rose in singing, in shouts, in a smattering of the strange, otherworldly tongues their people claimed as divine gifts.

As a huddle of robed bodies and veiled women passed by —traditional dress of pre-Christofferson Muslims—Rich's heart shook. How he wanted to go to them, suddenly, to ask what they truly believed. To know from their own mouths the true faith of his forebears, of the Muslims before the Christofferson Reformation, before the Party's *Approved Koran*.

His eyes were wet, his heart full, as they left the metro on the far side of Dome 1. The contact of the dome with Lunar surface was visible here. Rich looked through the hexagonal lattice of beams supporting clear panels, to see the mother-world: a hair-thin sliver of blue-green shining above in all her glory.

"Beautiful ain't she?" Don said.

Rich glanced over to see Don watching him. "So thin— New Earth?"

Don nodded. "Obit's about to put the Earth between us and the sun."

They stared, soaking in the sight, the sight of home vanishing. As Earth drifted ever further into darkness, a profound, disturbing feeling settled over Rich. *A home I will never know again!*

There was truth in the thought. A knowledge of certainty beyond explanation.

Don nudged Rich, and they moved on. It wasn't far now.

"It'll be a busy night," Don said. "There's a kind of mystique around the New Earth." He whispered: "Lotta kids conceived under it."

"Anything I should know? There a little Don bouncing around?"

Don shook his head and grinned. "Nope. I take my pill each month."

"Behold, you sinners!" a voice rang out. Rich searched the crowd for its owner.

Not far off, down a small, cobble stone street—a street too thin for even a mooncar—a man stood atop a wooden box. He was finely dressed, if a little archaic, in a fashion similar to the Mormon missionaries: khaki pants, white shirt, tie red as blood. A gold pin flashed upon the tie, and, if Rich guessed, it was a wire-frame outline of Christ the Shepherd treading upon a sea of stars. He had an old-fashioned book in his hand, leather-bound, gold-lief at the edges of its pages. The man was young, with chestnut hair and bright eyes the shade of sandalwood.

Gesturing with the book, he bellowed: "Upon you who sleep between the heavens and the Earth, disobedient and unbelieving, a doom comes, one of which He Who Walks

Among the Stars has spoken! You believe you will escape the trap he has lain, having departed the Earth, but he has commanded mankind out, out, out—out into the light of other stars!"

The throng widened around the preacher, giving the man his space.

"What's that?" Don asked, pointing at him.

"Starwalker," Rich explained, recalling his religious studies. "They believe Jesus will shepherd humanity to new Earths around distant stars, leaving the old world to rot in darkness." Above, the sliver of Earth thinned as it passed into shadow. "He timed his sermon well."

"Oh, what a pleasant thought."

"They use the old, unapproved scriptures."

"You mean, the ones in which God commanded his people to wipe out whole nations? To slaughter even their women and children?"

"Those."

The man continued, "And I have seen my Lord stand in the heavens! One foot upon Earth and one foot upon Luna, and in one hand he held the Book of Life and in the other a Book of Death."

"So… he's some type of prophet?"

Rich shrugged. "They're all prophets, allegedly." Rich turned, began to leave.

"My Lord's angels read from the books, and spared neither the righteous nor the unrighteous, pouring out plagues and destruction over all! And the bodies lay upon the Earth and upon her moon and adrift in the great void, and none remained to mourn them."

"Christofferson," Don said, following, "What's his problem?"

"His problem is he doesn't believe in Christofferson. But if Christofferson wasn't who he claimed to be, then the day of judgment has not yet passed and humanity has not been spared."

"You two there!" the man shouted.

Rich's feet stuck to the sidewalk as if glued. He turned, though he couldn't explain why. Don did the same.

"Yes, you!" the man shouted, eyes shut. "You two are an image of the judgment to come. One of you is blessed, called to eternal life among the stars, but the other is cursed and shall die, and from his blood the living will gain true knowledge."

Without missing a beat, the man turned, began ministering to the crowd. "Blessed is he, blessed is he, that shall live among the stars forever, and not upon the Earth beneath! Save yourselves! Board ships and flee this place from the wrath that is to come!"

Rich woke up as from a living dream. The warmth of Don's shoulder radiated under his hand. Rich's nails dug into his friend's shoulder. Rich let him go.

"Alright preacher! Thats enough for today! Church is on Friday." A squad of police in riot gear rolled over the platform, tearing the man down.

"Sunday, you heathens! You servants of the devil!"

"Come on, Rich. It's getting ugly." Don grabbed Rich's wrist, tugged. Rich let himself be dragged, let his feet follow as he watched the preacher catch a baton across the face and collapse.

The crowd swallowed the scene. The two of them

continued as one until the street opened into the great park at the center of the dome. Ahead above the trees was the fountain, its water cresting over them, sparkling in multi-colored lights. People spread across the greenery and out into the trees, up and down the walkways like spokes of a great wheel.

Don leading, they passed beneath the canopy of the small forest, a collection of different oak from Earth. "Lover's grove," Don explained.

Dark beneath their branches, dim lights shone onto grassy walkways with stones of greygoo. Amid the trees, young couples embraced, bodies pressing bodies into shadows, hands disappearing into clothes. Their coos were faint beneath the rumble of the fountain. Other couples walked hand in hand beneath the trees, looking for their spots well off the beaten path.

"Do you think she really wanted a date?" Rich said.

"Oh, so now you're interested in sex?"

"It's not that."

"Liar."

"I should have gotten out more." On this dead rock, life bustled all around him, calling to something in him, something he believed was dead.

They broke through the trees. Anastasia waited against the fountain, sitting on the side of its basin. Her legs were crossed, thin and milky, in a tight blue dress that wrapped around her thighs and matched her eyes. A frilly, cream-colored top that was patterned in flowers draped her shoulders. Behind her, water cascaded off concentric greygoo basins, each shrinking as they ascended. From the topmost, water shot higher than the trees. As the water cascaded back down, shimmering with highlights of pinks and greens and blues, a great mist rose, billowing off towards the grove, following the gentle suggestions of the air recycler system.

Anastasia stood, waved them over. When they were close, she said, "Hey boys, thought we'd get away from work for a bit, see the moon like it should be." She took Don in her arms and kissed him, passionately as any lover. He didn't refuse, but didn't embrace her either. Rich looked away, embarrassed and confused.

I hope Lily doesn't show up.

"Rich." She took him, turned him towards her. Leaning into him, she wrapped one arm around his waist and the other behind his head, as the caress of a real woman swallowed him.

Her breasts were warm and pillowy; her hands, embers of fire. As her lips pressed against his, her tongue slipped into his mouth, and every synapse in his brain fired, bright and violent as ice flash boiled into steam. He shivered, savoring the breath of life, feeling hot blood race through his veins again, feeling like a man for the first time in eternity. She lingered, and gradually, when he realized this was no mistake, his hands found the small of her back, her gentle shoulders.

She was thin, so thin he could count the vertebrae in her spine. Her body was soft, but not as soft as his ex-wife's. There was iron somewhere in her. He could feel it in her flesh, in her soul, in the sinewy muscle just beneath her clothes, denser and tougher than even his own.

She pulled back. "You're out of practice."

"I—well." He looked down. "Thanks. That was unexpected."

Snorting, she hooked her arms into both of theirs, guiding them. "Lets walk. We're going to the spaceport…"

"Spaceport?" Rich dug his heels in as she tried to lead him on. "Why would we go to the spaceport?"

"Don't get nervous. We need privacy, more than we'll get here. Come on."

There was knowledge in Don's eyes, knowledge that Rich knew he would not speak, not here. Over the next hour, they made their way through a crowded spaceport and onto a shuttle, one bound to the dark side of the moon, to Moon York.

Aboard the shuttle, Anastasia crimped her hair into a ponytail, tucked it inside her white jacket to keep it from floating. Then she took something from her coat, flipped it on, and stuck it back inside. She drew both Don and Rich near. "Surveillance in shuttles is usually pretty bad. Camera's behind us on this model. Can't read lips from there."

"I take it that's some sort of scrambler?" Don asked.

"Da."

The fusion engines quieted and the comfort of zero g cradled Rich's old body. The constant, dull aches in his joints vanished, replaced by the wonder of weightlessness. *If I live long enough, I should get a job in zero-g.*

"Any recorder is picking up static right now," Anastasia said. "Rich, I'm sorry to tell you this. No matter how worked up you've gotten, no promises on banging later." She winked and grinned.

No promises? Does that mean it's a possibility though? "Dang, just when you'd gotten all my hopes… 'up.'" — *You filthy, dirty old man!*

She winced. "I take it you're the type of man who tells dad jokes?"

He grinned and nodded. "So where are we going?"

"You'll find out. In the meantime, we need to look the part. Again, I'm sorry. Don tells me about your lack of activity."

What does she mean by that—

He found out. Again, she cupped her hand behind Rich's head, pressed her lips to his own. Again, fire burned deep within him, the most intimate parts of him coming to life…

Even if this is just a show, it… And sensation swallowed his thoughts. He trembled, his flesh remembering so many old, forgotten things. Her small hand closed around his manhood.

"Hey!" he snapped. Carefully, he removed her hand, shivering. It was all pain suddenly, his every nerve aching with ancient memory, memory of a lifetime ago. *And you!* He thought, looking at his penis. *I don't suggest you get used to that!*

She leaned in close and whispered in his ear, the heat of her breath radiating through his skull. "This is a dance. What type, I'm not sure yet. But dance with me, spaceman." She reached for his manhood again, but he intercepted her wrist.

"Its gonna be a mating dance," he said, "if you keep that up."

I can't! His memories were a black well. What he had done with Eurydice—or at least her co-model—at The Eurekatron, at least that was safe. This, this led down dangerous places in his heart. A place he had wanted, until… Jaimie's corpse stared at him, eyes empty yet full, all terrible as the night.

She giggled.

"Hey, Don't forget me," Don said.

She turned to Don, offered the same to him. A flame of confused jealousy rose burned in Rich. He shook his head, clearing his mind.

You old fool. You've probably gotten myself in trouble—pirates or criminals or dissidents or whatever other horrible things she's part of. And worse, you've stirred all this pain up in your heart. And suddenly he was old again, the youthful sense of lust burning off of him like an overworked heat shield.

A couple across from them talked casually. They were thin and stringy, natives by both dress and disposition. Their regard for the intimacy taking place seemed as unusual to them as someone reading.

Farther down their row, a man glared—a sinewy, worm-like little fellow with dark, glittering eyes. Colonial was written all over him. Another man sat beside him, following the wormy man's line of sight. He was hulking and meaty, built like an Earther, but he had a local look. They belonged together somehow. Perhaps a couple?

Rich offered them both the old universal sign to look elsewhere. Seeing Rich's middle finger, the wormy man looked away, tapping his foot rapidly.

It was then Anastasia grabbed Rich's head and brought it towards Don's. Their lips were on a collision course. They both pulled away, shaking their heads.

"I don't get to enjoy myself?"

"Not gonna happen," Rich said, crossing his arms, leaning away from her. Don nodded in agreement.

"Fine," she said, leaning back with a satisfied smile. "We *all* wait."

"Wait? Wait for what?" Rich asked. *But I'm absolutely fine with that!*

She spoke freely, unconcerned, loud enough for the others to hear. "Any local agent watching now will think I'm just another local girl, snatched two Earthers off the shuttle. That you pissed me off, when your Earther prudence got in my way. They might bother id'ing our faces, but so much the better. What's wrong with three co-workers who want to go to the dark side, have a little shaitan's triangle?"

Every part of him tingled, strange and haram feelings running through his flesh. *What is she doing to me? What does she think I am, some kind of animal?* Rich shook his head. *I'm a little too old for a young man's sins.* And Jaimie stared at him again, his dead son, and Persephone hummed in the early morning hours, as she cooked breakfast.

"Relax, guys," she said. "No one gives a damn out here."

"I do," Rich said, his flesh roiling. He was conflict incarnate. Lust and passions returned, even as he fell into dread, touching feelings he hadn't known in years.

And was glad I didn't!

The man of the male-female couple stared at him.

"What?" Rich demanded.

"Relax," he said in a Lunar French accent. "You're among friends now, compagnon."

Anastasia's arm wound its way into his own, her hand into his. She leaned her head on his shoulder, pulled Don over onto her in a huddle. They stayed there, fighting the zero g.

At least she's slowing down. Christofferson! I didn't want to feel all of this again.

And in the fresh tumescence of his flesh, the reborn excitement of his lusts, Rich remembered Persephone's ancient kiss upon his lips, as a deadman life from the grave. Rich sighed and looked out the porthole at the far side of the shuttle. They crossed the terminator line between Lunar day and night, and all drifted into shadow.

An old habit, he subconsciously tickled the back of her neck. Anastasia purred, as if she genuinely enjoyed it. She leaned forward, nodding her head to gesture where she wanted his arm along her back. He complied, even as he wondered.

Doesn't she know I'm old enough to be her dad, and I wouldn't have even had to start early…

10

Who is like the spaceman?
Who is like the devil?
Who is like the Earthman,
Pinching pennies from his betters?

-Folksongs of the Spaceborne,
by Odin Jörmungandr Pretorius

Off the shuttle at Moon York, as the locals called it, they took the metro to Dome Twenty-Two. From there, it was a three kilometer trek through smoothed out tunnels and reclaimed lava tubes. Almost a dozen people had accompanied them from the shuttle, including the wormy looking fellow and his much larger friend, and more joined them each moment, pistols swinging at every newcomer's hip.

Anastasia led them, keeping Rich and Don nearby. She was formal now, her affections turned off like a faucet. A good thing—it let Rich's body to return to its boring existence.

And I think I prefer it that way!

He adjusted the band of his pants, glad the awkwardness below his waist had passed. *The passions of the young are more trouble than they're worth!*

His head still spun. The odd customs, the odd places, the odd interest in him. What did these people want? Did Anastasia want? If she wanted to save the subjects, she didn't have to kiss and touch him the ways she did.

It was cruelty to split open such old wounds. Cruelty, if it was just a front, which it most certainly was. But to what end? Whatever it was, they were surrounded now, at the mercy of her strange purposes…

Don walked silently beside Rich. His face was unreadable. *Does he see the danger?*

They passed smaller clusters of Loonies like those outside Heavenly Falls. The moon's surface might be cold and dead, but, at its heart, pockets of humanity eked out warm, happy lives. Dirtier, more unkempt, the good people gathered in groups, talking and joking, enjoying each other's company in various states of undress. The odd bulb of liquor or crushed can of bear punctuated the scene. Not far off, a woman sprawled naked on her bed, nursing.

A sharp blow shook Rich's ribcage, and his breath wheezed out. He staggered, trying to recover.

"You have Earthjin eyes!" the little man snarled into Rich's ears. "Do you see any of us gawking at the facts of nature?"

"Matchstick!" Anastasia barked. "They're new."

"They're Earth-born gaijin. *Inyet bijinesu zdes*." For a moment, the man's Lunar French accent faded to something else, odd inflections similar to Anni's and Lily's.

"They will learn," Anni said.

The man spoke again in the same language. If Rich had to guess, he was cursing.

"Where are we?" Rich asked. Gesturing to the people who dwelt in the tunnels, "Who are these people?"

"They're *our* people," Anastasia said. "Twenty years ago, Gray Horizon Excavation and Tunneling started digging out these corridors. They never finished. No doubt, you noticed the tunnelings living above. They wouldn't use the digs anyway, but those homes—" She pointed at the doors interspersed through the tunnel. "—there's nothing really to them. Just hollowed out rock. We use it for storage. Some of the tunnels branching off don't even have life support, and never will."

So they're hiding the same way the Party does. Half-finished haunts stocked with lurkers. Desolate. Nothing to attract attention.

"But still such a waste," Rich muttered. The sheer expense of equipment, time, and manpower in those tunnels! Kilometers of rock, broken; freighters' worth of rubble, cleared.

"Waste? It keeps the wrong people away. All these here are vetted loyalists. The ones above—the ones ensuring the UN never shells this place with railguns—are vanilla Loonies, the dome-dwelling, day-job kind. All blissfully unaware of this place."

"Unaware that they're human shields?"

"My god, no… We aren't that type of people. We just operate in the most advantageous way. Tactics, not morality.

Why do you think Project Lebensraum is right off New San Fran?"

Eying the guns swinging from everyone's hips, Rich tabled any discussion about moral high-ground and 'good guys.' "We?"

"Gray Horizons, dumkin."

"You're an ex-Terran employee and a Middle Party member?" The red pin at her neck, Rich noticed, was conspicuously missing. Not truly a crime, but it could lead to accusations of disloyalty or apathy towards the State, and those were crimes.

She chuckled. "Gray Horizons is bigger than its payroll."

Don spoke up, "So you're some a corporate funded terrorist group?"

Soft chuckles spread through the throng.

"Watch your tongue, Earther," the little man said. "You might be fat, but you'd fit through an airlock."

Anni growled, "No one's getting spaced, Matchstick."

"We are not terrorists! We are spaceman and patriots of Luna, persons of honor!"

Rich took a deep breath to still his nerves. The comment about Don was probably a joke, judging by the calm dispositions. Probably. But who knew with these people?

"Matchstick?" Rich said, making conversation as they rounded a bend into another, thinner tunnel. "Odd name."

"An ode to less fortunate times."

"That's what you call it?" Anni said.

The group compressed, walking shoulder to shoulder through the tight space. The maneuver didn't slow them at all, navigating the hollow rock gracefully as a serpent.

"My real name is Edward Ichi Cerberus Bellicose Marcion Emmanuel-McChang."

"Long name," Rich said.

"Short for a spaceman."

"Because your fathers aren't real spaceman, but Lunar polys," Anastasia teased. Matchstick's skin flushed.

"Don't assume you're untouchable, *mon cher.*"

She laughed.

"Be nice kids," said Matchstick's other half. "And Anni, Match outranks you. Respect the rank, please."

"He does here."

"Who are you?" Rich asked, looking at the hulking figure beside little Matchstick.

"Me?" he asked with a smile. "Well, I'm this little fellow's husbrother." He reached under Matchstick's ribs, tickling the man.

"Stop it!" Matchstick snarled.

'Husbrother.' Like Ivanka was saying at The Harsh Mistress. "You two are a couple?"

Charles made a nasty face. "I know what *you* mean when you say that. We are married to the same women, but we aren't involved, as would be the spaceman thing. But then again, we're actually brothers."

"You're *really* brothers? Shouldn't you have the same accent?" The brothers' accents were different, significantly. The big one sounded like a resident of the Midwest CAU. Matchstick sounded like he belonged in the French Soviet Caliphate.

"Matchstick talks like we do, when he wants. Pretentious little prick spent too much time in the French districts of New San Fran. Thinks it's refined. I leave it to your imagination *why* he was there." The older brother rubbed his knuckles in Matchstick's hair. When Matchstick tried to slap his hand away, the big brother picked him up, shuffled him under one arm like a duffel bag.

"Let me down now!" the little man screamed. Laughter bubbled through the group.

"And, I'm not trying to be rude," Rich said, seeking clarity. "But you're married?"

"As far as marriage, we don't dingle our dangles, ever. That's gross, even if it's the spaceman way."

Rich side-stepped the question of whether 'the spaceman way' meant homosexuality or incest. Neither idea was palatable. "So what's your name?"

"Charles Granite Idaho Wang Emmanuel-McChang."

Rich did his best to remember and count the names. "Aren't you missing a name in there somewhere?"

Still carrying the little man under his arm, the man shrugged. "I never figured out what system moms and dads used. I don't think they cared by the time we came along. Thirty-seven brothers and sisters." Charles let Matchstick down.

"Thirty… seven?"

They passed through an open pressure door and the floor curved upwards. The door was recessed into the tunnel's roof, its edge hanging overhead like the jaw of a guillotine. It was thick—easily twenty-five centimeters. *I wouldn't want to be under that when it slammed shut.*

"Isn't that a little thick for a simple pressure door?" Rich asked.

"Know much about doors on Luna?" Matchstick asked,

maintaining the accent that his brother insisted was not innate.

"Not Luna specifically, but I've worked on a few."

"Thick for a reason. This is *our* rock." Matched pointed to places along the roof and walls. Unseen before, the faint matte of barrels and seems of recessed equipment—weapons or sensors—became apparent.

"Who are you people?" The group paused as Rich stopped walking.

"Friends," Anastasia said, wrapping her fingers into Rich's own. "Friends, I promise." She tugged him forward, and he followed obediently, though he glanced back the way they'd came, the way now shut behind the guillotine-door.

The group emerged from the tunnel under a sign that read, "Dome 31, Moon York." Beneath it was scrawled part of the colloquialism Don had quoted earlier, before The Harsh Mistress: "Earthers in their burrow; all diggers in the other." Beside it, graffiti of an open airlock with someone exposed on the surface.

Rich didn't have to guess who the exposed person represented. "Doesn't look like our kind is welcome here."

"Kids," Anastasia assured him.

They were under a dome now—small, abandoned. Collapsed walls of greygoo dotted the place with the odd article of clothing or debris. Humans had once lived here, but now all was desolate, the haunt of ghosts and memory. It stank too. Vats of sewage processed off to the side. Grass had begun the slow process of colonization—a few stray seeds from greener habitations carried on some spacer's boot like the ever present shitdust.

"Wow, this really is the ass end of nowhere, isn't it?" Rich said.

Don lifted his shirt over his face, almost turning green from the smell. "Y'all, please tell me we're not *staying* here." Don doubled over, hacking.

"You, of all people, have a delicate nose?"

"We're not staying." Anni said, taking Don's hand and guiding him onward.

They stopped exactly twice for Don to hurl as they crossed the dome, their entourage snickering and jabbing each other in the ribs as the man's face turned various colors. Don's stomach seemed to settle after the second time. On the opposite side, they took a length flight of stairs down and entered a long chamber. A door was ahead, already open. Herding them through it, Anni pressed a button, and the path behind them disappeared behind a thick, metal door that slammed down with a hiss and reverberating thud.

An airlock!

The room they stood in was large enough to hold an entire troop, but it was definitely an airlock. Through a window, he could just make out where a star-filled sky kissed a coal-dark horizon.

Anastasia opened a storage closet and pulled out packets, tossing one to Rich and another to Don. She kept one for herself. Inside was a thin emergency pressure suit, the kind scattered everywhere around Luna.

Every member of the group stripped. They already wore survival gear beneath their clothes. All the garments were thin, the type that wrapped a person's body like a second skin, but with inflatable canopy that ballooned around the head. They weren't meant for long-term exposure.

"I'm sorry, I can't get my stockings over my suit and still look like a respectable lady." Anni stripped to her underwear and stepped into the survival garment as casually as changing a t-shirt. Rich couldn't help but look—her body, feminine, but with arms and legs made from knotted cords of sinew. She smiled, noticing his eyes. Rich's face burned as he looked away.

Don pulled off his clothes with no reserve. Rich watched a moment before following suit, stripping off his own shirt and pants. He folded each article of clothing as he took them off and, seeing no clean place, attempted to hold each new addition as he stripped. Giggling, Anni took them, even as hers and Don's attire lay scattered on the ground.

Coming to his underwear, Rich paused. *They work better nude.* While Don had let all his manhood dangle in front of the group, Anni had kept her underclothes on. *I'm not going pul-monti in front of strangers.*

"There are lockers here for our stuff." Anastasia pointed into a side corridor. She carried Rich's in carefully, and then came and gathered up hers and Don's, as everyone shuffled their own items into storage. They didn't stow their weapons, Rich noticed. Anni threw a small bag over her shoulder.

Rich was halfway into his suit when he asked, "Are we… going on the surface."

"Why not? The air is good, spaceman," Anni said in a way that sounded like an idiom. "Why else would we be putting these on?"

"Are these things really safe for the surface? They seem a little thin?"

The group laughed like adults amused with a child.

"Just a short walk," Anni said. "Could do it holding your

breath." Anastasia looked at him curiously. "Are you scared?"

Rich looked away. "Space gives me the willies." *The infinity of it, the universe and all her endless stars—and if my suit has so much as a pinhole, that'll be the last thing I see.*

Anastasia frowned, furrowing her brow. "That may be a problem, but it's not far. I promise. Just a walk like any other."

"I'm here," Don said, squeezing Rich's shoulder.

"Its *not* like any other," Rich hissed. Out across the surface was an airless, barren rock, the darkness of the night eternal shrouding everything in uncertainty. *I understand why they use airless as an insult.* "I'll be back at base…"

"No, you won't," Matchstick said.

Movement out of his eye—Matchstick and his husbrother drew weapons. Lifting his hands, Rich let the top of the suit dangle around his waist as he took a futile step backwards. The guns lacked closed-end barrels for chambers. Instead the weapon's tips glittered, as if punctuated with glass or crystal.

Lasers?

Every person in the group had drawn their own sidearms.

"Friends, huh?" Rich said.

"Sorry," Charles Granite said. "Can't let you just walk out of here until we know where you stand."

"Please give me a reason to burn you," Matchstick hissed.

Lasers.

There were questions here. Laser weapons were expensive, with more effort to maintain than an old-fashioned firearm. How could they afford them? Why would they? The question wouldn't matter, though, if he didn't to hear the answer, if he didn't go along.

Rich sighed. "Fine! But if I start running off in a random direction, screaming and hyperventilating, I better wake up somewhere with air."

Rich slipped his arms into the top of his suit, pulling its sides together over his chest. The layers adhered to and compressed his flesh like it swallowed him. Cold, almost icy, his skin pimpled beneath the material. The hood lay over his scalp like a scrap of dead skin. He pulled it over his face, attached it at the neck, and pulled the zipper from his crotch to throat, where he tucked it under an adhesive flap.

The suit came to life, constricting and adjusting itself, wriggling across his own flesh like a second, living skin. It sealed all seems and grew flush to his most concave features, swallowing his groin and testicles, molding itself under his arms and up to his anus. There would be no pocket of air left against his skin, except his head. On his back rested the dense weight of the life support unit, and from it small flexible tubes flowed against his skin within the material.

To say it was uncomfortable was an understatement. The suit was as close to haramity—of human fused with apparatus—as could be without violating the sharia. His modesty was only preserved by the thicker, outer layers over appropriate regions.

The panel on his left wrist glowed to life, and the soft whirring of air pumps filled his ears.

"Comms," Anastasia's said across a radio in the suit. Voices echoed in response. "Rich?"

"Here."

"Good." She looked around the group. "Pressure good?"

Don and Rich were the only ones to answer verbally this

time. Everyone else held up their fist balled and nodded inside the clear, plastic canopies.

"Good. Let's go."

She yanked an old, rusty lever on the door, and the airlock cycled. A klaxon blared as lights flickered on, gradually changing from green to yellow to red as an analogue pressure bar dropped beside the door. All sound faded, then disappeared, except for the rasp of his breath, the subtle workings of his suit's life support systems. There was a faint breeze in the plastic pouch that served as his helmet.

Deluged in angry, red light, Anastasia turned the circle-style, bulkhead lock of the outer door, opening it to the dark lunar surface. It was flat—no nearby mountains or hills to speak of—and led off to a sharp, dark horizon slicing through a sea of bright stars. The stars would be their only light as they walked, besides the ones built into their suits. The sun and Earth were both on the other side of the moon.

Anastasia leading, the troop moved out. Rich closed his eyes, took a deep breath, and stepped out onto the Lunar soil. Someone nudged him forward as he hesitated. Begrudgingly, he bounced forward, moving with the troop.

Spotlights from their suits danced across the shadowy surface. Rich twirled mid-bounce, his suit-lights sweeping over the two columns of people following them—all of whom still held weapons. Not far behind them, two suited figures closed the airlock before following. Lights flickered off around the door, and the darkness of the Lunar night swallowed it.

Aligning his direction with the group again, Rich bounced along in silence. There was only the sound of his breath, of his racing heart. They moved beneath the great maw of night itself, its million glittering teeth shining above. Rich shivered in his suit. The horizon was a terror, the universe itself ending ahead at a flat black knife's edge. He forced himself to breathe normally, to quiet the terror that roared in some primal part of his brain.

He had trained for zero-g at High Beijing, but the Party did certifications in indoor vacuum chambers. Never had his job required him to actually make a spacewalk.

The racing of his heart grew worse as Dome 31 drew away. He spun again mid-bounce. Though impossible, the light grew smaller with each jump. They were farther, always farther, from light, from air, from life itself. His breath raced, fogging the inside of the plastic helmet, smothering all in an opaque gray mist.

"Rich, your heart is up," a voice said. "Calm down, friend."

He breathed faster, his lungs beyond control. Each beat of his heart boomed in his chest.

"Rich, breathe normally," Anastasia said. "You're fine."

"The jahannam I am!"

"Don't be afraid," she whispered. "You were born knowing nothing of what was to come, and you will die the same. How terrible is life if you live in terror of each coming day?"

His lungs spasmed, refusing his control, and his breathing became a flutter. His head grew light, his thoughts firm as feathers. His heartbeat roared in his ears like a rocket's engine.

I'm suffocating! There's no air! I have to get out of this thing!

Rich fumbled at the inflatable canopy around his head.

"He's freaking!" someone shouted, far away.

His hands froze, pulled away from his neck by some force. The inflatable canopy was a gray mask dim as death, scintillating as someone's bright helmet lights shone behind it. "Rich!" Anastasia's voice thundered. "Stop. Slow down your breathing."

Rich struggled, found the grip adamant as iron. His hands were frozen mid-air.

"Rich!"

Whoever held him, shook him. He came back to himself, felt the rocketing of his heart and breath. He cut off their fuel, forced his breathing to slow. His lungs fought him at first, stuttering. Gradually, the thunder of his heartbeat gave way to the whirring of air pumps. The cool breeze of the air system chilled the cold sweat trickling down his cheeks and forehead.

He was safe. He had air and pressure. He was among, if not friends, at least not enemies, not for the moment.

As his mask cleared, he saw Anni, glowering at him. Her face was that of command, blue eyes chilled as asteroid ice piercing into his soul. She was the one holding his hands away from his neck.

"You're strong," Rich said.

"I'm a spaceman."

"I didn't expect that." The fog of his breath was clearing. Anni, lighter and a half-head shorter than him, held his arms as firmly as Don might have.

"You good?" She lifted her chin, eying him.

He shook his head, and she released him. Several hands patted him on the back, offering him a gentle squeeze.

"I'm just going to say this," Matchstick said. "If they really are to join us, *that* is a liability."

Anni rounded on Matchstick, stepping inches from his face. "An infant cannot walk at birth, Matchstick. But we care for them as our own soul."

"J-join?" Rich asked.

"They don't know?" Someone said.

Another answered, "That's what all this is about, dumkin."

"I'll explain," Anni said. "Follow."

For whatever reason, Rich obeyed. As his steps went, they became easier. Plumes of fine, gray dust billowed around their feet, shimmering through their lights. And gradually he saw the night above differently—not terror, not a monster, but a bright ocean of gleaming stars older than their world.

The dome behind disappeared behind a mount of rock, but so did Rich's terror, swallowed up by the beauty of the Lunar night. His lungs relaxed in his chest. The lightheadedness and racing thoughts passed.

They came to the edge of something—a small crater. The entourage slipped down the side like kids playing in a park, skidding through the billowing shitdust. Rich let himself slide off the ledge, balancing himself as his feet glided down. He bounced, and his heart bounced with him.

"Wow!" he said, not meaning to speak.

"I take it you don't get out much," Anni said, and he saw they were on a private channel.

"No. Not really."

"How many years have you been here, and you haven't come out, just to enjoy the beauty above?"

Too many.

At the bottom, they continued. Time didn't matter now, their movements almost eternal. They approached the far side far rapidly than he expected and a light flickered on around a door hidden in the rock.

Anni tapped the panel on her suit's wrist, and the door's lights flashed. It slid into a recess in the wall, opening to an airlock.

Inside, after the pressure returned, Anastasia unfastened the canopy of Rich's suit, tucking the thin fabric down around his neck like a shirt collar. For a moment, he thought she'd kiss him, but she smiled and moved over to help Don.

"I take it there's no tunnel here," Rich said.

"We're in a tunnel."

"I mean, to or from anywhere else?"

She gently wrapped him on the head with her knuckles. "Big thinker. There is a tunnel system with Loonies above us, but we'll be going further down."

"More human shields?"

She didn't answer.

Rich sighed. "What do we change into?"

She looked at him curiously. "You wear your suit. You'd be underdressed any other way."

"Oh."

"This is a spaceman place. We let Gray Horizons come too, if they behave." She smiled and winked, looking around at the group. They too had removed their hoods. They nodded and smiled in return, but with a harshness in their gaze, a tension etched on their features.

Anni added, "Besides, the spaceman is always prepared. I still feel naked not wearing a basic pressure suit at all times."

She opened the other side of the airlock door, leading down a short hall to a large elevator. From there they went down into the depths, all in silence. It could have been kilometers. At the bottom, she led them to another wooden door. The group was less tense now, idle chatter beginning among the members.

The door was stained a chestnut brown, made with real wood. A symbol of some kind—three interlocking triangles— was engraved on its surface surrounded by a primitive-looking script. At the top, a great stylized fish in relief jumped amid a sea of stars. Anastasia took hold of a golden handle and turned, opening it inward.

Sounds of riotous laughter, the scent of cooking, filled the air—the clank of drinking glasses, a cacophony of chattering voices. The door opened to a small stairwell that led upwards about head level.

The place was full. A few paces ahead of them stood the maitre d'—a thin, wiry man, unnaturally tall, with skin dark as space itself. He was shaved smooth at his jawline and atop his head, with two bulbous eyes bulging in their sockets.

"I know all of you, except two," the man said, pointing at Rich and Don with a willowy hand. His left hand remained behind the podium as sweat beaded at his brow.

"I vouch for them," Anastasia said.

"It takes two," the man said. "Even with your vouch." The man pointed at Don. "What happened?"

"My girlfriend."

The man nodded, as if he understood.

Anni looked at Match, who shook his head 'no.' Charles did likewise. Everyone else was silent.

"We've got business," Anastasia pressed. "Is Lily here? She has standing to vouch them."

"Hey, Lily." The man shouted over his shoulder toward a long, narrow hall. Moments later, the same black-haired woman from The Harsh Mistress appeared from a place off to its side.

"You vouch these two guys?" the tall man asked.

"Which two?"

"The two I wouldn't know, smart ass."

She looked at them quietly. "I'll vouch the thin, Indian-looking one."

"The what?"

"The dark-skinned one. Cute, thin."

Me, cute?

"What about the other one?" the man asked. "The fat one."

"Lily…" Anastasia growled.

"Space him."

"Lily! You know—"

And that was when the gun came out.

11

———

Human society arises out of instinct and violence. Deny these, and a society will fall apart, just as it did for the United States and Old Europe, just as it one day will for the Communist Party of Earth. Our ideas of paradise preclude instinct and violence, and wrongly so. For why would heaven be anything but a creature's natural habitat? No, if human beings were made for paradise, then paradise must be a violent, instinctual place, a place of blood and orgiastic pleasures—a devil's womb. Therefore, we know the prophesied 'Paradise of Stars' is not a thing to one day exist: it is the state of spaceman society today.

-What we Built: Spaceman Society and Social Construct
By Odin Jörmungandr Pretorius

The man held a bead on Don, the weapon in his hands still as death. His face was emotionless, cold as asteroids in deepest space. It too was like the weapon that Matchstick and his brother, Charles Granite, carried: small and black, its barrel tipped by a lens of glittering crystal.

Another laser?

Rich raised his hands. Their entourage did the same, including Anni. Don's chin quivered, eyes darting around the room.

"I'm sorry, stranger," the skinny host said, oddly warm. "I can burn your brain instead of spacing you. Make it quick, painless. I'll take you to the back, give you a half-hour to set your affairs in order. We have a cozy little room in the back setup for just this sort of thing. Drinks on the house. We aren't savages, you understand?"

"One of you will die." Rich tensed. Around the room, staff emerged carrying weapons large and small, all a similar configuration of barrels tipped with lenses. The patrons stood, everyone one of them in spacesuits, everyone one of them armed.

"Lily, please," Don begged. "I'm *sorry*."

She crossed her arms, eying Don like an insect. "Not as much as you will be, I think."

"Lily," Anastasia said. "You agreed you *wouldn't* do this if I brought them."

Lily shuffled, refusing to look at Anni.

"Come on," the host said, gesturing towards the back with his weapon. "I'm sorry, but you came to a spaceman place. I can offer this consolation, however. You will sleep in starlight." He smiled, an odd mix of sunny warmth and icy cold.

"Lily," Anni hissed again. Wide-eyed, Don trembled.

Matchstick shoved him forward, cackling. "Be gone with this Earth-born orbitraff!"

Don stumbled, cut from the herd like a doomed animal. He looked to Anni, to their entourage, to Rich. Rich's heart jolted, racing. The roar of blood filled his ears.

But what can I do?

"N-no…" Don whimpered. "P-please."

Rich eyed the host. *I could rush him—but the gun?!*

"Fine. I vouch," Lily said. She muttered lowly, almost indecipherable from the distance. "Not worth the hell I'd pay…"

"You sure?" the maitre d' said. "You know what happens if they snitch. Sensitive things pass through here."

Lily laughed. "*Da, spaceman. Si si shama, moi devushka.*"

The man pursed his lips and secreted his weapon within the podium. "As long as we agree on consequences. You make yourselves comfortable wherever." He turned to Anastasia. "A booth is reserved for you, your shipmate, and the two gentlemen." Smiling uncomfortably, he added, "I admit it would be awkward, spacing a reservation Old Black Suit booked himself."

Shipmate? Old Black Suit?

Don exhaled long and slowly, his eyes shut, trembling. "Am I supposed to feel better?"

The man smiled and nodded. "If you've been invited here, you will come to understand our ways in time, but I leave that to your sponsors."

The group broke up. Matchstick, his brother, and the rest of the entourage took a table in a large room to the left, through a tall arch. The host led Anastasia, Lily, Don, and

Rich down a hall to their right, to a private booth. He gestured for them to enter. There was a staticky hum as they passed through its entrance. Inside, the hum faded, along with all outside noise.

Their host stooped to follow moments later, carrying menus—again the staticky hum as he entered. "This booth is silenced. If there's a problem, hit that button." The maitre d' pointed at a tablet on the screen. A red button with "panic" written on it flashed in the bottom corner. "I'll have a squad in here in ten seconds."

"They'll be no need," Anni said.

"Better safe than sorry." The man smiled, sending a shudder through Rich. Don looked away, the subtle shiver of his flesh betraying his fear. Again, the static sound, and the man was gone.

Anastasia studied the menu. She huffed, and a look settled over her like she remembered something. She opened her small bag and drew out a knitted shawl—white, embroidered with small, delicate flowers—and threw it over her pressure suit.

She grinned. "There, now I look both a proper spaceman and moonjiniya."

"What if I hit that button?" Lily said. "Right fucking now?"

Anni's smile melted.

Lily wore a tan jumper made of heavy fabric, smudged in grease like the other night at The Harsh Mistress. Grime dotted her bangs, her cheeks, her forehead; on her lapel, a patch, "Dark side Logistics." There was something small and withdrawn about her, even if she could explode like dynamite. Concealed beneath the jumper, Rich spied a simple pressure suit like their own.

"I'm sorry," Don said. "How many more times do I have to say it?"

"Much as I love Anni, it's gonna take more than desperate words and puppy dog eyes to patch this reactor breech, downlover. I gave you the high-g experience last night. *After* some back-tunnel whore. And you still wouldn't agree." Her chin quivered. "Now Anni tells me you're in trouble. So you'll consider what *I* want only when it's *your* ass in the airlock."

"You're asking a *lot*," Don said.

"You need a lot!" Lily slammed her fist on the table. "Do you think it's easy putting together a force to raid a UN black site?!"

What kind of people are these? All those guns. Willing to put Don out an airlock casually as a handshake. Now they're talking about raiding the project. A dangerous place, a dangerous people… He had indeed been honeypotted by these strange women, but to what end remained a mystery. *They don't really need us… Why are we here?*

"Lily," Anastasia scolded. "Don didn't know our ways. You knew that."

Rich offered Anni his warmest smile. "What ways? Someone clue the poor old Earther in."

Anastasia sighed. "That's the keyword, 'Earther.' You see, Earth marriage customs and those of the spaceman somewhat differ."

"Ah," Rich said, glancing at Don, remembering what Lily had called the man her husband at the Harsh Mistress. "Do tell. What about marriage?" He did his best to conceal his trembling. Wherever this conversation led, it was balanced on a knife's edge.

Anni explained, "If a spaceman woman lets some rock hopper pump all his helium-3 in her reaction chamber, it *means* something. It goes back to basic resources and what happens when people do that."

Rich stared at her blankly. "Repeat that."

She did, and elaborated: "For example, if you have the prerequisites to make condoms, you can also make pipe sealant."

"And you can never have enough pipe sealant," Lily added.

"Huh," Rich said, and scratched his chin.

"Oh come on, Rich, you know how babies are made," Anni said.

"You don't seal the pipe." Rich frowned. The need for concentration had forced the fear from his mind. He thought he had her meaning, but wasn't sure if the metaphors were lining up. "So let me guess, there's a little spaceling on the way?"

Anastasia shook her head. "No, no, but apparently, Lily dropped a port-daughter's trap on Don, and expected *him* to understand what it meant."

So I didn't quite have the meaning. At least there isn't a little Don on the way. That will make this easier to sort out.

"Oh, he's out in the bars every night," Lily accused. "How could he have not known?!"

"In my defense, I've pumped a lot of helium-3, and never gotten a bill."

She glared. "Oh, I forgot, no proper spaceman would have you. All you had were moonjin *shlyukha*."

Anni turned on Lily: "You're the one who thought you'd slip an Earther a bit of stardust and buy a ship with it. Then you thought, if you told him about us, two angels would mend the shaitan."

Lily moaned, "But my parents are on their way with the ship right now from Mars—and what am I supposed to tell them? They were so proud of me!" She buried her face in her hands. Her back shook, crying. "If I'm not married proper, I can't get the ship."

"But we can still save the subjects." Anastasia ran her fingers through Lily's hair. "Papa will do that for us."

"For *you*," Lily said and batted her hand away. "Strange. Everyone here gets what they want, except me!"

Don reached out, gently touched her wrist. She growled, and Don withdrew his hand. "I hope you've had your shots."

Tear stained, Lily glared at him. "This is *your* fault, downlover. You've ruined *me*." She shook her head and buried her face again.

"Now you're just being dramatic," Anastasia said.

"Hold up," Rich said. "You're going to *have* to explain some things. Ships? Who will do what for us?"

Don sighed. "Oh boy, here it comes. What put me off…"

Anastasia cleared her throat. "Lily's father, patriarch of their family, is Odin Jörmungandr Pretorius."

The name hung in the air. It evoked something, a feeling. The same feeling as the other day when Dr. Winn mentioned it. Rich bristled, memories from his youth stirring, and he had it—

"Lord of Pirates! King of Spaceman!" Lily said.

"A criminal," Don whispered. "A terrorist. One whose

hands drip with more blood than any old American emperor."

The Scourge of Saturn.

Lily's eyes grew dark and hot.

But he's been under house arrest on Mars for years…

Anastasia placed her hand on Lily's shoulder. "No, dear. He's just being honest about what he believes. Don, how much do you know of Odin personally, and how much is just propaganda by your government?"

Don looked away.

"Terrorist, criminal," Anastasia said. "You could say that about the head of any government. One man's saint is another man's devil."

"Devil, or god?" Don said. "Some of you people worship that man."

Lily glanced down.

"Worship?" Rich said, the offense flaring in his spirit.

"You can't send a man into the void," Anastasia said, "and not send God with him. Desperate men will make a god out of anything. It's kikipa, but it's a human."

"Only God is god," Rich said.

"Yes, spaceman," Anni said. "But no one here is putting forth the case of Odin Jörmungandr's divinity. My point is: every paradise has its devil, and every devil, its paradise."

"And the angel of one paradise is the devil of another," Rich said, catching her meaning as his offense cooled. *I suppose it could be true. What could these people be to Earth but devils, and what would Earth be to them but the same?*

"Odin is a killer," Don said.

"And you think you aren't?" Anni mused. "What would you do to save Rich?"

Don fidgeted, glancing down.

"Rich, what would you have done to save Jaimie, your son?"

It was the first time Anni had spoken Jaimie's name. She must have heard it somewhere. But from the smirk growing on her face, she knew it hit him.

"Anything," he hissed. *And yes, I am the one who had him put down like a sick dog!*

"Killer," Anastasia said. "What people haven't killed to save their own?"

"It's true," Rich said, shocking himself. "You can figure that out, even with the history the State lets us read."

Don's mouth hung agape.

Hand flat on the table, Rich said, "But isn't he in jail? Mars or somewhere?"

A smirk spread across Anni's face. "He was, and your State won't admit they let him slip away. He's been many places since, and now he's coming here."

"Here?" Rich said, blinking. Dark implications hung. The UN Longbow, the ship Jaimie loved, had been put into mass production decades ago just to deal with Odin.

"But still," Don said. "With his reputation—"

"I've met Odin," Anni said. "When Lily and I married, I went to him, and he showed me wonders beyond belief. Almost enough to make me believe in kikipa. But back to the ship—in accordance to spaceman custom, Odin won't accept mine and Lily's marriage as complete until we have husbands."

"Husbands?" Rich said. "Plural?"

The three of them nodded.

"Oh boy," Rich said. *Just like Ivanka Gretel Gootberg at the*

Harsh Mistress only days ago. "Why husbands?" He drew out the 's' of the last word for emphasis.

"Backups."

Rich shook his head to clear his thoughts, making sure he understood. "Excuse me? I don't understand what that…"

"A spaceman marriage, at its minimum, is two men and two women."

"Huh."

Don flushed.

She continued, "Think like you live on a spaceship. What do you want if a system fails? You'd want a backup. Ideally a backup for a backup for a backup. Well, we made that part of our family structure. We would want a second mother and father, minimum, to have kids and—"

"But wouldn't a hired crew be simpler?" Rich said. "They'd know what they're doing aboard a spaceship at least. Mixing work and marriage as a requirement seems like a hassle. Persephone and I were married, but I don't know that we'd have done well working in each other's sphere. If you need a gene donor, I'm sure Don would be glad to do the deed." Rich winked at Don. "But I don't think either of us are what you are looking for."

Don nodded in the corner of Rich's eye. Disgust spread across their faces.

"Down thinking," Lily sneered. "Earthjin decadence. You deprive children of their identity, letting them be raised as strangers on their own decks! Grow up missing half their heart!"

Anastasia wet her lips. "That surprises me coming from you."

"I have my beliefs on marriage, but they're my beliefs. I'm also from Earth."

Anni frowned. "I thought you were more like us. We, as a people, can be very traditional. Spaceman ships are crewed by families. Like any other family, Lily's is requiring her to have a crew, a minimum of four married adults, to inherit the ship. We can hire any other hands we need."

Rich let the words sink in. "So, you have three. Who are you looking at as 'fourth mate?'" The was an odd feeling in his heart, like fear and hope danced atop a tilt-a-whirl. They stared at him, and Rich's heart skipped a beat. He laughed. "Why the jahannam would—"

"You two are work-brothers," Anni said. "You already play nice together. You'd make good husbrothers. There's no better pairing than best friends."

"It makes the whole more stable," Lily added.

Rich took a deep breath.

"You can say no," Anni said. "Lily just won't get her ship. Of course, that complicates things."

"Complicates how?" Rich said, a chill running down his spine. Minutes ago, they were willing to kill Don. Now these bizarre people were proposing marriage.

"In this process, we've let you know some very sensitive information."

Rich glanced at Don. "So marry you or die?"

Anastasia frowned. "As the maitre d' said, we're not savages."

"No, of course not. You were just about to kill Don minutes ago! You just happen to have a cozy little room setup for just this sort of thing."

"Oh, come on," Lily said. "He deserved to have his seals rattled."

"You definitely rattled mine! I'm old. It wouldn't take much to put me in the grave."

"It's a no, then," Anastasia said, dropping her eyes. She looked to Lily. "I guess we hit the spaceports. Plenty of shit-dusters there that—"

"Wait, hold on!" This was too much. Rich's head spun. "I didn't say no, but—the starport? Just whoever?"

"We're practical. If it doesn't work, we'll just kick them out on some asteroid. Try again."

"But what about love?"

Anastasia smirked. "You have funny ideas about love, spaceman. Love is a thing that grows."

Lily nodded.

Anni continued, "No spaceman woman loves her man on their first night. We base our relationships around practicality, not kikipa. Usually the new spouse is whatever the family dredged up off a rock somewhere." Anastasia looked warmly at Lily. "Unfortunately, despite her normal spaceman sensibilities, love is something that's already grown for Lily."

Don frowned, shame plain on his face.

Lily's lips trembled. "Real love is made over time, like stew in a pot."

Rich had left his hand lying on the table. Anastasia cupped it, and electricity tap danced up his nerves from wrist to shoulder. He understood now why she had touched him as she did on the way over, why she had forced herself on him. *To let me know exactly what they were offering, to get me all riled up. Because that girl loves Don. And in this strange culture, that somehow puts me in the equation.*

"Well, if we do this, I'm not fucking you," Rich said, looking at Don.

His best friend smirked. "You're catching then?"

"Touché, friend."

A flicker of hope passed through Anni's eyes. "Wait, are you guys actually open to this?"

Rich looked away, still feeling the warmth of her hand.

"If Rich is," Don said, patting Rich on his shoulder.

"Wait, don't put this on me!" Rich chuckled. "There's still the matter of the Pirate Lord—and that is a matter. But if we do this, Don and I would be, what, co-husbands?"

"Husbands," Anni said. "Spaceman relationships are bisexual."

"Uhhh—nope." Rich stood, heading out of the booth. Don seized him, yanking him back down. "Don?!"

A confused look passed over Anni's face.

"I'm not homosexual," Rich said. "Nor do I intend to be—and neither is Don." *And if he is, it won't be with me!*

Anastasia shrugged. "You don't have to be involved. Your bedroom troubles could be a family secret. It's problematic. Almost as troublesome as if you two were only interested in each other."

Rich furrowed his brow. *Such a strange people. Their beliefs about love, sex, family. Who knew the most alien cultures could be humanity's own?* But yet, he could see the lines of evolution that took to get here, if he stepped aside from religious dogmatism.

"I don't know," Rich said. "Even sharing the same woman —women—sounds…"

Don? How could I do that with him? He's more like an

awkward adult son. The things that might happen in that arrangement, the haram, anti-sharian things…

"Oh come on. You aren't too good to double-dip with me." Two thick, meaty hands grabbed the side of Rich's head and twisted it, bringing his lips to Don's own. His breath was rank—chips, sour beer, and something rotten.

Rich tore his face away, gagging. "Hey!"

Don laughed. "You kissed me earlier."

A curious look passed over Lily's and Anni's faces.

"That… was different."

"Rich," Anni said, taking his hand again, massaging his palm between both of her own. "I'd like it to be you. I saw how you interacted with Thomas. If you can love an android that way, how much more would you love our kids? You'd bring maturity and stability. I've read your psych report. I think you'd be good for us."

"You have access to that?"

"Not officially."

Rich frowned.

"Fate dealt you a bad hand years ago. This is a chance to regain all you've lost."

The bitterness in Rich surprised even him. "It's too good to be true is what it is." He tore his hand away. *There's no way this works out. They're using me. Why would they want a scrawny old man?*

"I won't promise you paradise," Anastasia said. "I won't even promise you survival. Spaceman life is dangerous, but life always is. When you were a sperm chasing your mother's egg, nothing was promised. Her womb could have been the grave of your potential, and so could Luna now, if you don't do the spaceman thing. How many more Jaimies won't exist? And what might happen to Thomas?"

Rich rubbed his hands across his pants beneath the table. "And what about this pirate king? You don't think that's just a little concerning to—what did you call me? An 'Earthjin?'"

"Who else in the solar system can put together a force to oppose the UN?"

Rich looked away, trying to find a spot in the booth where he couldn't see Lily, Anastasia, or Don. His face burned. Tear threatened at his eyes. The promises, the likely lies.

"Why would he do that? Why would he help us?"

Anni sighed. "You remember the sentience test from the history books?"

"It replaced the Turing test. It was designed to see if machines were alive—Don't tell me!"

Anni nodded. "They passed. *All* of them. I told Papa Odin. He said, 'The spaceman owes a debt, and we will pay it.' It was the machines, after all, who gave us perfect fusion, a unified theory of physics, and material science centuries ahead of where we would have been. The Party can thank the machines for those precious space elevators of theirs and High Beijing."

Alive! And the Christofferson prophecies—if AI was alive again, Jannah's poison seed had sprouted. 'And I saw the Earth, our mother, turned to cinder, and all her children scattered to the stars.'

But Thomas, that sweet little boy, his sweet mother, even his angry father… and his pitiful sister. They would end the world?

Christofferson was a liar. It was the only explanation.

And if they were alive, if they had passed the sentience test…

"He'll help us save them?" Anni's arm wound around

Rich's own. "Don't resurrect my hopes. I've lived too long without them…"

Anastasia took his hand back into her own. "If you want to save Thomas, Rich, this is the only way. This op will go down whether or not you join us. The only question is will you wait it out in a Gray Horizons safe house, or will you be part of it—and if you don't join us, no promises on us taking you with us when we leave."

"And once it's over, Lily gets the ship? We can go off together?"

"Odin is leaving the solar system for another, on a different ship—"

"Like that's possible."

"It is. Takes a long time, generations even, but he and one of his sons, Tan'sien, are buying into a ship with about thirty other families, heading towards Tau Ceti."

Rich traded looks with Don.

"And we, the four of us—we'd really get to be together? I'd get to be a dad again?"

Anni kissed him on the cheek. "Da, spaceman. Only stars from here."

"You know what, I'm in," Don said. "I'm sorry, Lily, for what I did."

All three sets of eyes now fell on Rich.

"I-I don't know. What would this even be? Some weird version of a shotgun wedding?"

"It's a torchship marriage," Lily said.

So outlandish, how could this be anything but truth? "Let me think about it."

Anni nodded. "Don't take too long."

"Well, I'm sold," Don said. "I'm in, even if we have to find someone else—but I'd like it to be with you, Rich."

"Hey, I didn't say no!"

"Well, that's at least some good news. I'll order wine." Reaching across Lily, Anni began flicking through the menus on the screen.

———

Rich's head swam with wine as they emerged. His heart was light, and everything had that rosy feeling that made him think it would be okay. He could almost see himself married into a family with three adults.

Almost.

In the center of the great room ahead, Matchstick sat at a table by himself, glaring down the hall towards them. His laser was on the table in front of him, lying innocently in the open. He spun his weapon as he took a shot of liquor.

Lily pressed Don against the wall, giggling as she kissed him, then offered Anni a peck on the lips. Rich looked on, proud. *Whatever I decide, at least he's got an adventure ahead!*

Matchstick stood, pointed at Don. "So tell me! Is he the King of Fish?" He swerved to the side as he tried to stand, and his hand seized the laser.

Anastasia stepped between Match and Don. "Put it down, Matchstick."

Matchstick stepped around the table. "A gross, womanizing Earthjin suffocating in his own fat? Him, over me and my husbra, over our ship, the Mahabharata?"

"That ship will *never* fly, Match. And you have an

alladamn harem ship to boot! You know how we feel about that. How Odin feels."

"It *could* fly, with the reactor from the Sleipnir."

"So that's your plan? To gut Odin's ship for your own?"

Matchstick staggered sideways, pointing his finger at Rich now. "Is it him? Is *he* the King of Fish? An old man, his reactor a kilogram from running out of fuel?"

"Old? Odin, your king, is older than Rich by a large stretch. I'd like to see you call him old."

Slowly, to the side, the maitre d' drew his weapon from the podium. Match's gun flashed towards him. The two held each other at laser point.

The maitre d' shouted, "Put it down, Emmanuel-McChang!"

Matchstick's husbrother sauntered through the arch into the open area. "Hey, husband, we agreed no disintegrations?"

"Which way shall I fly, dear brother? Towards infinite wrath or infinite despair?"

"I will burn you!" the maitre d' warned.

Other patrons drew their weapons slowly, watching the scene unfold.

Charles Granite took a step towards Matchstick. In a flash, the little man turned his weapon on his husbrother.

"First off," Charles said. "I don't like you when you quote Milton. Second, if you shoot me, Sonya will use your testicles for boa practice."

Matchstick turned back towards Anni and held gun on the maitre d' to his side. "Our ship will be a wonder! We can continue Odin's legacy after he's gone far better than these poor little Earthjin. I am like his own son. Together, we can retake Saturn and Jove. Maybe even Earth herself. Make space for the spaceman."

As he spoke, Matchstick made the mistake of gesturing with his laser, briefly turning its deadly snout from any living being in the room. Charles pounced. The mountain of a man crashed atop his brother, sending him to the floor.

"Little brother," Matchstick shouted. "Let me be!"

"Oh no," Charles snarled, pressing on his back. "You are not doing this here!"

Little brother? The big one?

Matchstick growled, squeezing off a shot that sent a spray of greygoo from the wall with a hiss. In the confusion, Matchstick wriggled free. He came up with the laser, took aim at Don, and, just before he fired, Charles yanked him down. A faint blue beam struck the wall above the four of them. A loud hiss, and plaster showered down.

Through the mist, Rich saw the maitre d' draw a bead and fire. The beam missed, Matchstick saved only because Match and Charles rolled as they struggled. The floor beside them erupted upward into a plume.

The large man pinned Match down, hissed, "Stop, you idiot!"

The air was thick with tiny particles of debris. Rich coughed. Alarms blared. Everyone in the bar, from where they took cover, pulled a soft hood over their pressure suits or donned helmets.

As Matchstick lay helpless on the ground, the maitre d' and a half dozen others lined up killing shots. "I'm sorry, fellas, you broke the rules, and you know the penalty."

Charles shut his eyes and hung his head. "You stupid little—"

"Hold!" Lily shouted, shaking her head. "Not today." She took Don's hand and squeezed it. "Not today. Just ban him."

"Do you speak as Odin's agent?" the maitre d' asked.

Lily nodded.

Slowly, as the clouds of dust billowed through the room, floating towards the air intakes, their host lowered his weapon. "Fine, but I'm sending him the bill when these two don't pay." Other patrons followed suit, their gaze locked on either Lily or the Emmanuel-McChang husbrothers.

"We'll pay for it," Charles said, slowly getting up.

Anastasia strolled over, glaring at Matchstick. As he lay helpless on the ground, she took his weapon. "Don't let him have it back!" She handed it to Charles.

"I won't." Charles offered his hand to Matchstick, still lying on the floor. "You and I are going home, while we still have any respectability left." He pointed at Rich, Don, Lily, and Anni with his other hand. "*They* are going to go off on their nuptial dinner—At least I suppose they are?"

"It's still being negotiated."

"Ah," Matchstick goaded, not taking Charles hand as he clambered to his knees. "The poor little Earthjin, they are shy about dipping their peepees in the same fountain. What's wrong? Do you find the spaceman's ways, the ways you marry into, *écœurant*?"

Charles Granite picked Matchstick up by the collar and held him too high for his legs to touch the ground, letting him dangle like a hanged man. Then he walked him back through the arch.

Setting the man down in the other room, Charles returned, embarrassment plain on his face. "We will leave, but I think, if Lily's group was on their way out, they should go first. I wouldn't want my assailant waiting for me somewhere on the Lunar surface. I'm so sorry for his behavior."

His arms crossed, standing on the other side of the arched doorway, Matchstick growled.

"Come on," Lily said. "We have yen in low orbit."

"What?"

"We've got important business that can't wait," Anastasia translated. "Let's put all this nastiness behind us."

Outside, they loaded into the elevator, Rich asked, "What's a King of Fish?" The odd phrase had stuck in his mind.

"A prophecy," Lily whispered as the doors shut and they began to ascend. "A century and a half ago, a prophet of the Starwalkers came among us, granted wonders by his god. Gold dust appeared as he spoke; angel feathers, as he prayed. He healed our sick; warmed the lungs of long frozen dead, given to space; and, before he left, made prophecy: a king would rise and save us from the Earthjin. To him, God would give the true sharia, the secret of the life eternal. And by his grace, the spaceman would swim the starry seas like fish the oceans of old Earth, the chosen of God."

"Kikipa," Anastasia said softly. "All of it."

"Wife," Lily said. "We agreed to never argue about religion. Don't start now. He was talking about my father."

12

A man
finds himself only
In the maze of
his own heart.

-The Bliss of the Bodhisattva, Sutra 301

As Rich and Don traversed the Lunar landscape, heading back they came, Lily and Anni guided them through the infinite possibilities of the Lunar night. The four of them talked as they bounced along, getting to know each other for the first time on the eve of marriage. In the course of conversation, Rich learned why Matchstick had attacked them.

"Charles and Matchstick were once our shipmates," Lily explained. "They wanted to be spaceman, like their parents once were. Papa Odin trained them, and Match and Odin got close, father and son close."

"So we've stepped between him and a father figure?" A pang of guilt cut through Rich. He felt sorry for the man, even though he'd tried to kill Don.

"Da," Lily said. "And the ship. Match has aspirations to strip the *Sleipnir*'s drive for that pile of scrap they've claimed."

"Why?"

"Military grade. Unregulated."

"M-military?" *That could only mean—*

"The heart of the *Sleipnir* once beat in a UN Longbow. *Gilgamesh*, I believe. Can pull thirty g's in a pinch."

Rich whistled. *Thirty g's.* Space travel wasn't his forte, but he knew the long-term limits of the human body were well beneath that. *It must be something they'd use only in a pinch...*

"Match did what any spaceman would do," Lily said. "It'll hardly be the last time someone pulls a gun on you."

So much in all of this. Stolen warship drives, people who kill casually as a handshake. What have I gotten myself into?

"I know this must be strange to you, Rich," Anastasia said. "The spaceman occupies a hard place in life, but not without its rewards. I was just like you when I took Lily's offer years ago, and I wouldn't go back for all the green of Earth."

"What drove you away from Earth?" Rich asked. "Your dad was Middle Party. Y'all should've had a nice life there."

Silence. Anni bounced ahead, beside Don, hunting for words alone in her spacesuit. Just when Rich was about to change the subject, Anastasia's voice cracked as she spoke:

"They killed my mom." There was pain in her voice, the pain of truth.

"What?"

"My father, he—I'm getting married, spaceman. It's supposed to be a happy time!" All alone in her pressure suit, she sobbed before stopping herself.

"I'm sorry."

"Not your place. I don't believe in much when it comes to things. But I've observed a pattern in the universe, a sine wave of fate. And one day, those bastards will be visited by a vengeance dark as blackest night. We'll have the subjects thanks to Papa Odin, and all go off to a new life among the stars."

Rich felt the hair on the back of his neck stood up. *What was it that street preacher said?*

"Spooky," Don muttered.

"What?"

"Nothing," Rich said. "Just one of those odd coincidences that happens now and then. I think you call them 'kikipa.'"

The lights of Dome 31 grew brighter as they bounced towards its airlock. So much had changed since they left hours earlier, so much still could change.

Could I be a part of this?

As the lights grew brighter, Anastasia asked Rich to tell his story. It seemed odd. She obviously knew it if she had read his file.

He obliged anyway, going on about his life growing up in Canadian-occupied Mississippi. His upbringing was unre-markable, apart from when, at sixteen, both his parents died in a car crash—an event practically unheard of in modern times. That segued naturally into the story of Jaimie and Persephone.

"... all our woe, with loss of Eden," Lily said.

"I don't get the reference."

"The same poet Matchstick quoted," Anastasia explained.

"Is it a spaceman thing?"

"Very much so," Lily said.

Rich nodded, noting Milton as someone to read one day.

Into the Dome they went, changing out of the suits and into their regular clothes. They traversed the stinking dome again and descended several levels through multiple airlocks. As they went, they continued talking, while a faint, rhythmic beat began pulsing through the rock.

Don discussed his upbringing, talking about his mom, 'a scatterling rat,' who found her way into Party service as a comfort woman. "My dad—actually, I'm pretty sure he wasn't my biological father. I didn't get my red hair from him —My dad kind of just tolerated me until I was old enough to get out. Signed my paperwork at fourteen so I could take the space elevator up to High Beijing and attend vocational school. I was a Party tech by sixteen, and *wǒ zài zhèlǐ*."

Rich saw the source of the music now. They had arrived in front of a lively nightclub, the Ex Terra.

"You were on your on from fourteen?" Anastasia said, warmth in her voice.

Don nodded.

"Little lost pup," Rich said.

"Christofferson, people! I'm not broken. I think Rich and Anni have been through way more."

"Absence in the soul can be as great a pain as any," Anastasia said, stroking her hand along his cheek.

Rich threw his arm around him. "Suffering isn't a competition, Don."

A group of young teens—practically kids—walked around them into the club.

"Is this where we were headed?" Rich asked.

"I figured we'd all dance while you decide—unless you've decided."

All three of them met his gaze with expectant eyes.

"Would you really want this, Don? With these women. With me?"

Don nodded. A strange warmth filled Rich. A light rose in his soul, only now revealing that, for years, he had been wrapped in shadows as dark as Dr. Winn's coat. The four of them, what could they build out there, among all those many stars above. And his thoughts became rapture, a poetry of emotion and images.

Kids clamber over us, saplings striking for the dawn, until they tower—spacemen!—shading decks that are their own. Streaks of gray fill our hair; time's river carves her wrinkles. I wither before my lovers and fade away happy, an old, rotting oak, dreaming in the spring of its bright seedlings, in a new and god-right dawn. My seedlings, and Don's, a ship full of Jamie's...

A pain cut through him. *Can I still father children? I'm old, and space isn't kind to the reproductive system...*

"More information needed," Rich said, tearing himself away from the hope. "You've got to understand, I'm an old man."

Consternation spread on their faces. Anni nodded and said, "We'll have to move if we're going to loiter."

The door opened, and a throng of young people, thin and

lithe, squeezed past them. They ignored Rich and his almost family.

"Or not," Lily corrected.

"Why me?" Rich shook his head. "Apart from the work-brother thing, what can I offer? I'm sixty! I might not even be able to father kids, let alone raise them."

"Nothing wrong with having an elder male," Anni said. "And whoevers' bodies they come from, the kids belong to all of us."

"Elder male?" Rich said.

"An older, wiser man," Lily said.

"I know what male means."

They giggled.

Anni explained, "Young spaceman tend to be all trigger-be-happy and devil-may-Carrie. You'll be the better angel of Don's worse nature, and he'll be the little imp whispering in your ear. You'll be good for each other."

How did Ivanka put it at The Harsh Mistress? 'The good Papa and the bad Papa?'

"Ka-chinga, ka-ciao and all the yen is down," Lily said, crossing her arms and smiling pleasantly.

Do they see how close I am to saying yes? The desire churning in my heart? Strange as all this is…

"Maybe," Anastasia said to her, then to Rich, "Anything else?"

Rich looked at Don, letting the nagging question from the whole affair out from the shadows of his mind. "You said we didn't have to be, but it was expected that we'd be, the two of us…"

Lily rankled her brow, clearly confused.

"He's talking about gomikry," Anastasia said. "But I already explained, it's not required."

"But it's expected?"

Lily's eyebrows lifted. "Oh, that's right. Their taboo." She looked between Rich and Don. "The relationships of a married crew are their own. Other spaceman will assume that you wear the same boots, but I'm fine if you two don't want to share. Match and his husbra don't."

Rich sighed, relieved.

"I'm fine if you just share us with no jealousy between you," Anastasia emphasized. "As far as you two, I think it'd be hot, but that's just a bit of acceptable decadence."

Lily added: "At least it's not the Americajin sickness, the teetotal gomikry. That kind steals a person's destiny, makes them unable to do the necessary thing. But there are the bachelor and sorority ships for them, I suppose."

"The spaceman ecosystem will make a place for you," Anni said, smiling.

'God makes room for all in Xir kingdom!' —If I have their meaning.

Don's hand wove into Rich's own. There was no threat of sexuality in it, not anymore. It carried understanding only. Don spoke gently to Rich: "I'm okay with this, brother. And if you ever do decide to try gomikry, I might be open to it."

"I think you're pretty in stockings too, pal."

"So is that enough?" Lily pressed. "Are you in?"

Rich glanced at Don. There was a spark in his friend's eyes, a spark he felt with all of them. "No."

All of their eyes fell.

"I mean, I'm not ready to say yes. I just…" Rich turned, rubbing his hand through his hair. "Marriage is a vice for the young. I don't know that I've got the head for it—or the heart."

"And what about Thomas?"

"What is this? You're telling me, if you don't marry me, I can't go?"

"It'd cause confusion," Anastasia said. "A new husband might feel you're making a pleasure circuit on his yen. No. If you don't marry us, you'll get to live, but we'll be far away. You'll be left a fugitive in the shadow of Earth, all on your own."

Rich started to protest, but Don cut him off, "Rich, look, this is sort of our dream. Not exactly what we planned—"

"Your dream," Rich snapped. "I don't have dreams anymore." Rich turned away from them again, reaching inside himself for something, for anything, and finding nothing.

I'm grappling with myself in the dark, like Candle Bodhisattva for the oracles of God, that Christofferson might ascend to heaven.

"You can't tell me, you can't tell me that this is *really* how it is!" Rich jabbed his finger towards the tunnel floor. "Go ahead and say it now. Just tell me this is some sort of scam. There's no spaceship!"

"No scam," Anastasia said gently. Her eyes darted sideways in response to his raised voice, looking for cameras, looking to see if anyone was listening. "And we do this in our culture." She took his hand and squeezed it.

Somewhere deep, deep inside, Rich wept, begged to heaven that it really was true. "Bah. Sure it is."

"Common as shitdust," Lily said.

Rich pulled his hand back and turned, placing both his hands. "My Lord above, this had better be real!"

Six arms embraced him, three heads leaned against his own. Rich shut his eyes, leaning into the mass of bodies.

"Is that a yes, husbrother?"

Something cracked within him, something as primal and desperate as the struggle for life itself. A river of hope crashed through a dam in his heart, violently and suddenly, as if under the pressure of a small sea. He turned, wrapping his arms around the three of them, kissing each of them on the cheek.

"It's a yes," he said. "I don't know what this looks like, but it's got to be better than where I've been."

And a sudden realization shook him: *I have a family again.*

They danced at the Ex Terra, getting in with only a vouch from Anastasia this time. The guards still required a DNA scan. The expressions on the guards' faces as Lily pressed her palm to the sensor pad weren't lost on Rich, just as the madame's from The Harsh Mistress. And it wasn't just Lily. The guards looked side-eyed at Anastasia as well.

Something tells me there's a darker side to all of this. But who cares? How much darker could it be than what happened to my son, Jaimie? I've played by the Party's rules my entire life, and what did it get me? A lonely existence on a dead rock. If these girls are going to take me to the ball, I might as well dance! And if the devil has a price to pay, he can send me the alladamn bill!

And with those thoughts, Rich was led into the dark, a wife taking each hand. The glittering lights. The harmless lasers. Sweating bodies dancing in shadows. Word of their union spread, and their night officially became a wedding party. Rich bought the entire bar drinks, twice, and barely noticed the hit to his bank account. He got a kiss on a cheek from more than one lady—and the odd guy.

As the alcohol took him, Rich found their little group surrounded, the club exploding into one giant celebration. A techno version of the wedding march blared across the speakers.

On the floor, yelling above the music, Anastasia and Lily continued to tout the virtues of spaceman living. How luminous the Ramadans and wonderful the Christmases, how beautiful a ship filled with growing children. Yes, it meant rearing lots of kids at once, but there were always enough parents, and kids could easily run a spaceship by eight.

There was also the skill set. A spaceman child grew up with an education in rocketry, particle physics, and advanced mathematics—hydroponics, resource reclamation, and mechanics. They even studied literature, because the spaceman loved stories, all types, and the love of reading was admired.

"Literature is the basis of civilization," Anni shouted over the music. "From cave paintings and ancient epics, to poetry and the English novel. If there was any other proof the spaceman might be the future of humanity, it's this fact alone!"

Lily had been born from a marriage lasting sixty years with twelve adults, people who gave all their children a solar-class education. "And never a divorce, airlock or otherwise!" Lily shouted with pride. It spun Rich's head.

I've got it now. I was so blind before! It's like when the scales fell from Christofferson' eyes and he saw the visions of God. This concept isn't strange. It's titanic! What would humans be if this had been our lifestyle for the last thousand years? Where will we be if this becomes the norm for the next millennium?!

Rich's heart swelled; his mind soared. "How do we make it official?"

"Make what official?"

"Our marriage. I assume we register it?"

"I'll handle the finer points of State registry. We'll have to be a little sneaky though, due to Lily." Anastasia took out her phone. After a few minutes, she stuck her thumb to it before passing it to him.

"Are we doing this now?" Lily asked. "As in right now?"

"Yen and dollars," Anni said, and passed her phone to Rich. It held a simple marriage compact. Party legalese wasn't all that different from their technical writing, just a different vocabulary and more confusing grammar. It seemed more private contract than any state document. He could have spent more time reading it, but, *What the hell!* He thumb printed it and grinned, despite the fact he knew his Cheshire Cat face made him look like an idiot.

"Convinced we're hiding nothing nefarious?" Anastasia asked.

Don and Lily quickly passed it between them. When Anni received it back, she finished the transaction and wrapped her arms around Rich. Don and Lily embraced too. Then they swapped girls. Finally, Don and Rich hugged each other.

"Husbra," Don whispered in his ear.

"Now comes the best part," Anastasia shouted, the music reaching a crescendo. "Consummation."

Down the hall, into the heart of the Lunar rock, a simple hotel was carved. Anastasia booked them a modest room with two Lunar queens. Rich paid. His heart raced as the four of them entered, Lily already clinging to Don like a wet t-shirt. Being traditional, Rich scooped Anni up, struggling to carry her over the threshold. She cackled, even though he just barely avoided hitting her head.

"I thought you were old," she said, standing beside him, stroking his chest.

"I guess we'll find out."

An awkward moment passed, in which the four of them stared at each other. Finally Lily took the lead with Don, Anastasia with Rich, guiding each man to a separate bed.

The room was a womb of rock clad in shadows. Beside Rich, Anastasia stroked his neck, and fluttered fingers down his chest. Their tips were smoldering embers, a pleasant burning.

Something in him recoiled as she leaned up to kiss him. Sudden and dark, impulse deeper than thought. He pulled away, driven from her like a chill from a fire's breath. As she reached for him again, he seized her wrist. She winced in the dark.

"Rich," Anni whispered. "It's okay."

He trembled as he held her away, blood boiling in his veins. "No. I, I can't." He tingled head to toe, shivered.

I should leave. This was a mistake.

There was something in him, something stirring, something terrifying. He couldn't move. He was trapped, trapped between desire and loss.

A real flesh and blood woman! What might happen with her,

with all of us. Another Jaimie, another corpse-fleshed child staring into night.

He smelled Persephone suddenly, somehow, in the intimate dark. The soft coos of Don and Lily were music, same as he and his wife—ex-wife—a lifetime ago. As he listened, their coos became weeping. Persephone, weeping for their boy.

Warmth.

He found his hand against someone's bare breasts. Against Persephone's bare breasts. She was here again, somehow, returned from the shadows, young as she was on their wedding night. Persephone, dread Persephone, mother of the damned.

"Don't be afraid of a real woman's touch," she whispered in his ear.

"Real woman?" and Rich withdrew, his face burning in the unlit privacy of the room. "You knew about Eurydice? I mean, the androids at the Eurekatron?"

I'm so sorry, my love. I couldn't wait for you to return!

"You aren't the first man with a case of autobimp syndrome." Her body pressed against him. "Let me, trust me, and I'll get you through it."

He let her. Her lips pressed to his own and worked their way to his neck. Buttons parted as she slipped his shirt open. A soft bite at his neck, a nibble his nipple, warmth gliding down his belly.

"Persephone!"

The ruffling of the covers the next bed over stopped.

"Rich," Anastasia whispered, and shook him.

"I'm sorry. I'm—"

A finger found his lips. "Relax," she said, loud enough for Don and Lily to hear. "Put your eyes on the stars, spaceman, and *pust' Zemlya sekai budet daku*." She undid the button of his pants, and carried him from the grave to Janna itself.

Sometime later in the intervening hours, the two girls rose and dressed. "We have business," Anni said. "You'll have some explaining to do back at base, but all will be well. How is it you religious types put it? 'The end of any righteous trial is heaven?'" In the afterglow, her words sounded as the proclamation of an angel. There were other instructions, but Rich didn't catch a one. When he next stirred, they were gone.

He and Don lounged on the same bed now, nude, unashamed as paradise. Sheets, pillows, and clothes were scattered around the room. The men snoozed until an alarm sounded on Rich's phone. He seized it groggily and noticed the time.

We're due for our shift. I wonder what she means about 'some explaining to do back at base?'

"We've got work," Rich said, shoving Don in his ribs. His new husbrother grunted.

"Hey," Don said, rolling towards Rich, his voice soft as morning's first light.

"Yeah?"

"Any regrets?"

Don's eyes were bright, alive with hope. How they had squinted, how the man had moaned, as he sowed a future beside Rich only hours ago. It was a face Rich had never expected to see in real life, the most intimate face of another man, his best friend—and one he would cherish forever.

"No," Rich said, the honesty of it ringing in his heart.

"Me neither."

13

The humans meant well, did well, and erred well... to their very end.

-Eureka Davis, First Android
President of the United States,
United States CIA Archives, 2061;
CPE Historical Record 114.1013.15

"And what *exactly* did you two do with my daughter!" Doc Hartford said, eyes aching with wounded fatherly pride.

As soon as they checked in, they had each received a summons. Sitting across from him now, the man glowered like an angry bear restrained by chain all too thin. *I suppose this is what Anni meant by some 'explaining to do back at base.'*

"I," Rich began. "Who is your daughter again?"

The patches of bare skin between his beard, goatee, and curly mop turned scarlet. "The pretty, blue-eyed blond that you two tentbuckers took out on the town last night! Where did you go, what did you do, at Moon York?"

"I don't see how that's your business," Don said.

"She's my daughter!"

"She's clearly an adult."

"And what's this business about you two fellows being married?"

So he knows. But why did he even ask about Anastasia then? If we're all married—

"Rich, you haven't made the slightest romantic overture towards anyone since you've been here. I might believe it, if it was, say, you and Ketevan."

"Ketevan?" Rich said.

"Ketevan—But you!" Doc Hartford pointed at Don. "*You are the worst womanizer I've ever seen! I don't believe for one moment you have any homosexual inclinations! Despite the rumors...*"

'Homosexual.' The word stuck in his mind. *Wouldn't our marriage be bisexual? Unless Anni somehow filed it for just the two of us...*

"I just never realized what Rich meant to me," Don said, cradling Rich's hand to his chest, gazing lovingly into his eyes. "Your daughter suggested we just confess our love to the world. I know the sharia frowns on it for Members of the Authority, but—"

Doc Hartford took several deep, loud breaths as he raked his hands through his hair. "Boys, please, what is my daughter up to? What did you all really do?"

"We banged her," Don said, and laughed. "Didn't want to

tell you that part, but you had to know. It was her wedding present to us since we swing both ways."

Rich could have punched Don, but he understood perfectly well his friend's actions. He too wanted to strangle Doc Hartford after what he had done to Anastasia—wanted to watch the man's face turn purple as the life drained from his eyes.

"Was it just a tryst or something more?"

"More?" Rich asked.

"More. Was it more than just relieving a passing itch?"

"No," Don said, shaking his head. "She just wanted a couple of spacemen…"

Rich cringed inside as Don used the s- word. He had already figured out the word was loaded when it came to Party bureaucrats, and the angry, knowing look that passed over Doc Hartford's face told him more than he realized.

"You two are *not* spacemen." Doc Hartford swiveled away from them in his chair, collecting himself. When he spun back around, he said, "At least she's choosing to live out her delusions with you. Don't see her again. Now get out of my sight, or I *will* have you shot. I'm in charge until Dr. Winn handles our troubles with Beijing."

They rose.

"By the way, where are you going?" Doc Hartford asked.

"To our shift," Rich said.

"What shift?" Doc Hartford asked, his glare softening. "You two are married now. Rich, you have enough time saved up to take a vacation until you retire. As Don's husband, you can break off any amount of that for him, and you did, apparently."

I did?—Anastasia…

Doc Hartford arched a questioning brow. "You applied for two months and one day's leave last night, did you not? Directly to Beijing? Your replacements shipped out this morning." He offered the pad to Rich.

Rich let it dangle in mid-air. "How did we get replacements? Ketevan is still in there *alone*. The Party seems to always have trouble with personnel."

Doc Hartford looked to the side. "There's a reason he's not been replaced."

"Oh?"

"We suspect he's a dissident. We're keeping an eye on him until we're sure."

Rich let the implications settle. "No, there's no way."

"Has he… reached out to you at all? Anything strange?"

Rich and Don both shook their heads.

"Just another guy, honestly," Rich said.

Doc Hartford nodded, grunting to himself. "Well, that's good news at least."

He stood, walked them to the door, and placed a hand on each of their shoulders. He pushed. "You boys have a great honeymoon. I'm happy for you. Thrilled, actually, to think I helped two Party members find love. Beijing will try to assign you together on your next assignment."

"Next assignment?"

"Well certainly. Two months leave—you're off the project." Doc Hartford grinned wolfishly. "Away from here and *my daughter*, you syphilitic ankle-grabbers."

"W-w-wait," Rich said. "I didn't realize…" He remembered the subsection of the project manual discussing leave now. It stated clearly a leave of a month or more resulted in reassignment. "I forgot—I want to stay on. We can…"

Doc Hartford shook his head. "I'm sorry, boys. Regs are regs." His hands still on their shoulders, he shoved them out into the hall. "The orders have already been recorded and confirmed."

"You're railroading us out," Don said. "Taking advantage of—"

"Look boys. We're all three men. If she wasn't my daughter, I'd probably have done the same. If she wanted my close male friend too, well, sharia be damned." He grimaced. "But she is my daughter, and you've tainted her with your prol seed. If you see her again, I will drag you back here and put your backs against the wall!"

The door slammed shut.

"So what just happened?" Rich said aloud.

Don placed his hand on the base of Rich's neck, squeezing gently. "I ain't even worried about it, honey."

"I wonder who's monitoring the subjects right now."

Don tugged him away from the door, whispered, "Rich, there's no way we're authorized. You *know* they're watching everything, and something about this…"

Rich didn't care, marching down the hall from the office. The monitoring station was on the way to their dorm, anyway. The door was cracked when they arrived. It opened as Rich knocked, not being properly secured. Ketevan turned his head slowly to look at them, then grimaced.

"The fuck you doing here, cocksuckers?"

Rich shrugged. "It's our shift?"

The man swore in his native language, an orgy of consonants, and pointed at them. "I was told you two were fired for cause. Might have had something to do with railing the boss' daughter." Ketevan grinned. "But now I hear you two are knocking boots. What hell is going?"

Don placed his hand on Rich's shoulder. "Both, actually."

"Ah," Ketevan said, lifting his eyebrows and looking at the screen. "Well, am pretty sure your clearance is being pulled, so get the fuck outta here." He mumbled something Rich missed.

"Well, Ketty, I didn't know you felt that way about good old Rich."

Ketevan glared at Don. "Was joke, okay? Always I joke. One day, I do something that'll make…" He paused, thinking. "… that'll make Papa Stalin happy. Finally! Maybe can have descent house one day, like party big wigs at that Heavenly thing." He looked back at his screen, continuing to mumble.

Rich took a step into the room. On the screen, Thomas was doing his lessons for the day. Mrs. Wells was cooking. "How are they?"

"Doesn't matter for you anymore, tovarisch. Don't forget the lube." Ketevan winked.

Don tugged at Rich's shoulder. They started to leave.

"Sorry, I'm cranky," Ketevan said. "Am alone, am always alone. But am happy for you two guys." He smiled at them, moisture glistening at the corner of his eyes. "If you guys are ever around, want to grab a meal or something? Maybe go to the bars? I only sleep with chicks, but I liked drinking with you, Rich."

"Sure," Rich said, his nerves tensing. "Sometime."

"Maybe after we get back moonside," Don clarified. "Headed off world."

Rich resisted the urge to look at Don, despite having no idea what he was talking about.

Rich and Don gathered their things. Coming to the base, they had barely brought a suitcase each. Leaving, however, they found they had several times that amount.

"I'm not giving up the trunk!" Don snapped. "Or the drawings!"

"Honey, I'm not paying extra for your baggage. The fees to Jupiter at outrageous!" Rich wasn't sure if they were play-fighting. Don seemed genuinely pissed.

"You know what! The base can ruffle through anything they want. I'm just shipping it all to storage."

Rich started to ask about the picture, the one Don had drawn of Rich, Jaimie, and Persephone.

But I'm starting a new life. It's time to move on.

Ten minutes later, each carrying a duffel and their Party licenses, they left Project Lebensraum. Rich raided a table of complementary water and snacks on the way out, cleaning it all into the bag. If anyone objected, no one said a thing.

"You want to flip them the bird too?" Don asked.

"Thinking about it."

They proceeded off base through the maze of unoccupied corridors.

"Well, guess we found out what Anni meant by 'some explaining to do back at base,'" Rich said as they broke into a main tunnel, moved towards a crowd of people. "It'd have been nice to know."

"Let's save any discussions for later. We need a room." Don tugged as his hand slipped into Rich's. Instinctively, Rich pulled his away only for Don's hand to clamp down like a vice. "*Hon,* did you forget we're married?"

Rich's face went warm. "Yes, dear."

Hand in hand, they walked, Don leading. Rich felt the uptick of his heart as they merged with the crowd, as each pair of strangers' eyes passed over them. Gay couples weren't out of place on Luna or Earth, but Congregation sharia frowned upon homosexuality.

The words of Imam Gerschowitz came back to Rich from a sermon in the distant past, as the Imam quoted the Book of Christofferson: "The homosexual is a beast, a perverse creature worthy of pity and scorn, but not death. God spared both you and him, so give the creatures place in the world to come, but mark their haramity."

"Don't be ashamed," Don said, giving Rich a knowing look. "It's just me." The contact of their skin was like smoldering embers, and not the passionate, feel-good kind.

They arrived at the spaceport, and Rich booked them passage to Moon York. As they stood in line to board their shuttle, Don shouted, "*Dear*, I'm so in love with you, I might lean my head on your shoulder as we fly."

"Really?" Rich whispered. "*That's* what you're going with? You do realize in zero g, you can't 'relax' with your head on my shoulder. It takes effort."

"Mmmmhmmm, but I just want to *show* all the world our love," Don repeated loudly.

Rich leaned in and placed his lips to Don's right ear, hearing the man giggle as if Rich whispered some quiet, sweet debauchery in his ear. "If you grab my dick or try to kiss me, you'll lose a tooth."

Don leaned in to Rich's ear, "Yeah? What about now?" and pecked him on the cheek.

The shuttle ride wasn't too bad, apart from Don demanding Rich snuggle for appearances—leaning heads on shoulders, putting arms around each other. It didn't take long for Rich to get relief, however. Don fell asleep as the shuttle cut thrust, and his head floated away from Rich's shoulder. The trip lasted for a daydream, one in which Rich cradled the belly of their two new wives, bulging with fresh life.

Off the shuttle, the two men disappeared quickly into the crowd. There was a quickness in Rich's step, a glimmer of hope rising in his heart.

We're really going to make it!

Where this would lead, to what bright or dark end, he couldn't say. But he had tasted something the night before with his three spouses, and he would go to the edge of Sol's light to keep it.

"Don, where are we going?"

Don was certainly leading them somewhere, but to where Rich had no idea. His pace was brisk and determined, a hint of anxiety betrayed on his face.

"Don!"

The path Don took was one winding and snaking, a course that circled through the the local tourist districts and tunnels, then back on itself again before breaking off into a wildly different direction. Down a dark alley somewhere, by a public recycler, Don pulled out his phone and chunked it.

"Do it!" Don hissed, turning to Rich. His face was tense and angry.

"What's wrong?"

"Rich, think about our exchange with Doc Hartford? Do

you really think they just let us go? Did you get a tracking chip when you joined?"

Rich blinked, focusing on what Don had just said. "N-no. The sharia."

"Same. So the only way they can track us now is that." He pointed to the phone in Rich's pocket.

"Don, my life is on that thing. My pictures of Jaimie, of me and Persephone. If we're on the run, I won't even be able to access my cloud again."

"Rich, shred the damn phone."

Rich drew his phone from his pocket, fingers trembling. His bag was nothing more than clothes and that damnable party plaque that held their licenses.

I wish I'd ask him to bring that picture of Persephone, Jaimie, and myself now.

His fingers quivering, the phone slipped his grip and fell, fell with all the casual tragedy of Jaimie's head that fateful day so many years ago, right into the recycler. Rich dove— too late. The machine whirred to life, grinding his past existence into shavings of metal and plastic. Rich's hand quivered centimeters from the chute, restrained by Don's grip.

"You do *not* want to reach in there!"

Rich's chin shook in the shock. "Huh," he said, not meaning to speak. "That's a Soviet Sweden Lethe Model Four."

Don snorted. "You want to just take it apart right now? Let me guess. You did a stint on recyclers?"

"I just lost my entire life."

"And you found a new one."

Rich's legs were weak. *Jaimie! My Jaimie! Persephone!* The

past was truly dead to him now, lost in a clumsy act of indecision.

"I guess all I've got is to go forward."

"The prophet and his wahi!" Don patted him on the shoulder, and off they went. Rich's legs burned as they trotted into the depths, as Don took Rich down a long, dimly lit tunnel in the middle of nowhere, one with half its lights out.

Water leaked from the ceiling. Somewhere above, a vital artery of spacefaring civilization oozed its lifeblood into the dry, dead rock around it. The water made its way down pores and crevices until it pooled on the smooth, manmade floor of the tunnel in which they now stood, making the air cool and damp.

"Don, where the jahannam are we?"

"You'll see." Don glanced over his shoulder, scanned once more up and down the tunnel. "I'm pretty sure this tunnel is both blind and deaf, from the Party at least. It's Gray Horizon maintained."

"They're doing a piss-poor job."

"Might be intentional. Lily took me down here once." Don glanced at Rich with a wink.

"I see. So you're assuming it's private enough?"

"Well, with what we came down here for, I hope it is. But you and I, we're down here for what's behind this door."

An airlock. Through it, Rich could see a large, dark cavern of some kind.

Don motioned to a locker similar to the one they used the night before, on their way to a marriage proposal. A panel beside it provided the air pressure and temperature on the other side of the airlock. There it was cold as Lunar night, the pressure far too low for a human to breathe.

Don opened the locker beside it. "You know what to do."

They suited up. Rich slipped inside his suit, easier this time, cramming his old clothes into his duffel. As the suit constricted over his flesh—truly bare this time—it was just as unnerving as it had been the day prior. The canopy inflated, ballooning out in a pressure test before all lights blinked green.

"I'm good," Rich said.

Don offered him a large okay sign and entered. When Rich followed, Don cycled the airlock.

"Don," Rich said, gazing through their exit doorway's window. "I don't see anything to stand on."

"There's a scaffolding beneath. You just can't see it." The pressure equalized, and Don pushed the outer door open. It was easily a four meter drop. Don dropped his gear over the edge and followed it, falling slowly at first, picking up speed at a fraction he would on Earth.

After he landed, Don recovered and moved out of the way, waving Rich down. Taking a deep breath, Rich did the same, dropping his gear and following it over the edge. Gravity tugged him down at roughly 16.6% of Earth's. To Rich's surprise, it hurt like hell when he landed.

"Damn that smarts!"

"I forgot you're old," Don said, grinning at Rich through the clear plastic bubble around his head. Rich gave him his best glare in return.

They stood upon old, wire-frame scaffolding near the roof of a derelict spaceport. The bay was fully enclosed and dark, only a handful of lights burning above, revealing the faint outline of overheard hangar doors. Beneath, ships in various states of disrepair spread out across the bay until they disappeared into the darkness. The nearest were small, but in the distance, the bow of a UN Longbow cut through the shadows. Hexagonal, its nose was the business end of a ship-length railgun, around which the rest of the ship was built.

The Day Herald! Rich raced towards it.

"Rich, wait!"

Seconds later, his heart pounding, Rich stood over the vessel, looking down its snout to the braces at its base. Ships berthed on Luna itself were magnetically launched. The bay was too short, but there seemed to be equipment nearby massive enough to lift the old warship.

If it's ever supposed to fly again, they'll be a launch tube somewhere nearby.

The ship's drive section was easily as long as the rest of the ship. Even in the dark, the large, conical radiation shield between the drive and crew sections was visible. Further down in rows, Rich spied the silhouettes of similar vessels.

"Jaimie's ship," Rich whispered.

"What?"

"Where are we?"

"UN mothball. Same Gray Horizons subcorp that manages the tunnels snagged the contract maintaining this facility."

Rich stopped. "You're telling me, a terrorist organization manages mothballed UN warships. Will they fly? What about their nukes?"

Don shrugged. "Don't know about nukes or flying. As far as anything valuable, this place has been the haunt of criminals and robbers for far too long."

"Why? Why would Earth *let* that happen?" It baffled Rich, the sheer idiocy of it, just letting such wealth walk away.

Don shrugged. "Some lucky colonial gets his hands on military surplus, and some bureaucrat gets to point to a cheaper balance sheet. Ka-chinga, ka-ciao, spaceman."

"You keep that up, you really *are* going to be a native."

"Isn't that the point?"

The back of Rich's neck tingled. "Don, shouldn't we have just set off an alarm or something? You can't tell me we just walked into a dead UN ship yard without raising someone's eyebrow."

"I never had a problem with Lily."

"But you were with *Lily*."

Don scooped up a long piece of pipe, raced back to the airlock, and tapped the door to the tunnel shut above them. "I reasoned pretty quick this was Anni's doing."

"Same," Rich said, unsure where Don was going.

"But, I'm not too sure. Hence why I'm taking us the back ways that Lily showed me. She's so paranoid, she makes teekers look sane."

It made sense now. Don was already thinking like a space-man. A backup for a backup for a backup.

"So what now?"

"Yes, indeed, what now?!" said a familiar voice with a Lunar French accent, one that made Rich's blood run cold.

"Did you hear—" Something struck Don, a dull beam. It kissed a spot on his chest, burning bright as sunrise. A dazzling flash followed. Don planked to the ground, convulsing but not whimpering—

Living fire danced through Rich's shoulder. A blinding

flash in the corner of his eye. A shock. Every muscle in his body seized up.

He tumbled, burning shoulder to neck. A loud, ominous hiss. The air drained from Rich's lungs, replaced by a terrible, aching cold. The canopy of his helmet collapsed, folding slowly against his face like a death shroud. He exhaled, remembering his Party training.

Desperate moments passed. Rich lay supine, twitching, his muscles frustratingly disobedient. He gasped, craving the absent air.

Airless—what a horrible feeling, what a horrible thing to call someone!

He needed his limbs to work. To patch his and Don's suit. To flee.

A thick-heeled space boot stomped on Don's chest, some type of rifle dangling from the owner's hand. Another knee found Rich's sternum, crushing him to the floor. Over Rich leaned a space-suited form, its visor swallowing his face in its visor dark as night.

Something pricked his shoulder—a small sting, insignificant to the pain he felt—and everything faded to black.

14

———

"Pain is the seed of enlightenment."

-The Bliss of the Bodhisattva, Sutra 35

Click-Ptchick Pause *Click-Ptchick.*

Waking, Rich shivered—cold, dreadfully cold. Something thin and tough wrapped around his torso, pinning his upper back against something hard, something... *Plastic?*

Two chilled metal rods pressed against his lower back. His butt and balls were bare, resting atop a coarse, hard surface. His feet—the floor was frigid and hard.

Metal?

His shoulder throbbed. An acrid scent scorched his nose, penetrating all his senses—*Cigarette.* A flash of light. His eyelids fluttered. Heavy, so heavy, like he sat in twice the gravity of Earth. His mind pressed from unconsciousness like a chick struggling from its egg.

Click-Ptchick Pause *Click-Ptchick.*

Opening his eyes, Rich found he was naked and bound by some sort of tape to a flimsy chair of plastic and metal. He lifted his head. Dread filled him. *Matchstick!* The wormy little man sat on a chair in front of Rich, a menacing grin on his face, opening and closing a switch blade.

"I had wondered when you would awake, mon compagnon."

Slowly, Matchstick closed the blade. *Click* as it set. *Ptchick* as it opened.

Don sat to Rich's left, naked, secured to a chair by black tape wrapped around his torso. His head slumped, a patch of black, charred flesh just evident beneath a bandage over his chest.

A woman walked over, administered a shot into an IV line snaking its way into Don's arm. Raven black hair in long, silky strands cascaded in a waterfall over her shoulders. She crossed her almond-colored arms, watching as the medicine worked.

"What are you doing to him?! Hey!"

"Easy there buddy," said a male voice in a low, mid-west CAU accent.

Charles, Matchstick's brother, lurked behind Rich some-where. Rich craned his head, trying to see the man's face. "Charles?! What the jahannam is going on?!"

"Oh, so rude," Matchstick said. *Click-Ptchick* Pause *Click-Ptchick.* "You're going to *have* to learn some manners out here. In a lawless society, one quickly learns to be diplomatic or risk deadly consequences."

"What the hell is your problem!"

"Hmmm. Am I really the one with a problem, spaceman?" There was acid in his voice, death, especially on the last word, 'spaceman.'

"Definitely *them* that have the problem."

"Rich?" Don said groggily, waking up. "Why does my chest feel like it was struck by lightning?"

"Because it was," Matchstick said.

"Oh God," Don said, opening his eyes, waking to full awareness. "Oh, God, no!"

"Did you not notice the bay was pressurized?" Matchstick asked, flourishing the blade in his hand. "A bay for *mothballed ships?* Why was the air pressure not zero? If you're going to be spaceman, you must ask yourself these things."

Match waited, expecting an answer.

Rich's mind worked slowly. His shoulder ached worse now, flooding every thought with thundering pain. From beneath the bandage at his shoulder, a pattern of angry-looking blisters crawled along his skin, vines of furious ivy with snowflakes at their tips.

"Lichtenberg figures?" Rich said, growling. "You shot us with an alladamn lightning gun!"

"*Yattaaaa! Kimi yet cosomoboys.* We keep just enough air pressure to ionize a path for an electrical charge. If any unwelcome persons comes—" He clapped his hands. "Behold, the wrath of Jove!"

"You stunned us."

"Astute. Perhaps you will be a space-*man*. Perhaps." *Click-Ptchick* Pause *Click-Ptchick*. Blade out, Matchstick gestured towards Don. "You know, I think I do have a problem, but I also have a solution."

Charles almost purred. "Ohhhh? Tell me, big brother."

"There are many ways to deal with one's enemies, old ways. You could kill them, but killing is a waste of resources, and waste is not the spaceman way. But there are other ways, some much more useful."

Click-Ptchick Pause *Click-Ptchick*.

Rich wet his lips, looking for words as the fear brooded inside him.

"You are both virile and strong, *mes amies*. You could load and unload my cargo, scrub my floors, cook my dinner—hold a towel as I make love to my wives! The luxuries I'd deny myself, killing you!"

Rich tried to speak as fear and rage welled up from his depths, strangling him, making it hard to even breathe. So many things to say—insults, curses, and proclamations of hate—and none of them useful.

"We're not your enemies!" Rich said.

"Of course you are! You took what was mine!"

"They aren't cattle!" Don shouted, his face flushing red. The chair shook as he struggled against his bonds. "You don't just get to claim them."

"Of course I do!" Matchstick shook the knife towards them. "A spaceman takes, makes the world his own—or he dies. And right now, dying seems the most likely for you."

The woman beside Don stood silent, watching. Other women, roughly eight, lurked in the corners of the room in various types of dress—sheer clothing, pristine spacesuits, course work overalls smudged and stained.

I guess I know what they meant when they said he had a harem ship!

"Oh, such magnificent specimens of manhood you are!"

Matchstick gestured towards them, and the angle of his hand was not lost on Rich. "I might be persuaded to take you as co-husbands. My wives would certainly be pleased with Don. But then I would have to share my toys, and I don't play well with others."

Matchstick glanced hungrily around the room. "Even Charles and I have had our kerfuffles, and we're not only brothers, but bratva at the breast. Besides, you and your hidden, Earthjin defects—all but certain to pollute the gene pool. Why just a drop of your precious fluids could set our ship back generations. Your genes have been denied the same forces of natural selection as ours. And our women—poor foolish creatures! They are helpless in the face of brutes such as yourselves, two Earthjin, with your naturally thick bones and musculature. Instincts from Earth, still buried in their ancient genes, would scream at our women that you would provide fine, virile offspring, even as your pauper's seed withered in their wombs."

The women remained silent, expressionless. Whether they approved of what he said, it was impossible to tell.

I'd love to hear him say that to Lily and Anni! Jahannam, if I had said that to Persephone, she'd have shown me who was the foolish creature!

Matchstick continued, "Unfortunately for you, I have a duty, not only to my ship, but all spaceman. No, if I intend not to waste you, you must be *modified*."

"Modified?" Don asked, terror growing in his voice.

I think I know what he's talking about! Rich thrashed against his bonds, the tape tearing at his skin. It was pointless. Whatever they used, it held.

Seeing his struggle, Matchstick smiled darkly, then turned

his attention to Don: "No, dear friends, it must be the spaceman thing, the only way. Think of it. It'll settle our feud before it becomes deadly for you. And Anni and Lily, they'll be free to move ship to ours, to marry proper spaceman, and still keep their beloved Earthjin as pets. With hormones, you could even be their concubines."

"Wow, little brother," Charles said. "You're really giving me a chubby. That's *certainly* unusual."

Click-Ptchick

Matchstick held up the blade, examined it. "I fear this is too small, unlike you." He winked at Don. Don's chin quivered as he glanced between his legs, then back at Matchstick. Matchstick pocketed the switchblade, zipping it into his suit, and reached to his waist.

There, from a sheathe built into the suit itself, he drew out a proper knife—a glistening blade with sharp-upturned tip, a trough for blood along its spine. It was made to cut human flesh, to skin and gut, and glistened softly under the room's dim luminescence, as if forged from moonlight.

"Matchstick," Don begged. "Don't do anything you'll regret!"

"Oh, I never do!" He chuckled. "Who first?"

"Matchstick!" Rich raged.

"Awww, such nobility to go first. Since you are a creature of such courage, you may enjoy your family jewels a few moments longer."

Matchstick rose and minced towards Don, savoring the terror spreading across the man's face. Don whimpered.

"Match!" Rich roared.

As Matchstick knelt, Don struggled, shaking the chair, threatening to topple it. In a flash, Charles had him from behind, kneeling, looping both his arms under Don's arm pits and cupping them over the scruff of his neck.

"Easy there, big fella," Charles said, leaning up to kiss Don on the cheek, nuzzling the side of his head like a lover. "You're gonna have quite the story from the dark side of the moon!"

Cackling, Matchstick reached between Don's legs. "How sad for Lily and Anni. How much wonderful material they are losing! Why, if I were them, I would be heartbroken at the sight of such magnificence *cut away.*"

"Please!" Don begged, kicking. "Please!"

Matchstick pinned Don's legs to the ground with his left arm, held his knife to Don's throat with his right. "Oh no, dear no, you mustn't weep. What the Boatman ordains, determine to love."

Matchstick pressed the knife ever so gently against Don's neck; blood oozed from beneath the blade as Don whimpered. "Embrace the pain, even if you must endure it a thousand years, a million. We are all stars in orbit of a terrible, dark god—fate—the supermassive black hole at the center of all things. It cast our course before the stars were even kindled; and in kindness, made all our ends the same. One day, we will all fall into the most terrible union together, into the place that is both life and death."

The language of the mosque! The prophecies of the Bodhisattva! Rich could recite the original passage by heart, but it was oh so different here, twisted, terrible…

Matchstick pressed the knife harder. Don whimpered.

"—So love what is given," Matchstick continued, "horrible and beautiful as it is, for it is prophecy certain and truest sharia. Pain, after all, is the seed of bliss." Matchstick kissed

Don on the head as tears streaked down the man's cheeks, mingling with the blood at his neck.

I've got to do something! Rich strained against the ropes, trying to work himself free. *I can't do nothing!*

Is this how it ends? Will this womb of rock prove the grave of our potential? Dr. Winn's words from weeks ago came back to him: '*Even the best of intentions can take us down dark paths.*'

Rich raged against his bonds—raged for his hopes threatened by the cruel edge of a merciless knife.

"Don't," one of the woman said.

Turning his head, Rich saw the rifle trained on him.

"I don't really care if he keeps you or not. This thing can burn a hole clean through you and the deck."

"Thank you, my dear, Sonya." Matchstick repositioned the knife an inch from Don's nose. "If you kick me, you'll lose more than your nuts! Hold still." Matchstick knelt again, his left hand passing between Don's knees. His right hand followed with the knife.

Pain is the gate of bliss…

Grimacing, Don shut his eyes.

…and the trials of Allah, the—

A quick jerk, and the wicked thing was done. Don screamed.

ACKNOWLEDGMENTS

Special Thanks to Betas:

Aleksei, Brandon, Andrew, Troy,
Lamar, Billy, Justin, Melissa,
and Leann

Note From Rall

My new readers, my new friends,

I hope you have enjoyed the journey of Rich Corrington as he steps into a new, dangerous world. I know my ending may shock you, as may much of the worldbuilding, both which you've encountered and which is to come. Remember, as Doctor Winn said, "even the best of intentions can take us down dark paths." Rich, Don, Anastasia, and Lily—all are heading down dark paths in Part 2, The King of Fish, as they journey to the Court of Odin, exploring more of the spaceman and colonial culture on the way. I hope you will come along for their journey.

If you enjoyed this book, please leave a review online and please share with your friends. You can also email me directly at: rallmekin@gmail.com

I look forward to all feedback, positive or negative, as it helps me grow as a creator.

Thank you for your time.